W9-CJF-453

# The Time Tree

Enid Richemont

LITTLE, BROWN AND COMPANY
Boston • Toronto • London

First U.S. edition, 1990

First published in Great Britain in 1989
by Walker Books Ltd.

The characters and events in this book are fictitious. Any similarity to real persons, living or dead, is coincidental and not intended by the author.

Library of Congress Cataloging-in-Publication Data
Richemont, Enid.
The time tree / Enid Richemont. — 1st U.S. ed.
p. cm.
"First published in Great Britain in 1989 by Walker Books Ltd." — Verso t.p.
Summary: The summer after their last year of elementary school brings changes in the friendship of Rachel and Joanna, as past and present worlds seem to merge and a mysterious girl dressed in old-fashioned clothing appears and disappears at their secret place in an old tree.
ISBN 0-316-74452-2
[1. Time travel — Fiction. 2. Friendship — Fiction.] I. Title.
PZ7.R39839Ti 1990 89-39449
[Fic] — dc20 CIP
AC

10 9 8 7 6 5 4 3 2 1
HC

PRINTED IN THE UNITED STATES OF AMERICA

*For Polly and Justine*

# chapter one

It was summer.

It was August.

It had been their last year in elementary school and they already sensed that nothing would ever be quite the same again. Perhaps that was why they loved the tree so much.

To Joanna and Rachel, the tree was just like a great house full of rooms.

Their favorite room was the one they called the attic. It was not so very high up, but it was well hidden and quite difficult to reach, and there was enough space on it only for two or, possibly, three people. It was their secret place and they felt quite private about it.

That was why it was so disturbing — the feeling of being watched.

Rachel and Joanna were best friends and they had always thought they could tell each other anything, but this was different. How could you talk about a vague prickling at the back of your neck? How could you admit to a feeling that every word you said, each gesture that you made, was being heard, noted and considered by an invisible audience? It simply sounded silly. And a bit childish. Secretly fearful of losing sight of each other among the vast corridors of the big middle school, they had recently become very wary of their friendship and neither was prepared to take the risk of making a fool of herself.

So they said nothing, but the feeling lay between them just the same — too heavy and oppressive to be ignored. They tried. They really worked at it, sitting astride their branch, swinging their legs and making up unlikely stories about their teachers.

"Wouldn't be surprised if he liked . . . You know . . ."

"And what about Miss Hoskins? Did you see that blouse she was wearing?"

And, their thoughts elsewhere, they giggled self-consciously, without much real amusement.

But it was all nonsense, wasn't it? It had to be. This was their secret place and no one could possibly be watching them. To begin with, it would not have been easy for someone to have climbed up much higher. Anyway, no one could have gotten up that tree without being spotted and they had both been sitting there for ages and ages.

And so they went on eating their chocolate, flicking through the pages of an old magazine, folding a piece of paper into a fortune-telling game and telling outrageous jokes — furiously acting as if nothing at all had changed.

*The girl could not take her eyes off them.*

*She watched them, fascinated but terrified, not daring to move for fear they would attack her.*

The tree was in a wood.

Once it had been a wild wood, which had covered many acres of land. Foxes and badgers had lived in it. Deer and wild pig had been hunted on it. That was a very long time ago. Now the little of it that was left had been tamed and enclosed in a park. Now you could not walk through it without catching glimpses of neatly shaved lawns and richly patterned flowerbeds and, farther away, the metallic glint of the swings and slides in the children's playground.

There was a lane that went past the back of the wood. The lane was not supposed to be the entrance to the park. That was some distance away, along streets and through the big, green-painted iron gates. Near those gates was a sign that told you at great length, and in very small print, what you could and could not do in this open space, among these winding paths and smooth lawns, on the round boating lake and the sports field, in the playground and the little wood. Someone had spray-painted a silly face over the words. Nobody minded. Nobody read them anyway.

Behind a tangle of blackberry bushes and stinging nettles lay a broken-down fence. That was the way in for the people who knew about it, for the kids who lived there. That was the real way in.

*The girl frowned.*

*She was puzzled by their blue stockings, their loose shirts and their funny white shoes, but they did not fool her with those boy's garments. What were they? Traveling players? For what honest maid, she wondered admiringly, would deck herself out like that? Even the Gypsy wenches showed a little modesty.*

Of course there was nobody watching them.

So they each began thinking, uncomfortably, that perhaps it was something else that was wrong.

Perhaps something had happened to their friendship. Perhaps they had simply stopped being best friends — people did, after all. These things happened. For they could each think of at least four people whose own parents didn't even live together anymore. People could stop loving each other. People could even stop liking each other. Nothing was forever.

And the whole idea was silly.

They were ten years old, nearly eleven, and pretty sensible, and they knew that no one could possibly be watching them every single time they went to the tree. After all, who would bother? What did they get up to that could possibly attract such undivided attention?

So, maybe, they had come to the sad point where there was nothing further to say and nothing more to share. At that moment this idea was far more disturbing than the remote possibility of someone spying on them.

Suddenly the tree with its attic branch seemed like nothing but childish nonsense and they decided to go home.

*They disappeared into a green mist.*

*The girl watched them go. She was sorry that they were leaving, for they were curiosities and even stranger than herself. Curiosities seldom came her way, but when they did, she found them oddly comforting.*

*Freaks she had seen at fairs, but these were not freaks. She would have liked to have come closer to them, to have put out a finger and touched their hair, their skin, or the fabric of their clothes, but she dared not. For anything might happen.*

*Even the people in her own village had been known to attack her, and these were strangers.*

Rachel and Joanna walked down the lane.

It was really a country lane, trapped inside the city, where roses, grown wild, ran amok over the sagging fences of neglected gardens, and long-forgotten apple trees dropped their small, wizened fruit to ferment in the gutters. The lane dipped between the dark side walls of two gaunt buildings. Then it opened out, astonishingly, into a street of tall Victorian houses, whose windows were often boarded up and whose porches now bore the names of many occupants. It was a long, boring street, its boredom lessened only by the possibility of a chance encounter with an attention-seeking cat. And today all the cats were inside, or around in the back, asleep in the shade.

The two girls crossed the bridge over the railroad. Main Street was full of afternoon shoppers, and Rachel and Joanna moved, in a dreamlike and oppressive silence, past the exhausted young woman with the screaming baby and the gang of punks, too hot to be aggressive, whose tough masks were already melting in the sun. This was where Rachel lived — in the bottom half of an old house in a leafy suburban street near the shopping center. Joanna lived one stop away on the subway.

At the turnoff for the station, Jo announced awkwardly, "I really ought to go home now."

"Not coming back to my house?" Rachel felt almost relieved.

"Not this time."

"You're coming tomorrow, though?" Rachel asked quickly, suddenly fearful of a refusal.

Jo grinned and nodded, and the tension was instantly broken.

"Two-thirty, OK?"

"See you."

# chapter two

Anne sat under the table, thinking.

At that moment the table marked the boundaries of her private world, its edges defined by the four carved legs. She played idly with the rushes on the floor, pleating the stems into elaborate shapes or weaving them into little plaits. The summer heat had made them stale-smelling. It would have helped if she had brought in sweet herbs from the garden. That was one of the simple tasks they gave her, for they disapproved of idleness, even in a fool. But it felt so good to be sitting alone in the cool shade of her table house that she did not care.

If her mother had been around, she would have chided her for such infantile behavior but, happily for Anne, she was not. Today she was far too busy. Anne's older sister, Kate, was to be betrothed, and to no common yeoman either, for Thomas was a lad of noble birth — a Gentleman, no less. At fifteen, Kate, with her smooth, high forehead, her carefully plucked brows and small, delicate mouth, had brought much honor to the family. Thomas had persisted in his courtship in spite of the existence of Kate's lackwit sister, in spite of the muttered warnings from the good-wives of the village, and their father was very proud.

"But she comes of good stock," he boasted, "and she is fair and virtuous. As for Anne — accidents can happen in the noblest families."

Anne sighed. It was sad to be nothing but a burden — a burden and a shame.

Her father, not noticing her, sat down at the table and began to write. Anne knew what he was doing; she had already peeped at the columns of numbers in the big ledger. Honor did not come cheaply and she knew that he was working out the cost of the banquet and the cost of the sewing women, too, for they were all going to look very grand. There was much talk of farthingales and French hoods and starch. Even she, Anne, was to have a special gown, although her mother had sniffed and said that it was good money wasted upon an idiot.

And they reminded her daily that she was to be silent at the feast, to smile modestly but say nothing, lest she shame them.

She squatted, watching the shifting and flexing

of the heavy leather boots, aware of her father's concentration and wishing for the impossible — that she could help him a little, for she knew that her existence brought him nothing but woe. And she thought again about the maids in the tree — if maids they were. They were able to write. Many times she had seen them writing things down in their small books. Anne sighed. If only she could write, she thought, she could tell people things. There was much locked away inside her that she wanted to say. But who would waste precious time teaching her?

Wistfully she fingered the lines of the carvings on the table legs, pretending they were letters.

Joanna walked up the hill past the parking lot. The sky was gray and white. It looked like rain.

She shivered. Would it be the same today?

Over the past few months the differences between herself and Rachel had seemed to grow, and little things, which once would not have troubled her at all, had suddenly become irritating. Rachel's family, for instance, always seemed to be so infuriatingly well organized, making her own, by comparison, look totally chaotic. And Jo was always forgetting things, while Rachel never seemed to lose anything at all.

But then people had to be different, didn't they? It would be so boring to have a best friend who was exactly like yourself. And anyway, she liked Rachel. She liked her smooth, fair skin and her blonde hair (fashionably cut these days by one of her mom's friends). And she always took Rachel's side whenever she was teased, and suffered with her whenever she started blushing, which she did so readily. (Joanna herself did not get so easily embarrassed.) Suddenly she made up her mind.

I'm going to say something, she thought, about the feeling of being watched. I know it's going to sound silly but I'm going to say it just the same.

She dawdled past the Indian fabric shop with its shimmering saris and the thrift shop with its wire baskets full of exciting offerings. Sometimes they bought clothes there. They would pool their pocket money and come away with their loot — a velvet jacket, threadbare but interesting; a crumpled T-shirt with an unusual slogan or, once, a sequinned and gold-threaded skirt that someone might have worn to a fancy dress party and then discarded. And they shared everything because that way they each had twice as much.

Joanna was late.

Rachel was waiting.

She had been waiting for some time, nervously, not even certain anymore that Jo would turn up. Occasionally she would stand on tiptoe, trying to pick out Joanna's ginger ponytail from among the crowd and quickly ducking down again to make herself inconspicuous. Waiting for people made her feel self-conscious. She hated it.

And she began thinking, all over again, about the previous afternoon. She remembered the heat and the prickly feeling that someone was watching them. They couldn't go through all that again today.

She came to a decision.

I'm going to tell Jo, she thought. It's going to sound crazy but I'm going to tell her just the same.

But when they saw each other they were so relieved that they hugged and forgot everything.

"What have you brought?" asked Rachel.

"Just some money; didn't have time for anything else. Thought we'd go to your big supermarket."

"OK."

They walked up the street arm-in-arm, as if nothing had ever been wrong.

Rachel's big supermarket was the kind of place that sold everything — even beach umbrellas and garden chairs. It was the kind of supermarket you could lose people in, and they did, several times. Soon, the sappy, sentimental music began to make them feel giggly and they started to fool around, dancing down the long, almost empty aisles.

When they came upon the trayful of Special Offer Oversize Bras, it was simply too much. They picked through voluminous lace-trimed constructions in tea rose or baby blue and held them against their chests.

"Mine's bigger than yours!"

"Mine's D cups — look!"

"Well, mine's F cups!"

"That's nothing . . . mine's a Z!"

A woman glared at them disapprovingly, which only made them choke and splutter with laughter.

Sobering up with difficulty, they managed somehow to put together a couple of cans of soda, some chocolate bars and a few bags of chips before staggering out into the street, still nudging each other and giggling.

But halfway to the park they suddenly became serious.

"Listen," said Joanna boldly, "I think someone was watching us — yesterday afternoon, when we were up in the tree. I mean, there wasn't anybody around but I could sort of — feel it. Look, I know this sounds silly —"

"No, it doesn't," Rachel said quickly. "I was going to say exactly the same thing to you."

It was out at last, and they both felt better.

"What shall we do," asked Joanna, "if it happens again today?"

They each thought about it.

"Challenge them," said Rachel at last. She sounded quite angry.

"How?"

"Call out. Yell. Tell them we know they're there and then see what happens."

They went on up the lane. A boy came skateboarding toward them, twisting his shoulders in an arrogant gesture, showing off. When he drew level with them, he made a face at Joanna and mouthed, "Carrothead!"

They ignored him.

At the top of the lane they ducked under the fence into the wood. And there was their tree. They climbed it defiantly. No one was going to spoil this afternoon.

Anne always felt proud of herself for being able to find the right place each time. After all, there were plenty of saplings in the forest and one looked much like another. A fool and an imbecile she might be, but she knew how to read her path from the shape of a bush, a scattering of yellow-lipped comfrey or a beech stump smothered in ivy.

And now she had her reward.

For the maids were there.

Oh, but she had waited so long.

She supposed that she must be brave, too, for she knew that not everyone would have dared venture as deep into the forest as this. Rogues' and vagabonds' country, people called it, but that did not trouble Anne. Any place beyond the safety of her own garden walls could be dangerous for someone like her.

She knew that she was a freak. She knew that her presence offended people, that her shadow falling on the wooden pails might sour the milk, that even her passing might cause one or two of the old women to make the sign against the Evil Eye before turning their heads away.

But it was the children she feared the most.

For she could never tell when they were creeping up behind her until her hair was painfully tweaked, or a stone was lobbed. And then they would snigger behind their hands and mime the noises that she made when she tried to protest.

"Moo! Moo! Moo!"

"Wallawallawalla!"

But the forest was kind. It offered her no harm.

The brambles didn't pick on Anne because she was different: they would have scratched anybody. And as for vagabonds, she had never seen one.

She had only seen two strange maids up in a tree.

Rachel and Joanna sat on the high branch, listening. Not talking. Listening.

"It's happening again," whispered Joanna.

Rachel nodded.

"Ssh!" she said. "Let's see if they give themselves away."

So they sat, absolutely still. Listening.

A twig snapped somewhere above their heads. They looked up sharply. Bits of twig and tree droppings scuttered through the leaves. A pigeon flapped noisily and rose into the air.

"They're up there!" Rachel said. Her face was pale and her mouth felt tight and stiff. She was not often angry, really angry, but she was angry now. Something very precious to both of them was being ruined by this stupid game played by some jerk who obviously had nothing better to do.

"Let's tell them," she said, and she began shouting. "Come on down! We know you're up there!"

But there was no response. No one shouted insults back at them. No one pelted them with orange peel or candy wrappers or chewing gum. There was no sound but the rustling of leaves and the distant voices of the little kids in the playground.

Rachel stood up, holding on to the trunk.

"I'm coming up to get you!" she yelled.

Joanna was horrified.

"Rache, you're not serious! The branches up there could be really brittle. It's a very old tree."

But Rachel's mouth was set in a hard line.

"They managed it!"

"We don't know, do we?" said Joanna desperately. "We don't know for sure. There's probably no one up there at all."

But Rachel had already started climbing and she could do nothing to stop her. A touch might have meant disaster. She felt helpless and frightened.

# chapter three

To the watcher they were a source of perpetual amazement. Maids they undoubtedly were, and nearly grown — about the same age, in fact, as herself; yet they clambered about in the tree like a couple of lads. They even dressed like boys. Her mother, she knew, would have thought them immodest and probably wicked, which was partly what made them so attractive.

She was watching the one with the shorn blonde hair and the round fair cheeks climbing farther up the tree. Impressed by her daring, Anne feared at the same time for her safety. Higher up, the branches were thinner and some of them looked brittle. It was not safe. She would surely fall.

Under Rachel's weight, the stout-looking branch unexpectedly creaked.

Shocked, she grabbed at the solid trunk, digging her nails into the rough bark. Down below, too far down, she saw Joanna's frightened face.

"I'm OK!" she called out, but she did not feel it.

The trick, she told herself, was to climb just a little at a time and not to look down. She bravely hauled herself up to the next fork. It was a big tree, wasn't it? There were plenty of footholds and she could always climb down some other way. Besides, she was angry; she was not going to give up now.

"I'll get you!" she yelled, to keep up her spirits, but the only response was the faint droning of a distant airplane.

Suddenly the wood she was standing on cracked, sending a shower of splinters pattering through the leaves like heavy raindrops. Instantly her right arm shot up and found a small overhead branch that dipped and swung.

Anne could have told her that the branch was going to break. Anne could see that the wood was rotten — the sudden crack came as no surprise at all. She had learned quite a lot, trotting curiously after her father as he tended the trees on his land, watching him prodding and poking them and pruning away at the dead wood. But this tree was in a forest and had never been cared for.

And already the girl's grip was weakening. Sooner or later, she was bound to fall.

Anne could not see the ground, but she guessed that it must be a long way down. The maid would surely be killed, she thought, or, far worse, crippled — like the boy in the village who sat all day, watching with bitter, old-man's eyes while the other children played.

The red-haired one had begun to climb now, shakily, trying to help her friend — oh, but she would only make things worse.

Anne could see that it was useless. She clenched her fists in a rage; she did not want that maid to fall but she did not know how to stop it from happening. What could she do? What did she know of tree climbing?

Why, she could not even be sure that what she was seeing was really there. How could it be? A tender sapling with its first slender branches and a great oak gnarled with age occupying the same space? That could not be.

Even a poor fool like Anne could see that.

Rachel clung to the branch with one hand, not daring to move, too mindless with terror even to reach up with her other arm. The sharply ridged bark scraped against her flesh and made her fingers sting. She felt her fingers slipping. She was going to fall. She knew she was going to fall.

Just inches below her feet was a swelling in the trunk, a solid foothold, but Rachel could not see it.

All she could see was a small red beetle moving slowly, slowly, across a green leaf, like a speck of dust. Time seemed to be running down. Time, for her, she knew, was about to stop altogether.

Anne kicked off her wooden shoes and bunched her skirts in a knot around her hips.

She had to do something.

Joanna could see the foothold.

"Rache, move your right foot down a bit. Your *right* foot, Rachie! There's a place just below you."

Rachel waved her left foot about aimlessly, treading air.

Joanna could not bear it any longer.

She clambered fearfully up the next bit of tree, squeezing the trunk with her knees and digging her toes into the bark, but when she reached out, her fingertips just missed the rubber of Rachel's sneakers.

There was something solid beneath Anne's feet and she did not waste any time questioning its reality.

For she could see quite clearly now what had to be done, and she could do it.

It was easy.

She was just below the fair girl, behind the curve of the tree. Her left arm was wrapped around its trunk, and her bare toes curled over the tickly bark of a stout branch.

With her right arm she reached out and guided the waving foot to a temporary harbor. Then, as the girl dropped heavily, she grabbed her, supporting her around the waist and hauling her to safety.

Then the red-haired girl took over.

It was extraordinary.

Suddenly someone was there and it wasn't Joanna. Someone was helping, holding Rachel, guiding her down. Rachel caught a glimpse of curly brown hair fringing a white lace cap. Intense dark eyes seemed to meet her own — brown eyes under dark lashes.

But a fancy collar and piled-up skirts still made Rachel think ungratefully, What silly clothes.

Then the vision was gone and she couldn't make it come back. She could see nothing now but Joanna's white face. "It wasn't me," Joanna was saying. "I tried but you wouldn't listen. I didn't help you — it was her . . . some girl in a fancy dress."

"I know," Rachel said quietly. "I saw her too."

"Then where did she go?"

Rachel shook her head.

"I don't know but she probably saved my life."

"But why . . . ? How could she . . . ?"

"I don't know . . . I mean, she just sort of . . . vanished. I mean, I tried to say something but she just wasn't there anymore."

They were both still shocked. They each wanted to go home.

With unusual caution, they scrambled shakily to the ground. It was beginning to rain. They ducked under the fence and hurried down the lane. They did not speak much, for the appearance of the strange girl in the tree was still bothering them.

The horror of Rachel's climb seemed less vivid now than the memory of those dark, frightened eyes.

The slip had been nothing, really: it could have happened to anybody. They agreed not to mention it at home. Parents fussed.

But the girl . . .

She was a mystery.

They couldn't have made her up.

If they had both seen her, then she had to be real.

# chapter four

The weather turned wet and for the next few days Rachel and Joanna did not see each other. Rachel went to a movie with her older sister. Jo baked a cake and quarreled with her brother. They quarreled because the weather had kept them both indoors and they were sick of the sight of each other. Mark fooled around on a guitar and played records very loudly, which irritated Jo. Jo watched television and made a lot of silly phone calls, which irritated Mark. Then they each said some extremely unpleasant things. Finally Jo had had enough. She slammed the front door and ran out into the rain to walk off a combination of rage and hurt feelings.

While she was out walking, she began to think yet again about Rachel's climb and about the strange girl in the tree. The girl bothered her; how on earth had she done it? One minute she had been there and the next she had simply vanished. It suddenly occurred to Jo that it might have been the girl who had been watching them — that would explain why she had disappeared so promptly. Disappeared? The word made Jo feel vaguely uneasy. Disappeared was silly. People didn't disappear, like rabbits into a magician's hat. She had just slipped down through the leaves and run away.

But with all those floppy skirts?

That evening she called Rachel.

"I wonder why she picked on us?" said Rachel. "I mean, there's nothing unusual about us, is there? And what about her? I mean, did you see her clothes? Weird . . ."

They both giggled.

A second later they stopped, feeling guilty. Whatever she had been doing and however she was dressed, she had saved Rachel's life.

"Perhaps she was lonely," said Joanna thoughtfully. "She didn't seem to be with anyone."

"I'd really like to see her again," said Rachel. "I ought to thank her anyway."

On the following day the sun came shining out of a cloudless sky, as if it had never rained at all. Frayed tempers were miraculously mended and people lined up in the street to buy ice cream.

Mothers gratefully made sandwiches and directed their restless offspring toward parks and swimming pools. Rachel's mother had meant to take the two girls for a picnic on Hampstead Heath, but at the last minute the car wouldn't start.

"You could," she suggested, "take the sandwiches over to the park."

Rachel groaned.

"Let's not go to the park," she said. "It'll be full of little kids."

But they did, and it was.

Half a dozen small boys were playing noisy war games all over their tree. The girls gave up and walked out onto the grass to eat their picnic. Afterward they lay flat on their backs, like everyone else, rolling up their jeans to let their legs tan. They turned over, pushing up their T-shirts in order to toast their backs. They leafed through magazines and dozed. Ladybirds and small insects scuttled over their hands.

At the end of the afternoon they stood up, their hair full of bits of grass, and sleepily wandered over to the tree. The boys had long since gone home.

Cautiously, Rachel and Joanna climbed onto one of the lower branches and sat there, swinging their legs.

* * *

The festivities had gone on for two days and the preparations for much longer.

They wanted to impress, but they were not a wealthy family. It was Mother who had rushed, pink-faced and sweating, from supervising the making of the great pies and ornamental jellies to check on the fit of the girls' dresses; who came with damp and spice-smelling fingers to flatten Anne's unruly curls beneath the richly embroidered cap; and who fussed as much over the correct starching of their ruffled collars as over the niceties of mounting the peacock on the spit so that, later, its unsinged tail could be spread open at the table like a great jeweled fan.

Anne moved about, stiff and awkward in her new clothes — an open gown of fox-brown brocade trimmed with black and a long turquoise petticoat — like a starched and ruffled doll, who smiled but never spoke, for if she had opened her mouth she would have shamed them all.

Unlike her graceful sister, all dimpled smiles and modest blushes, Anne was not a child to be proud of, and she knew it. She knew, too, that she was lucky to have survived to the age of eleven, for she would always be a burden to her family and would never marry. A child who could only make noises like the beasts in the barn was like something from a menagerie; she was a freak, a monster — possibly even a witch. Why, even the wet nurse who had fed her as a baby had been known to declare openly that it would have been better if she had not lived.

Perhaps she was a witch and those wanton maids in the tree were her familiars, her evil spirits. At the end of two days of primping, posing and pretending, Anne was exhausted and did not care; better to have friends who were evil than no friends at all.

Unnoticed, she slipped out of the house, rustled through the kitchen garden and, moving slowly in her heavy skirts, crossed the meadow and entered the wood.

It was the same feeling again. They both had it. They were being watched.

"Do you think it's her?" whispered Rachel.

Joanna nodded.

"What do we do? Call her?"

Joanna shook her head.

"If it's her, she'll be too shy. Maybe," the idea suddenly came to her, "she's some sort of refugee and doesn't speak any English." She sighed. "I don't know what we do."

They sat in silence, thinking.

Then Rachel said, "This is going to sound a bit silly but could we will her to come out? Like the time we all willed Miss Shelton to drop the chalk."

Jo giggled.

"And she did," she said. "We could try."

At the beginning they could do nothing at all. They kept on catching one another's eyes and laughing. Then, gradually, the game became more serious.

Come out! they thought. Come out! Come out!

And come she did.

Anne did not enjoy being the focus of other people's attention, and she could always tell when it was happening.

She did not have to watch lips making words. Someone had been calling her. She had felt it. She was sure of it.

No one was going to creep up on Anne.

She turned round to catch them.

Then something extraordinary happened.

For there she was, sitting on the branch of that big old tree, and she had no idea how she got there. Leaves brushed against her cap, and her feet in their new little pointed shoes were swinging in the air.

And the two maids were so real and so close that — if she had dared — she could have reached out a finger and touched them.

She came very gently. Brown eyes blinked through the leaves, then a pale face formed around them, like smoke. Her dark curls had been scraped back under an embroidered cap and the pleated lace ruff round her neck made her head look like the center of a flower. Her ridiculous skirts — golden-brown and turquoise — swelled around her like a ball gown or something from a Christmas pantomime, the rich fabric caught up in places by twigs. Her thin hands, emerging from narrow, white-ruffed sleeves, were twisting nervously in her lap.

Rachel and Joanna stared at her in open amazement.

At last Jo said, hesitatingly, "Are you part of a theater group or something?"

Neither of them wanted to consider any other explanation.

The red girl was speaking to her.

Anne watched the red girl's lips very carefully. She had taught herself to do this when she was still very little, so that strangers did not notice, sometimes, that she was deaf.

She picked out the word "theater."

Of course. That was the explanation. She smiled — no devils these, but masquers, mummers, come to perform on the village green. Tumblers, perhaps — that would explain their strange costume.

*   *   *

The girl had smiled but she was clearly nervous; her fingers plucked at the fabric of her skirt.

They tried to reassure her.

"I think your dress is very beautiful," said Rachel. The ruff made her think of pictures of Elizabethan clothes she had seen at school, and she added tactlessly, "Is it very old?"

Anne understood. Anne was offended. Anne was furious. Old? Her gown? When her father had just spent a small fortune on their clothes?

Automatically she protested, forgetting, as she frequently did, that her mouth would not make words like other people's.

# chapter five

It was a language, but not foreign.

They could even pick out one or two words which might have been a funny kind of English.

The girl was trying to tell them something and they couldn't understand. No wonder she looked cross.

The odd thing was, it reminded Joanna of something — something she had heard not so very long ago.

If she had been able, Anne would have left at that moment, run away, gone back to her forest and her sapling, but she seemed to have no choice.

In some mysterious way, the two girls had called her and held her. Why? Were they restless? Did they need a fool to amuse them?

She watched their faces, waiting, like a dog accustomed to abuse, to see what they would do. She waited for them to snigger and point their fingers at their heads and mouth insults. At least there were no stones for them to throw, and acorns did not hurt so much.

But they did nothing.

Perhaps they were frightened of her.

Perhaps, when they had recovered from their shock, they would climb down and run away, making the sign of the cross against the Evil Eye as they ran.

Joanna remembered now.

She nudged Rachel.

"Saint James's?" she whispered.

"Oh. Yes. Could be . . ."

Last term, their teacher had taken a small group of them to visit a school for deaf children. They had learned that these children, because they could not hear the sounds that other people made, had never had words to copy when they were very little. They couldn't, without help, even hear the sounds they made themselves, so that their words seemed to come out all wrong. But, like everyone else, they wanted to talk, and talk they did, chattering away like monkeys. And if you gave them time, if you really listened, really concentrated, you could begin to understand what they were trying to say.

Could it be? Was it possible that this girl had the same problem?

"Listen. I'm going to try something," said Joanna.

Feeling very silly (it was only a guess and she might be wrong), she opened her mouth and let out an ear-piercing shriek.

The girl neither blinked nor flinched. It was obvious that she had heard nothing at all.

"You were right, then," said Rachel. "Clever old Jo!"

The two of them felt instantly protective. No wonder, then, that the girl was shy, that she disappeared whenever people were around. She was probably desperately lonely. And maybe she did herself up in all that fancy dress in order to draw attention to herself. After all, if you couldn't hear anything, it might be difficult to believe you were there at all.

When Joanna touched the girl, gently, on the shoulder, she felt her stiffen. She addressed her carefully, remembering to flex her lips as she spoke.

"I'm Jo," she said. She pointed to Rachel. "Her name's Rachel."

She picked up the notebook in which they wrote down odd, private thoughts and things they didn't want to share with other people, and she unzipped her pencil case and took out a shiny ballpoint pen.

"Will you write your name for us?" She offered

the pen and the book — open at an empty page.

The girl took the things warily, as if they might bite, and sat, looking at them, turning them over and over in her hands, and examining them minutely, as if she had never seen anything like them before.

Rachel and Joanna watched her. They were puzzled. The pen was cheap and ordinary. A notebook was just a notebook. What kind of home did this girl come from? Obviously she wasn't putting on an act.

For that matter, what kind of parents would send her out dressed like that?

"Maybe she's some sort of Gypsy," whispered Rachel. "The clothes look . . . sort of . . . real."

But Joanna didn't care.

After all, she was just a girl. She looked about ten, maybe eleven. She could have been in their class at school.

"Look," she said. She took the notebook out of the girl's hands and brought out some felt-tipped pens. Carefully, she drew pictures of the two of them — Rachel with her sleek, short hair in bright yellow, and herself with a russet ponytail tied back with blue-beaded elastic.

When she had finished, she labeled one RACHEL and the other JOANNA. Then she said the names aloud, taking care over moving her lips.

* * *

Anne could not believe it.

They did not find her evil or frightening.

They did not think her a fool.

It had to be a dream but it did not feel like one. If it was a dream then she wanted to go on dreaming it forever.

At first the two maids had been so unreachable that it had felt quite safe to pretend that they were her friends.

But now they really were.

She stared at them, puzzled. Could they not see what the others saw? What kind of people would not think of her as evil, or else a poor fool to mimic and torment? From where had these maids come? What village? What town? What . . . other place?

If it were hell itself, she thought defiantly, she would go there willingly.

She picked up the writing stick the red girl was offering her and she drew another girl on the next page, a maid whose new leather shoes made two neat little points below her modest skirts. It was the first time she had ever made a drawing and she held the pen clumsily in her fist, like a very young child.

She pointed to the picture, and back to herself.

"Anne," she said.

* * *

The girl said, "Aah."

She had to be saying her name.

Rachel came out with the only girl's name she could think of with the single sound Aah.

"Anne?"

The girl smiled delightedly. Her smile had an unexpected radiance, like sun coming out of cloud. Her whole face changed.

Then Rachel took the notebook and wrote underneath the girl's drawing A-N-N-E.

"That right?" she asked.

Anne frowned.

"That's your name, isn't it? Anne?"

The girl stared at the letters, fascinated.

"Aah," she said, and nodded.

Rachel was curious. She handed Anne the pen.

"You do it now," she said.

Anne stared at her and shook her head. People did not usually try to teach letters to fools except in jest.

It was clear to Rachel that the girl did not even know how to write.

"Go on," she said. "Try . . ."

Were they laughing at her? Anne wondered. She would show them.

She studied the shapes of the letters, the straight lines joining at sharp angles. She thought about the carvings on the linen chest, which she had so often traced with her finger; they were much more complicated than this.

With the greatest concentration, she carefully copied the letter A.

"That's good," said Joanna.

"That's super," said Rachel. "You've made an A. A for Anne. A for apple."

Encouraged by their approval, Anne copied out the rest of the word. Then she wrote it again. And again. Each time it became easier.

"Try my name now," said Joanna. "That's much more difficult." And she wrote it out. J-O and J-O-A-N-N-A, for Anne to copy.

Anne stopped looking for reasons and explanations. She was enjoying herself and she just wrote. She wrote A-N-N-E and J-O and R-A-C-H-E-L, over and over again. Sometimes she made mistakes, but when she did, the others were not angry or scornful — they just giggled. Then one of them would guide her hand and she would get it right.

It was like a game. Anne had never played a game, for no one would play with her.

Rachel suddenly looked at her watch. Anne noticed it for the first time and stared at it, her eyes round with amazement.

It was getting late.

"We've got to go home," Rachel said.

"Where do you live?" asked Joanna, suddenly awkward.

What a silly question.

"Why, here, of course."

Rachel asked an even sillier one.

"Where's here?"

Here? Why, Finchley village — where else could it be? Finchley village, not a day's ride from the great city of London where the Queen lived.

And her fingers curled around the slender young limb of a sapling.

And the great tree had gone.

In shocked silence, Rachel and Joanna packed up their things.

"She really was there, though, wasn't she?" said Rachel at last. "I mean, we couldn't both have imagined her, could we?"

Joanna was thinking about it. She was thinking hard.

They climbed down the tree and began walking home.

"We both saw her," Joanna said at last. "We both touched her. She was real."

"But she just disappeared. I mean, she disappeared like a . . ." She didn't want to say it but she made herself. "Like a ghost. And those clothes . . ."

"They weren't a Gypsy's."

"They were real, though."

"Yes, I know."

They had turned the corner and walked halfway up the road before Rachel said it.

"I thought ghosts always wore white things. I though they were transparent."

"There is a sort of transparency about her," said Jo. Then she added boldly, "Anyway, I think she's pretty. I think she's beautiful and I don't care."

# chapter six

She remembered most of the letters, and all the important ones. A-N-N-E made Anne. Her name.

The next afternoon she grubbed around in the garden for a chalking stone and across the dark timber frame of the house, around the side where she hoped no one would notice, she tried out an A. Then, boldly, she added two Ns and an E, and suddenly there it was — ANNE — standing out clear against the brown wood. It made her feel real, seeing her own name in letters: ANNE. No one could ignore that.

She stepped back to admire her work. A-N-N-E. All stick letters, she thought, and no curlicues; it looked very plain. With great daring, she tried out an embellishment or two, like the ones she had seen in broadsheets and manuscripts — a squiggle here, a curly leaf-shape there.

When she had finished, she felt quite proud of herself.

* * *

Joanna and Rachel developed an unexpected interest in historical costume, for, as Joanna had to admit, with awe, "It isn't *where* she comes from — it's *when.*"

So they pored over reference books in the library and found that dresses like Anne's had been quite ordinary in the sixteenth century.

"The sixteenth century?" Rachel gasped, and held up four fingers.

"Four hundred . . ." she whispered.

"Doing a school play?" asked the librarian, curious.

"Maybe . . ." They exchanged glances and giggled.

Silly kids, thought the woman frostily. Probably up to some mischief; better keep an eye on them.

"Four hundred," repeated Rachel as they sat down at one of the polished tables, and Joanna let out an impressed whistle before clapping her hand over her mouth.

The woman at the desk frowned.

"Sssh!" she said. These two were trouble. She had known it the minute they had come through the door.

"Shakespeare . . ." whispered Jo. "I mean, she might actually have seen him."

"Quiet, *please!*" snapped the librarian.

"And imagine not being able to read or write at her age, though. Didn't they teach them?"

"Probably thought she was a loony."

"Well, she isn't."

The woman stood up. Her spectacles, on a thin gold chain, winked at them malevolently from the frilly shelf of her chest.

"If I have to speak to you two again it will be to tell you to leave. This is a study area, not a playground. Look at the notice." The words SILENCE PLEASE were printed in large letters on a glossy card pinned to the wall. "Can't you read?"

This was too much!

Faces pink, they rushed outside, to collapse in giggles downstairs.

Anne went back to the forest the very next day. She wanted to show off to her two friends, persuade them, perhaps, to come with her to admire her letters, but the sapling stubbornly refused to change. She wondered if she had found the right place. It felt right, and she had followed all the signs — anyway, how could she not know her own special little tree?

The next day she tried again, but it was still the same. Then she began to wonder if — wanting friends so badly — she had just made them up. Perhaps she was as lunatic as they thought her.

But the letters were real enough.

And she had already tried out some of the others — a J and an O and an R (that one had been difficult). And a C.

Kate, already playing the goodwife, the mistress of a household, found her covering the beams and even some of the red bricks with chalk marks.

"Oh, Anne!" she chided. "What foolery is this?"

Then she looked more closely.

"Why, Anne," she exclaimed. "You have been making letters! Who could have had the patience to instruct you?"

She went off at once to tell Mistress Latymer.

"My poor fool making letters?" cried her mother, shaking her head in total disbelief. "The very idea! She can't even say her own name." Nevertheless she ran out into the garden to see.

But when Anne became aware of the fuss she was causing, she fled in embarrassment.

"How," Rachel casually asked her mother, who worked in a nursery school and might well be expected to know such things, "do you teach kids to read and write?"

"Same way as you were taught . . . lots of pictures with words underneath them so you learn the words for things . . . alphabet books . . . big letters. Why?"

"Oh, just wondering."

"How," Joanna asked her mother, "would you teach someone as old as me to read and write?"

"Do you know someone like that?"

"Not really."

They spent the following few days preparing for their next visit to the park — reading, collecting things, putting things together. In the thrift shop they found an alphabet book, brightly colored and full of animal pictures. Joanna's brother was scornful.

"Just about your level," he commented.

They rummaged through their own bookshelves for forgotten treasures of their infancy. Rachel's mother was amused.

"Having a second childhood, you two?"

"That's right," said Rachel.

Anne tried yet again.

Tucking up her skirts, she ran through the kitchen garden, which was heady with the fragrance of summer herbs, and slipped unnoticed through the gate. She crossed the meadow where dreamy cows stood deep in buttercups and clover.

And where the meadows ended, the forest began.

* * *

Rachel and Joanna met with a feeling of suppressed excitement.

The plastic bags they had brought held an odd collection of things: an alphabet and several picture books for very small children; an old-fashioned children's textbook with funny-looking people drawn on yellowing pages; a couple of cheap sketch pads and notebooks and an amazing assortment of pens and colored pencils.

It was a day gray with clouds, and chilly for mid-August. They were counting on the weather to keep the kids away from the park. When they got there the tree was empty. They sighed with relief and began to climb.

She ran to the place where the sapling stood.

From the moment she touched it, she could feel them calling her: *Anne . . . Anne . . .*

And she looked up into the great tree where the two girls sat, swinging their legs.

"Anne!" they were saying. "Anne! Come out! Come and play with us! Anne."

And she came.

There she was, sitting on the branch beside them.

"She's come!" said Jo delightedly. "Oh, Anne, we thought we'd never see you again!"

They looked at her. She was wearing a grubby blue gown, very different from her previous grand dress with its heavy skirts. Her bare feet were dirty and her curls spilled out from under her white cap.

She said, "I have been making the letters you taught me. I have made good progress — see."

The words were garbled but their meaning became clear when she reached for the notebook and pen.

A-N-N-E, she wrote, and J-O and a backward R. She watched their faces anxiously.

They praised her lavishly.

"Good, Anne, good! Very good! Fantastic. You're really smart!"

Then they got down to the serious business.

They opened the alphabet book. Anne looked at it in amazement. The one or two printed books she had seen had been in black and white. This was bright with color — who had illuminated it? And it seemed to be written for children, but what overindulged child would own such a treasure? Surely no one less than a prince? She put out a hand and touched the fabric of Rachel's jeans. It felt rough, like the clothes of peasants, and there were patches on the knees. How any wandering player — which, in faith, these probably were — could possess a book of any kind astonished her, but a book specially made for children? They had probably stolen it. She did not care: they were her friends. She stroked the paper reverently.

Joanna turned to the first page.

"Look, Anne," she said, "an ape. A is for ape." The ape in question swung merrily from a tree branch, waving a banana.

"Write it down," ordered Rachel. "Go on . . ."

And write it she did, forming the letters with painstaking care.

"B is for butterfly. C is for cat . . ." They went slowly through the book, turning the pages. "G is for giraffe." Anne's eyes grew large.

"Monster," she said.

"No, giraffe." They were beginning to understand her a little.

"Giraffe?"

"An animal with a very long neck — see? It comes from Africa," explained Rachel.

But Anne went on looking baffled.

"It's sort of yellow — look — and it has these brown spots."

"Like you," said Rachel. Joanna grabbed a handful of leaves and threw them at her and they burst out laughing. Anne did not like them to fight, but when they laughed she laughed with them.

They gave up on giraffes.

"G for girl, then," said Rachel, drawing one on

the page, "if you don't go for giraffes." But Anne, challenged, carefully lettered G for GIRAF in red pencil across the paper.

Jo and Rachel were delighted. She was learning. She was learning so quickly. They had never done anything so satisfying before.

Today they would not get much beyond the alphabet, but next time they could make a start on one of the books.

# chapter seven

For the two girls it was beginning to feel like one of those pretending games they used to play when they were much younger.

But this was real.

Wasn't it?

"Perhaps we should tell someone about her," Rachel announced as they walked up the lane. "The people at that school we went to."

"Don't be silly. They won't be there during vacation. Anyway, I don't think she'd come out if anybody else was around."

"How do you know? She might . . . and they could teach her properly — I mean, they had all that equipment, remember? Microphones and stuff."

"You must be crazy! You know where she comes from, same as me!" Joanna sighed. She was beginning to be tired of Rachel's obsession with doing things properly. She didn't want to follow someone else's rules; she wanted to work things out for herself.

But the question of Anne's reality went on bothering Rachel. If she could not be properly helped, she said to herself, then she could not be properly there. Perhaps, in spite of everything, they had really invented Anne. Rachel knew all about inventing people: there had been, for instance, Philip, her imaginary boyfriend. Even now, the thought made her blush.

"You mean she's a ghost," she said crossly, to cover up for her pink cheeks.

"Don't call her that!" Joanna was furious. "What do you think we are? To her, I mean."

Rachel was shocked. She hadn't thought of it like that. Immediately she tested herself for reality, checking out the weight of the plastic bag bumping against her leg, the out-of-reach itch in the middle of her back and the scratchy texture of the bark as she climbed the tree. Oh, she was real all right. She felt angry with Jo.

They were suddenly disliking each other, but all the same they had something to do.

Sitting as far apart as the branches would allow, they each separately began to call Anne.

Anger was something Anne could smell. She did not need words, sounds, raised voices.

Anger. Irritation. They were tired of teaching

a jolt-head, a beetle-head. She pointed to herself.

"Anne," she said. "I come not well . . ." and she began to fade.

They protested.

"Oh, no," said Rachel. "Don't go."

"It's not you," said Joanna. "It's us. We had a fight but it's over now." Her lips moved too quickly for Anne to read but her gestures were warm and welcoming. They still wanted her.

She remembered the wonderful books and the writing sticks. Not trusting her own memory, she pointed questioningly at the bag.

"Write?" she asked, but when they gave her the exercise books and the crayons, she drew two round faces with down-turned mouths. The two girls giggled self-consciously.

Suddenly Joanna had an idea.

CROSS, she printed, and she stuck out her tongue at Rachel to show what she meant. ANGRY, QUARREL, FIGHT, she wrote. Rachel, catching on, thumbed her nose at Joanna, and between them they pantomimed their quarrel so convincingly that it seemed as if it must have been a joke in the first place.

And Anne, relieved, drew two more faces, this time with smiley mouths.

HAPPY, they wrote, and SMILE, stretching their lips with their fingers, waggling their heads and clowning.

ANGRY, copied Anne, and frowned so severely at them that they shrieked with laughter. SMILE, she wrote and grinned at them. Then, watching their faces for approval, she added something of her own.

A MERY PASSUN.

"A merry what?" They listened carefully to the sounds she was making. A merry pattern? A merry pastime? Rachel worked it out first. "A merry passion? Laughing? Giggling, you mean?" She mimed it and Anne nodded excitedly. "A merry passion!"

Joanna tried it out. "We are in a merry passion," she declared.

"We are very passionate!" Rachel couldn't resist it.

Anne laughed with them. She could not understand their jest, but she knew that their laughter did not exclude her. She could feel their amusement bubbling warmly all around her and it made her want to be part of it.

They had brought things to eat and extra things for Anne. They laid out apples, chocolate bars, three Danish pastries and three bags of potato chips. The sight of the little feast made Anne sad. They gave her so much, her two friends, and she could offer them nothing in return. It was not that she hadn't tried. She had brought them fairings — gilded gingerbreads and folded ribbons — but when she came through, she found that her hands were always empty. On her return, she would see her gifts lying in the grass at the base of the sapling.

"Have an apple," said Joanna.

"Wait." Rachel had remembered something from their visit to the school. "Ask for it, Anne. Ask."

Anne was puzzled by this request but she wanted to please them. She asked very politely.

"I prithee let me have it."

The sounds made little sense but the meaning was quite clear. It was very important, Rachel had remembered, for deaf children to communicate, and for other people to listen. Anne had tried.

But when she tried to bite the apple, which was, after all, her reward for trying, nothing happened. Her teeth did not even dent the skin. It was nothing but a jest and she threw it back at them.

Joanna caught it. She was puzzled.

"What's wrong?"

Anne shook her head fiercely. "Not real," she said.

Joanna turned it over and over in her hands. There was nothing wrong with it. It was just an apple. She took a bite out of it and juice ran down her chin.

"It's OK. Look." She handed it back.

Anne tried again but it was like trying to bite into smooth marble. Only then did they realize that she could not eat their food.

Hastily they finished up their snack. It did not taste so good now; they had been looking forward to sharing it with Anne and they had chosen their bits and pieces with great care.

When they brought out the chips, Anne screamed. Wood shavings! So they were demons after all. Demons or magicians.

"Wood!" she said. "Wood!" Wood shavings, she thought, and shuddered; a mouthful of splinters! But no, it was another of their harmless tricks; why should she care?

"Only chips," said Joanna.

"Potatoes," said Rachel, scrunching up a handful of them and offering them for inspection, but Anne had already gone.

"Frightened by a potato chip!"

"It's not funny," Rachel said. "How do we know she'll come back?"

And when they picked up the notebook they saw that all the silly heads had disappeared.

"Look," said Rachel, "everything she's written, too. All gone."

"It's as if she's not allowed to leave any marks in our world."

"She can't eat our apples."

"She can't eat any of our stuff, can she?"

"She's just a ghost."

"Don't start that again, Rachel."

"But what's the point?"

"Of what?"

"You know."

"I don't know. We've got to, that's all. I mean, she remembers things, doesn't she? And anyway she's a friend and I really like her even if you don't."

"But I do. Jo, don't be silly — you know I like her just as much as you do."

"Tomorrow, then."

"OK."

# chapter eight

It had not been fear that had sent her back.

Even as Anne's fingers closed around the smooth limbs of her sapling, she was thinking that the splintery golden shavings of such alarming appearance were probably nothing more deadly than fritters or thin spice cakes.

No, it had not been fear.

It had been something else.

And she regretted her rude departure, with no proper leave-taking, for she would gladly have tarried with Jo and Rachel, but she seemed to have no choice. For the time she spent in their company was not like ordinary time. It was more like a gift from some good fairy who had supped well from her family's occasional night offerings of bread sops and soured cream. Everyone knew that fairies' gifts were not made to last — that the crock of gold would soon turn back into autumn leaves, and the fat cheese into the yellow face of the moon reflected in a duck-pond.

She knew already that she could bring nothing back with her save what remained inside her own head.

But within the blackness of her curtained bed, she could gloat over these treasures which she could not see, practicing her words over and over, making letters on paper in her dreams.

Even here, in the byre, she could practice them in secret, while her hands went on pulling rhythmically at the pink teats of the dairy cows. HAPPY. I AM HAPPY. KATERIN IS MOR HAPPY. CROSS. I AM CROSSED. ANGRY. FIGT. I WIL FIGT YOO WIV MI SORD.

Anne's family liked her to be able to perform simple tasks, for that way she could be less of an embarrassment to them. And so she had been taught how to card wool, how to keep the floor rushes fresh with sweet herbs and help the hired women around the farm, for idle hands, they said, even upon one of so little wit, might well be used by the devil. Anne did not mind. She enjoyed milking; she enjoyed being with the slow, patient cows. Their wordless voices, she often felt, ruefully, might not be too unlike her own.

She carried the pails of warm milk into the kitchen and found her sister, Katherine, crimping and decorating a pie, her eyes heavy with secrets, her ring flashing and all the kitchen wenches fluttering around her like doves. Anne watched her cutting little birds out of the pastry, running the point of a knife around a wooden mold. It looked easy — much easier than drawing things on paper — and she wanted to do it, too.

She patted Kate on the shoulder, silently holding out her hand for the knife, but Kate irritably shook herself free. Suddenly Anne could see Rachel's lip-words inside her head: Ask for it, Anne. Ask. Ask . . .

Of course.

She put on her best manners.

"I prithee let me try." But nobody listened.

She said it with greater force.

"I prithee, Kate, let me do it." Still no one bothered to listen.

Furious suddenly, she snatched up the knife and carved five letters across the rolled-out pastry.

ANGRY

This time Rachel had organized them. She could be quite bossy sometimes but she did get things done. Apples and cookies were disposed of long before they called Anne, and when she finally came through, book, pens and crayons were waiting for her in neat little piles.

"More reading today," Rachel announced. She was really enjoying playing teacher.

Anne looked from one to the other. Yesterday they had seemed like two strangers who didn't like each other very much. Today the warmth of their friendship enclosed her like a soft woolen shawl.

"A better humor," she remarked boldly, for the morning's happenings had made her bold, but when she saw that they did not understand what she meant, she said, "Happy. No more strife," and they grinned at each other sheepishly.

Then Joanna opened the book. It was a new one, and they were rather pleased with it. Feeling that some of the others were rather shabby, they had pooled their spending money and bought a cheap reading primer.

The first part consisted of nothing but games: things like matching shapes and finding two identical mice or sheep or turtles in a row. They felt a bit embarrassed presenting such infantile stuff to someone of their own age, but Anne was fascinated. Next, they got her to crayon over dotted-line letters. Already she recognized most of them, so she tried, instead, to make them beautiful, choosing her colors with great care.

Then came a story with pictures.

"Look," said Joanna, and she read aloud, pointing to each word. " 'The old woman made a gingerbread man.' " She took pains to pronounce the sentence very carefully.

And Anne read the words, looked at the picture for confirmation, and understood.

" 'The gingerbread man ran away,' " read Joanna. " 'The gingerbread man saw a horse.' "

Anne's eyes sparkled when she saw the horse and she held up three fingers.

"Three?" said Rachel, feeling slightly envious. "One, two, three?" And Anne nodded. "You lucky thing!"

" 'He saw a cat.' "

Anne looked pleased. She held up four fingers this time. She was really showing off.

"Four cats?" said Joanna, and Anne nodded.

"Mice," she said. "Mice. And rats." To show them what she meant, she drew a collection of them with black whiskers and long, wiggly tails. Then she remembered something.

"Mine," she said. "Meg."

She pointed at Joanna's hair.

"A ginger cat? Carrots? Like her?"

Anne nodded.

Then she pointed at her own white cap, and patted her chest.

"White? White, too?" They were enjoying the guessing game.

"A white shirt-front!" shrieked Joanna.

"Stick," demanded Anne, reaching out for a felt

tip. Then she remembered her manners. "I prithee . . ." and she drew a cat and colored it orange, leaving the white bits on its chest and paws. Underneath the drawing, she carefully printed MEG, and got it right.

"We've got a cat," said Joanna. "He's called Fred." She drew a silly-looking cat in black crayon, leaving out the white bits as Anne had done, and wrote FRED underneath it. Then as an afterthought, she added, A BOY. She pointed out a boy in the book. Then she pointed to the three of them.

"Girls."

Anne nodded wisely.

"Babes," she said, pointing to her own stomach. "Soon."

"What?" Joanna was horrified.

"Silly! She means Meg. Meg's pregnant."

"Ooh, kittens!" said Joanna, feeling a little foolish.

They got back to the lesson, and turned to a page of sentences, each one beginning with "Here is a."

" 'Here is a . . .' "

Anne looked at the picture. "Tree!" she shouted triumphantly.

"Write it," said Rachel.

They tried the next one.

" 'Here is a . . .' "

"Bauble!"

"No, silly, it's a ball. A b-a-l-l, Anne. Write it!"

" 'Here is a . . .' "

It was a house, if they said so. Apart from the chimney pot, it was nothing like any house Anne had ever seen, but she wrote it down obediently: HERE IS A HOUSE.

" 'Here is a . . .' " They should have left this one out, but it was the next sentence and they were trapped.

"Car," said Joanna, before she could stop herself.

"What . . . ?"

They did some quick thinking.

"A chariot," said Rachel.

"Don't be stupid!" said Jo. "A coach, Anne. It's like a coach."

"But it doesn't have any horses."

They were talking nonsense. She could read some of their words but she could make no kind of sense out of what they were saying. A coat was something to wear; this small, lozenge-shaped object looked like a painted bead, and what horses had to do with it all left her quite speechless.

She was still trying to work it all out, frowning, as she walked back through the meadow.

*          *          *

Rachel sighed.

"Oh, well . . ."

"We did lots, though, didn't we?"

"Almost half the book."

"She learns really quickly."

"But nothing stays. I mean, all her funny drawings and those colored letters she did — they all go away. She can't even take them back with her to show her mother."

"Maybe her mother doesn't care that much . . . maybe she's embarrassed by her . . . I mean, her voice is funny and she can't hear anything anyone says."

"Well, she's got a cat. And three horses. . . . Things can't be that bad."

# chapter nine

The lessons were becoming almost a routine.

Although they could not share their secret with anyone (for who would believe them?), it was beginning to seem perfectly natural to go along two or three times a week to teach a deaf girl from another century to read and write. Of course, they never did express it quite like that or they might have started doubting themselves. She was Anne, simply Anne; she was their friend and they loved her dearly. They were so fond of her that they were gradually allowing her to become an extension of that close friendship which had started five years ago when they first sat next to each other in kindergarten. Instead of two of them, now there were three — Rachel, Jo and Anne.

But it was not always easy.

One of the frustrating things about it was that, outside of the tree itself, Anne appeared to have no existence in their world at all. They longed to take her home with them sometimes and share more things with her but they could not. And their respective families seemed so remote, like an ongoing legend which they could only imagine.

"I'd swap my brother for you, Anne," said Jo one afternoon after Mark had been particularly irritating.

Anne frowned. "Swap?"

"Exchange. Give."

Anne's face lit up.

"My sister Kate." And so well did she mime her sister Kate that they could almost see her there, fussing over the set of her lace collar, polishing her betrothal ring against her petticoats and admiring the blue glitter of the stones, delicately tweaking at a raised eyebrow with little grimaces of pain and rehearsing all her coy glances in a hand-held mirror.

Not to be outdone, Jo took the exercise book and drew quite a good caricature of Mark with his exaggerated, gelled hairstyle.

Below it, she printed, HERE IS MY BROTHER MARK. She hesitated, wondering how to turn "He is an arrogant creep" into the sort of words Anne would understand. Finally she added, HE IS PROUD AND FOOLISH.

Anne grinned and reached out for the pencils —

it was her turn. She drew them a picture of Kate in all her betrothal finery, with her stiff high ruff and with an enormous ring on her finger.

HERE IS MY SISTER KATE, she wrote very carefully. She paused. Then she added, SHE IS TOO CUMLY.

Now it was their turn.

"Cumly?"

Anne traced the oval of her face with her fingertip, and simpered.

"Vain?"

Anne shook her head.

"Proud?" It was still not quite right. "Pretty? Attractive? Beautiful?"

Anne nodded vigorously. "Yes, yes."

"But you are very — cumly — too," Rachel protested.

Anne, amazed, blushed and turned away, for no one had ever said that of her.

She stood on tiptoe and examined her reflection in the small round mirror on the wall. Anne? Comely?

Fool she had often been called, and lackwit and sometimes Anne-the-Curst when she railed against that wall of silence which cut her off, not only from other people but even from the sound of her own fury. But comely?

And yet . . .

These days Anne moved with a different step. Even her father had noticed it.

"Why, the child has a little grace after all," he said wonderingly.

And each day she worked at her writing, making the letters wherever she could — with a stick on the bare earth, with chalk on the flagstones, or the dark beams or red bricks of the house — until finally, exasperated, they cut her a quill and found her an old, wine-stained ledger for her scribblings.

Rachel and Joanna were uneasy.

Their spare time was being increasingly gobbled up by activities to do with their new school. Although it wouldn't start for another week or two, the incoming students were invited to come to an orientation day so that they could get to know the layout of the building.

Rachel's mother pinned up the school checklist and ticked off each item as they bought it.

Joanna's mother lost hers and they had a screaming argument about it. "Who cares, anyway?" said Mark. "You don't need half the junk they tell you to get."

They went together to a preterm sale of school uniforms, and Jo's mother, who made stuffed toys for a factory, took in seams and turned up hems so that the things fitted the two girls perfectly.

They had a dress rehearsal.

"Stylish!" sneered Mark.

"Oh, shut up!" said Joanna, but Rachel just giggled.

Jo put her name on the waiting list for the School Drama Club.

Rachel, who already played the recorder in a music group, signed up for flute lessons.

It was scary but exciting, waiting for the beginning of the new term.

But Anne . . .

What was going to happen when school did start and they could get to the park only on weekends?

They tried talking to her about it but they could not get her to understand. School? That was only for boys. Rachel and Joanna imagined things must have been very different in Elizabethan times but they didn't really know.

And you grew up more quickly then, they supposed.

They thought about Kate, who was only fifteen and soon to be married. There were times when, compared with Anne, they felt like children.

# chapter ten

Anne wondered if they were still her friends, for they had come less frequently of late. And even when they were sitting beside her in the tree, they seemed . . . different.

For in the last few days, they had begun to take on a sort of transparency — almost as if they were ghosts. She did not want them to be ghosts; she refused to believe that they were. Ghosts did not have red hair tied up in bunches. Ghosts did not blush. And you could not play games with a ghost, or giggle so much that you nearly fell out of the tree. Oh, Anne knew what ghosts were like. They had skulls instead of heads and they scared people.

Rachel and Jo did not frighten her. They were real. They were her friends and she wanted to stay with them. If she could have chosen, she would have stayed with them forever.

She loved them so much.

And since their appearance, on that magical afternoon, her life had changed and she had no desire for it to change back. She was no longer prepared to be the family lackwit, the poor imbecile, the fool.

She was no fool — she knew that now.

She could write her name. She could read letters.

She was Anne.

Hopefully, she ran her fingers over the sapling oak. At last, she felt the girls calling her, "Anne . . . Anne . . . Where are you? Come out and play." But now the call was so weak that she could scarcely feel it.

And the space through which she looked to find her two friends was no longer clear but like a muddy pool and, even when she passed over it, things still appeared as blurred and smudged as a mummers' painted scenecloth after a rain. Even the thick, solid branch on which she was sitting felt light and insubstantial, as if it had been made out of paste and gauze.

The others had noticed the difference, too.

"Oh, Anne," said Joanna, squinting, "you've gone all funny."

Well, so had they, but Anne did not want to think about it. For the faces of her two friends had already begun to drift and melt, like reflections in troubled water, but they were still there and that was all that mattered.

And she had so many things to tell them. She took a deep breath; she had been holding her news all morning and now she could say it.

"Kitlings," she announced proudly. Earlier that day, she had come across Meg's new babies stumbling around blindly in the yellow straw of the barn.

But the girls did not seem to understand.

After she had said the word over and over again she lost patience with them, so she reached for a pen and drew a mother cat with five tiny cats sitting beside her in a row.

"Oh, kittens!" they shrieked.

And Anne vanished.

She could feel herself going and she was furious.

She had spent only minutes with them. It wasn't fair. She panicked and grabbed at things — branches, twigs, leaves, even — but it was like grasping at air.

Anne was gone.

She had stayed for such a short time. They hadn't even started her lesson. What was wrong? Had they said something to upset her?

For about ten minutes, Rachel and Joanna sat there numbly, refusing to believe that Anne would not, at any moment, reappear, with some incomprehensible explanation, even though she had never done such a thing before. They tried calling her again, screwing up their faces with concentration, but there was no response. They had always known when she was coming because of the feeling of tension, the slight tingling in the air around them. Now there was nothing. Nothing at all.

At last they gave up. And there seemed to be no point in hanging around, so they packed their things and climbed down.

All the way home they kept asking each other if it had been something they had said or something they had done. Was it because they had not understood her funny word for kittens? Was she offended? Had they hurt her feelings by being simply two more people who couldn't understand what she was trying to say?

"Perhaps it was just too much for her," said Joanna.

"But she was learning so quickly!"

"Look," said Jo. "Let's leave it for a week. Give her time to digest it all — I mean, imagine learning to read and write at our age. It must be a bit of a shock."

* * *

It was over.

Anne knew it.

She had always known that the fairies' gift was bound to wear thin and been aware that the time she was allowed to spend in that enchanted place was limited. But now, suddenly, there was no time left and she knew that she would never see Rachel and Joanna again.

She began to cry. It had been a cruel jest to offer her the things she wanted most, only to snatch them away. She kicked at the sapling. Who wanted a sapling? She wanted the big tree. She wanted her friends.

And the very thought of going back to the house appalled her. She would never go back. She would stay here, in the woods. She would become an outlaw or a wild woman.

When it grew late, Katherine said, "But where is Anne?"

They searched the house, the garden, the barns and the byres but there was no sign of her.

At last, in desperation, they began to look for her in the fringes of the forest.

They did not have to look far.

There she was, lying under a young tree, clutching at handfuls of nothing at all and sobbing her heart out. Her mind, they could clearly see, had gone at last. She had finally lost even the modest half a wit with which they had so grudgingly credited her. Mistress Latymer thought of the lunatics in the Bedlam Hospital and shuddered. Not that, she thought. She is, after all, my daughter, my own child.

They pulled Anne to her feet and tried to talk some sense into her, but she would have none of it. Crying like a baby, she fought them, tugging at Kate's hair and pushing her mother away. And all the time she was babbling, in that strange, animal tongue out of which they could sometimes pick the odd word or two, some nonsense about a Jo and a Rachel. But there was no Joseph in Finchley village and the only Rachel was a wanton wench and no fit company for Anne.

Inside the house she broke free, but when she found that they had locked the doors, she hid herself in a store cupboard.

"Nay, let her be," said Mistress Latymer. "Let her cool her heels and her passions. In quiet her reason may be restored."

"A sound whipping might restore it faster," muttered one of the hired women, for it was well known in the village that Philip Latymer was far too mild when it came to family discipline.

And down in the kitchen, they shook their heads in despair.

"The maid has a devil in her," they said. "Far better if she had never been born."

* * *

Joanna and Rachel spent a great deal of the following week preparing Anne's next lesson.

This time, they considered very carefully how much they should teach her, and how long each lesson should be. And they resolved to try even harder to understand all the things she was saying, for each of them knew how awful it felt not to be understood.

They also resolved not to get too excited or to giggle when she was with them.

Maybe Anne was not used to that sort of thing.

For a whole day, Anne lay with her face turned to the wall, saying nothing and scarcely moving, as if she were grieving for someone lost.

They had sometimes seen young widows in this sort of state, but never a child.

And Katherine and Mistress Latymer picked armfuls of rosemary and pulled up garlic bulbs and hung them in bunches around her bed, so that the heavy curtains began to smell more of the kitchen than a bedchamber. And they brought in a priest to help them pray. They prayed that the evil spirits which had so clearly possessed her should depart, for she was not too young to be hanged as a witch and, in their own, odd way, they were fond of her.

The herbs were effective and the prayers were heard.

Anne recovered.

But after that, they kept a careful watch over her, not letting her stray far from the house, for who could say what evil she might have met with in the forest?

One day, her mother found her making letters in the old ledger. She was amazed at Anne's bold penstrokes.

"If you must write, then you shall!" she declared with sudden determination. "There are those who would say I am half-crazed myself to do it and I don't know who will teach you, but we will find you a tutor. And praise the Lord you have a little wit."

On the following Monday, Joanna and Rachel went back to the tree with their collection of books and pens and pencils and all their good intentions.

They climbed up to the attic branch and waited.

They waited for a long time, but nothing happened. There was no feeling of being watched, no tingling in the air, nothing. Nothing but the hum of distant traffic and the yelling of little kids playing.

"Let's concentrate, then," said Jo at last. "Let's start calling her like we used to."

So they each closed their eyes and thought about Anne. They thought about her pale face and her dark, frightened eyes. They remembered her thin, nervous fingers shyly twisting a loop of fabric in her long skirt. And they remembered her smile, and her funny, funny voice.

Come out, Anne, they thought. Come out. Come out and play with us. We love you . . .

But when they opened their eyes, all they could see were flakes of blue sky between brown-scalloped, rustling oak leaves. Sunlight suddenly flickered silver and, for a moment, they were convinced that something was happening, but nothing did.

They tried again and again, with increasing hopelessness; they did not really expect her to come, and she did not.

Toward the end of the afternoon, they felt the lower branches of the tree shaking violently. Anne . . . it had to be. They waited, crossing their fingers and holding their breath.

At last, two grubby faces appeared through the leaves.

"Get out of our tree," shouted one of the boys, "or we'll bash you!"

And without another word, they left.

# chapter eleven

They found her a teacher, and life, for Anne, slowly changed.

For even if she could not say words properly, she could write them. Best of all, she liked writing her own name — ANNE — and decorating it with squiggles and flourishes. And she insisted on cutting the quills herself, picking out the very best goose feathers and carefully slitting and shaping the ends.

When her family noticed this unexpected eagerness for learning, they offered her, out of curiosity, more. Secretly, they were beginning to feel quite proud of Anne. She was becoming almost an asset — and a performing pet was, after all, easier to live with than a gibbering idiot. They set her to sew and embroider with the women, who exclaimed (to Anne's fury!) at every stitch she placed accurately upon the linen. Her father, not to be outdone, tried teaching her to add figures together, then found to his amazement that, for Anne, two and two quite clearly made four. By the end of that year she could even pick out one or two mistakes in his accounts, for Philip Latymer was no mathematician. Soon he began deliberately seeking out the quiet company of this once-rejected daughter; things just seemed to come out right when Anne was around.

Now when people made jests about her daughter's speech, Mistress Latymer would chide them.

"My Anne makes more sense than many I could name in this household," she would retort.

And she began to boast of Anne's prowess to the women.

"Anne's no fool," she would declare proudly. "She can read and write with the best of them. . . . Of course," she would take good care to add, "it is only to be expected: she comes of excellent stock . . ."

Rachel and Joanna went on trying.

They tried the next day and the day after that, closing their eyes and concentrating, calling Anne, Anne . . . but nothing happened.

Nothing ever happened and they began to feel a bit silly. The whole thing was becoming a bore. Anyway, the holidays were nearly over and there were more important things to be thinking about, like the big, slightly scary new school. Perhaps it had all been nothing but a summer fantasy that had run away with them.

Just before school started, Rachel organized her things and tidied up her room. When she came across the alphabet book, she threw it into the dustbin and the picture books she dumped in a bag to take back to the thrift shop.

One day, Anne decided to make herself a sampler.

And why not, said her mother.

A waste of money, some of the women muttered. Materials were expensive and it was family wealth squandered on the whims of a poor fool — she should be well content with the scraps and remnants she was given. But these days, Mistress Latymer listened to no one.

The linen was purchased and set up on a small frame, and Anne's mother showed her how to catch it to the webbing so that it could be stretched. She picked out the silks. Yellow, the child had asked for, and brown, holding a marigold against a scrap of brown velvet, to show them exactly what she wanted. And scarlet and mauve.

And a fine waste of money it was turning out to be, whatever Mistress Latymer might say to the contrary. The women could see quite clearly that Anne's head was still stuffed full of sick fancies, for no beast, neither heraldic nor natural, could possibly be as distorted as the creature she was making. And besides, no one with any understanding of how such things were done would ruin the symmetry of the piece by extending the neck of the beast up into the neat bands of stitch-patterns and the little garlands of flowers.

But Anne did not give a fig for what they thought. She was making it for herself.

The women watched, with benevolent amusement, as the design grew. The animal's face, for instance, with the grin of a man, could only, surely, have grown out of a fevered imagination. The child had even drawn in her own name — such wanton pride! — and was carefully filling in the letters with small satin stitches. In short, it was not the least like anyone else's sampler, but then, what could you expect of a child like Anne?

Anne took great pains over the words, lovingly making each letter. Her friends would be proud of her, she thought wistfully.

She missed them . . .

Many times, when people were looking the other way, she had sneaked out to the forest. She wanted, at least, to thank them.

But each time, the sapling remained a sapling, no matter how much she willed it to grow, and the only big, old trees were the ones that had always been there. And already they were beginning to seem like a dream, the two girls in the tree, but it was a dream much too precious to lose. She wanted to hold it in some way, preserve it for herself forever.

The work was nearly finished. There was just enough room.

Standing at the embroidery frame, she stitched in the two small figures in their blue stockings, with the tiny tree beside them. And above them, all brown-spotted and glorious in yellow, straddled the wonderful Giraf animal, pushing its neck boldly into the flowers, and smiling, as she remembered it smiling in the bestiary.

Now it was told.

# chapter twelve

It was an icy afternoon in mid-February. Outside in the street, the bare branches of the plane trees were dangling their dark, frozen fruit against a cold blue sky.

Inside the museum, Rachel had dutifully covered three pages of her notebook with notes and sketches and now she was restless. One or two people were fooling around; others had gone wandering off in search of soda, snacks, postcards or restrooms.

Down behind the last display case, Joanna was doodling over the project title, INVESTIGATING HISTORY — illuminating it with orange and pink felt-tips. She sighed. What a boring teacher! What a boring afternoon! What a boring way to spend a couple of hours in the middle of town. She considered, for a moment, investigating the windows of the tantalizing shops up the road, but Miss

O'Connor had said four o'clock at the main entrance and there simply wasn't enough time.

These days, the two girls did not see nearly as much of each other. Ever since Jo had been given a tiny, walk-on part in the school play, she had become totally hooked on acting, and Rachel, with a secret crush on someone in the Junior Orchestra, kept staying behind for extra flute practice.

Last summer was a half-forgotten dream — something to do with leaving elementary school, something to do with a childhood they were both outgrowing.

Joanna, restless, decided to wander.

On her way out, she spotted Rachel.

"Want to go for a soda?" asked Jo.

"No chance." Rachel pointed at a plastic-wrapped scroll sticking out of her bag. "No money. I bought one of those posters."

"Oh, well," said Jo. "In that case I'll find the Costume Court and look at some clothes."

"You would. I'll come with you."

They turned right and wandered vaguely up the main staircase.

"This where it is?"

"What?"

"The Costume Court, stupid."

"I'm not sure," said Jo. "I lost my map."

"You can borrow mine."

This irritated Jo and she immediately changed the subject.

"What's down there?"

"Let's find out."

It was pottery, which was a bore, but farther along and around a corner there were little rooms they could look into, each one furnished in the style of a different century.

"Look at that chair!"

"Imagine living in a place like that."

They lingered over the Elizabethan room with its heavily curtained bed.

"Imagine sleeping in that thing — you'd get nightmares."

But Jo was staring at the portrait that hung above the linen chest.

"Maybe she . . ." She stopped herself quickly. "She's got problems," she said loudly, moving away to point at a shiny porcelain nymph with yellow hair and a sorrowful expression.

"What sort of problems?"

"Spare tire — look! And look at her stomach." There was no one watching so she ran her finger over the cold curve. "Needs a good diet!"

They began to giggle.

A uniformed attendant appeared unexpectedly from around the corner — a solemn young man built like a wrestler.

Joanna grabbed Rachel's arm.

"Quick!" she whispered. "Up there."

They clattered up the stairs. It suddenly felt good to be doing something together again, something secret and mildly silly — a little like that old tree game they didn't talk about anymore.

"Yikes!" said Rachel.

"Him Tarzan! Me Jo," muttered Joanna, beating her chest with her fists, and they started giggling again.

They seemed to have the whole place to themselves up there in those dimly lit galleries, where the white glitter of winter sunlight was softened by canvas blinds to a honeyed gold. But soon the silence became too much for them.

Jo started fooling around.

She reared up, waving her arms.

"Me Tarzan!" she announced, leaping about and scratching her armpits. "Watch out! I'm coming to get you!"

It was a perfect place for hide and seek, with its rows and rows of tall wooden frames on polished chests.

Rachel squealed and ran, ducking into one of the aisles.

Joanna waited, listening.

The silence returned.

Then Rachel snorted.

"I heard that," called Joanna.

She started to weave in and out between the aisles, but Rachel had cleverly slipped away and was already creeping up on her from the other side.

Baffled for a moment, Jo began fiddling with the wooden frames.

"Hey, Rache," she said, looking in the wrong direction.

Rachel jumped out at her, grabbing her by the shoulders, "Got you!" she said.

"They come out," said Jo, shaking her off. "Look . . ."

The frames held pieces of embroidery displayed under glass. Jo showed Rachel how each piece could be pulled out by its wooden handle and looked at.

"Oh," said Rachel.

So for a while they amused themselves by browsing through the pieces, dreamily pushing them in and out without really looking at them. The silence closed around them again. Suddenly they wanted to talk in whispers. It was so very peaceful . . . it was as if they had all the time in the world; it was as if the whole museum had become their own private attic.

"Oh, look at these," said Rachel.

Jo read the label.

" 'Sixteenth century.' " She felt excited, which

was funny. Dates, apart from birthdays, did not usually interest her.

"You see?" said Rachel. "So we don't need to look anywhere else, do we?" She had no idea why she had said that.

And at once they began to flip out the frames, one after another, like a huge and heavy pack of cards, aware that they were looking for something, but pretending, all the time, that they were not; giggling nervously and making flippant remarks as if it were still a game.

Samplers. Just bands of white stitches over off-white linen. Well, fine, if you were a needlework teacher. Fine, if you liked that sort of thing, but they did not. Samplers with colored flowers. Well, those were a bit more inspiring. They picked out pansies and honeysuckle, roses and daffodils.

"Funny," said Jo, without thinking, "that the same flowers were around when — "

"When Queen Elizabeth was on the throne?" Rachel said quickly. "Yes, it is, isn't it?"

Samplers with beasts — now, they were more fun. Lions and unicorns, porcupines and rabbits, serpents, dogs and cats, butterflies, and even a caterpillar. But so what? Nice animal pictures you could find in any library. Better ones than these. It was a long time ago, the sixteenth century. It had nothing at all to do with Rachel and Joanna.

"But we still haven't found it," said Rachel.

"Found what?"

"Oh . . ." Rachel went very pink, "I dunno. You know . . ."

After this pointless conversation, they were ready to give up. Then one of the frames caught Jo's attention.

"Wait a minute," she said.

Slowly, she pulled it out.

They looked.

It was quite a small sampler and very worn at the edges, but there was something about it that bothered them, something that did not quite fit.

They read the label. It was difficult to understand.

COLORED SILKS IN SATIN, HOLBEIN, CROSS, BUTTONHOLE, ALGERIAN EYE, RUSSIAN DRAWN AND OVERCAST FILLING STITCHES ON LINEN BASE. A VERY RECENT ACQUISITION AND SOMETHING OF A CURIOSITY. THE GIRAFFE MOTIF WOULD SUGGEST A MUCH LATER PERIOD, BUT THE NAME AND DATE (AGAIN, RARELY FOUND IN SAMPLERS AT THIS TIME) ARE UNDOUBTEDLY GENUINE.

A giraffe.

They had not immediately recognized the faded yellow and brown animal in the center of the sampler, but now they could clearly see its quite exceptional neck poking incongruously through the uneven bands of roses and violas, and its silly face smiling its ridiculous smile.

THIS EXTRAORDINARY IMAGE, they read, COULD ALMOST HAVE COME OUT OF A MODERN CHILD'S PICTURE BOOK.

"Oh," said Rachel.

"Really," said Joanna.

Then they spotted the two little figures with blue legs, standing beside a tiny tree. And the hair of one had been worked in bright yellow silk and the hair of the other in red.

And across the bottom, with careful stitches, the maker had embroidered her own name.

ANNE LATYMER. AGED ELEVEN.
ANNO DOMINI 1598.

# The Sacred Marriage Rite

# The Sacred Marriage Rite

*Aspects of Faith, Myth, and Ritual in Ancient Sumer*

Samuel Noah Kramer

Bloomington
INDIANA UNIVERSITY PRESS
London

Library of Congress catalog card number: 73-85090
Standard Book Number: 253-35035-2

Published in Canada by Fitzhenry & Whiteside Limited, Don Mills, Ontario, Canada

Manufactured in the United States of America

**To Cyril Gadd**

the *ummia* of London and Ur

# The Patten Foundation

MR. WILL PATTEN of Indianapolis (A.B., Indiana University, 1893) made, in 1931, a gift for the establishment of the Patten Foundation at his Alma Mater. Under the terms of this gift, which became available upon the death of Mr. Patten (May 3, 1936), there is to be chosen each year a Visiting Professor who is to be in residence several weeks during the year. The purpose of this prescription is to provide an opportunity for members and friends of the University to enjoy the privilege and advantage of personal acquaintance with the Visiting Professor. The Visiting Professor for the Patten Foundation in 1968 was

SAMUEL NOAH KRAMER

# Contents

# *Illustrations*

# *Preface*

For close to a century now, the scholarly world has known of an ancient Mesopotamian fertility cult whose major protagonists were the shepherd-king Dumuzi (commonly known as Tammuz from the biblical form of the name), the outstanding prototype of the "Dying God," and his loving spouse Inanna (also known by her Semitic name Ishtar). But until quite recently very little concrete, definite, authentic, and trustworthy data relating to this Dumuzi-Inanna (or Tammuz-Ishtar) cult were available to the cuneiformist, and almost none at all to the anthropologist and historian. It is only now, with the identification, publication, restoration, and translation of a varied assortment of Sumerian literary works inscribed on scores of clay tablets and fragments scattered throughout museums the world over, that it has become possible to present a fairly comprehensive and reasonably reliable account of this cult, and especially its central core, the Sacred Marriage Rite. This book represents a pioneer effort to collect and interpret this Sumerian material for the historian, anthropologist, and humanist.

The first two chapters are introductory; they set the stage for a fuller appreciation of the role of the Sacred Marriage Rite within the framework of Sumerian history, culture, and literary achievement. The third chapter treats the origin and development of the rite: its psychological motivation, historical background, and transformation over the centuries. Chapter four presents translations of the Sumerian poems concerned with the courting and wooing of the sacred couple, as well of those that shed some light on the marriage ceremony itself.

As all these texts reveal, the Sacred Marriage was a jubilant ceremony accompanied by rapturous, ecstatic love-songs of the type collected in the biblical book commonly known as "Solomon's Song of Songs." The fifth chapter sketches the contents of more than a dozen of these Sumerian love lyrics, and points out their resemblance to the biblical book in style, theme, motif, and occasionally even in phraseology.

But love and passion notwithstanding, the marriage of Dumuzi ended in bitter, ironic tragedy, at least as far as Dumuzi was concerned. The first half of the sixth and last chapter presents the full, revised text of one of the most intricate and imaginative Sumerian myths, "Inanna's Descent to the Nether World," a tale that ends with the torture, death, and resurrection of Dumuzi. The second half of the chapter sketches the contents of several additional myths concerned with Dumuzi's tragic death, and concludes with a summary statement of the possible parallels between the Dumuzi myth and the Christ story as told in the gospels.

This book is an expanded version of the Patten lectures delivered at Indiana University during the fall of 1968; were it not for this unique and valued opportunity provided by the Patten Foundation, *The Sacred Marriage Rite* might have had to wait many a year for its preparation and publication.

It is a profound privilege to dedicate this work to my friend and colleague, Cyril Gadd, for many years the Keeper of the Near Eastern and Egyptian collections in the British Museum, the savant or *ummia,* to use the Sumerian word for it, whose researches and publications over the past fifty years have illuminated virtually every aspect of Mesopotamian history and culture. It was while working together on the joint publication of his copies of the Sumerian literary tablets and fragments excavated by Leonard Woolley at Ur that we discovered several pieces inscribed with parts of "Inanna's Descent to the Nether World," the myth that sparked my interest in the Dumuzi-Inanna cult in the first place. One of these tablets provided the long missing denouement of the myth, and thus made possible the revised translation and interpretation presented in the sixth chapter of this book.

Finally, sincere thanks are due to Jane Heimerdinger, Research Assistant in the University Museum, University of Pennsylvania, who helped with the preparation of the manuscript; and to Gertrude Silver, whose nimble fingers completed the typescript in record time.

S.N.K.

# The Sacred Marriage Rite

# 1

## The Sumerians: History, Culture, and Literature

Ancient Sumer is a land roughly identical with the southern half of modern Iraq, from the region of modern Baghdad to the Persian Gulf. It consisted largely of a bleak, wind-swept alluvial plain formed by the silt laid down by the Tigris and Euphrates rivers over the millennia. Its climate is hot and dry, and its soil, if left to itself, is arid and sterile. But with the help of irrigation, the collecting and channeling of the rich silt-laden overflow of the Tigris and Euphrates, it can become immensely fertile and productive; no wonder that most scholars identify it as the biblical Garden of Eden. Here in Sumer flourished man's first high civilization; it had its roots in the dim prehistoric past and in one form or another continued to well-nigh the beginning of the Christian era.

The existence of Sumer and its people, the Sumerians, is entirely a discovery of modern archaeology and scholarship, a kind of unexpected and in some ways disconcerting bonus to historians of man's past. The ancient Hebrews and Greeks knew the land as Babylonia, and its inhabitants as the Semitic-speaking Babylonians; the archaeologists who first began excavating in the region over a century ago were of the same opinion. In the course of the decades, however, as the excavated artifacts and written documents multiplied, it became ever more evident that the Babylonians were not the first settlers in the land, nor its most creative. Preceding them was a people who, according to the written documents, called their land Sumer, and who spoke an agglutinative language that was neither Semitic nor Indo-European.[1] It was the Sumerians who were responsible in large part for one of the most creative eras in the ancient Near East, one fraught with profound significance for the history of civilization as a whole. It was Sumer that saw the rise of man's first urban centers with their rich, complex, and varied life; where political loyalty was no longer to tribe or clan, but to the community at large; where lofty temples and ziggurats rose sky-high, filling the citizen's heart with awe, wonder, and pride; where technological inventiveness, industrial specialization, and commercial enterprise found room to grow and expand. It was in the cities of Sumer that an effective system of writing was first invented and developed, bringing about a revolution in communications that, not unlike the electronic inventions of our own day, had far-reaching, unforeseen, and unexpected effects on man's economic, intellectual, and cultural progress. Sumerian ideas, techniques, and invention were diffused east and west, leaving their mark on virtually all ancient cultures, and to some extent even on that of our own day. The history and culture of this "cradle of civilization"[2] will be very briefly outlined in this chapter.

## *History*[3]

Sumer, or rather the land that came to be known as Sumer during the third millenium B.C.,[4] was first settled about 4500 B.C.[5] The earliest settlers in Sumer, however, were not the Sumerians, but a people known archaeologically as Ubaidians,[6] that is, the settlers responsible for the cultural remains first unearthed in the mound known as Al-Ubaid,[7] and later in the very lowest levels of a number of tells throughout ancient Sumer. These remains consisted of stone implements, such as hoes, adzes, querns, pounders, knives; clay artifacts, such as sickles, bricks, loom-weights, spindle whorls, figurines; and a distinctive, characteristic type of painted pottery. These "Ubaidians," therefore, were enterprising agriculturists who founded a number of villages and towns throughout the land, and developed a rural economy of considerable wealth and stability. They did not, however, long remain the sole and dominant power in ancient Sumer. Immediately to the west of Sumer lies the Syrian desert and the Arabian peninsula, the home of the Semitic nomads from time immemorial. As the "Ubaidian" settlers began to thrive and prosper, some of these Semitic hordes began to infiltrate their settlements both as peaceful immigrants and as warlike conquerors. There are good indications that as a result of the cross-fertilization of the "Ubaidian" and Semitic cultures there came into being the first relatively high civilization in the land, one in which the Semitic element was probably predominant.[8]

The Sumerians, themselves, probably did not arrive in Sumer until the very last quarter of the fourth millennium B.C. Their original home is still quite uncertain. To judge from a cycle of epic tales now in the process of restoration and translation, the early Sumerian rulers seem to have had an unusually close and intimate relationship with Aratta, an as yet unidentified city-state in Iran, to the east of Sumer. The Sumerian language is an agglutinative tongue, and this may point to the general area of the Caspian Sea. But wherever the Sumerians came from, and whatever type of culture they brought with them, this is certain: their arrival led to an extraordinarily fruitful fusion, both ethnic and cultural, with the native population, and brought about a creative spurt fraught with no little significance for the history of civilization. In the centuries that followed, Sumer reached new heights of political power and economic wealth, and produced some of its most significant achievements in the arts and crafts, in monumental architecture, in religious and ethical thought, and in oral myth, epic, and hymn. Above all, the Sumerians, whose language gradually became the prevailing speech of the land, developed a system of writing into an effective tool of communication and took the first steps toward the introduction of formal education.

The first ruler of Sumer whose deeds are recorded, if only in the briefest kind of statement, is a king of Kish by the name of Etana who probably ruled at the very beginning of the third millennium B.C. In a document written centuries later, he is described as "the man who stabilized all the lands." It may thus be inferred that he held sway, not only over Sumer, but over the lands surrounding it—in short, an embryonic empire builder.[9] Probably not very long after Etana, a king by the name of Meskiagsher founded a dynasty at the city of Erech, and extended his rule from the Mediterranean Sea to the Zagros Mountains. His son, Enmerkar, conducted an expedition to the city-state of Aratta, for the purpose of obtaining some of its metal and stone;[10] according to the Sumerian epic poets, its rulers had Sumerian names, it gods had Sumerian names, and its people spoke the Sumerian language. Aratta's importance lay in its metals and stones; it was reputed to be the home of the most skillful stone and metal workers of those days. The fame of Aratta was so widespread in Sumer that the word Aratta came to mean "honored," "celebrated," in the Sumerian language.

One of Enmerkar's heroic heralds and companions-in-arms in the struggle with Aratta was a warrior by the name of Lugalbanda, who succeeded him on the throne of Erech. The victories and conquests of Enmerkar and Lugalbanda sparked the imagination of the Sumerian poets and minstrels to such an extent that a whole cycle of epic tales grew up about them. Four of them have been recovered and restored only quite recently, and at present they are our most important source of historical information for these early days.[11]

By the end of Lugalbanda's reign, however, the power of the city of Erech was seriously threatened by its northern neighbor, the city of Kish. The last ruler but one of the "Etana" dynasty, Enmebaraggesi by name, was not only a successful leader in war but the founder of Sumer's holiest shrine. On the military side he was noted for his defeat of Elam, the land directly to the east of Sumer. As a religious leader, he was the first to build a temple to the Sumerian air-god Enlil, in the city of Nippur. Since Enlil was the chief Sumerian god, the "father of all the gods," Nippur became Sumer's religious, spiritual, and cultural center.

Enmebaraggesi's son, Agga, tried to carry on in his father's footsteps. But by this time, Ur, the biblical Ur of the Chaldees, was ready to take over the rule of Sumer as a whole. Its first king was Mesannepadda, who is said to have ruled eighty years. Mesannepadda and the dynasty which he founded were powerful rulers in firm control of important sources of raw materials outside of Sumer. The tombs of the royal cemetery at Ur, which probably date from this time, were filled to capacity with weapons, tools, vessels, and ornaments fashioned of gold, silver, copper, and semi-precious stones.[12]

Ur did not long remain the capital of Sumer. A short time after the death of Mesannepadda, Erech once again came to the forefront as the leading city of Sumer, this time under the rule of the great Gilgamesh,[13] whose deeds won him such wide renown that he became the supreme hero of Sumerian story and legend. Poems extolling Gilgamesh and his deeds were written and re-written throughout the centuries, not only in Sumerian, but in all the other more important languages of Western Asia. Gilgamesh became the hero par excellence of the ancient world: an adventurous, brave, but tragic figure symbolizing man's constant but hopeless drive for fame, glory, and immortality—so much so, that Gilgamesh has sometimes been taken to be a rather legendary figure who lived long before Mesannepadda of Ur.[14]

The next great "empire builder" concerning whom we have any information is Lugalannemundu, a king of the city of Adab. He is reported to have ruled ninety years, and to have controlled an empire extending from the mountains of Iran to the Mediterannean Sea, and from the ranges of the Taurus to the Persian Gulf.[15] Not long after him, a king of Kish by the name of Mesilim became the dominant ruler of Sumer. According to his own inscriptions he built temples at both Adab and Lagash, far to the south of Kish. In fact Mesilim, who probably ruled some time about the middle of the third millennium B.C., was responsible for the first known case of political arbitration. A bitter border dispute between the two Sumerian city-states Lagash and Umma was brought before him as the overlord of the entire land, and he proceeded to arbitrate the controversy by measuring off what seemed to him a just boundary line between the two cities. He even had an inscribed stele erected to mark the spot and prevent future disputes.[16]

But Sumer's strength was waning. Its cities were exhausting

themselves by their incessant struggle for superiority and control, and soon a Semitic conqueror would appear on the scene. In Sumer's final spurt of power it was the city of Lagash which played a predominant role. One of its rulers, Eannatum by name, actually succeeded in extending the sway of Lagash over Sumer as a whole, and even over several of the neighboring states. His success proved ephemeral, however, and in a short while Lagash was reduced to its former boundaries. The Lagash dynasty is memorable more for its literary achievements than for its military campaigns; its archivists were the first to prepare commemorative inscriptions written in a style which marks them as man's first attempt at history writing.[17]

The last of this Lagash dynasty was a king by the name of Urukagina, noteworthy as man's first known social reformer. According to one of his inscriptions, one in which the word "freedom" appears for the first time in history, he put a limit on the oppressive powers of a greedy bureaucracy, reduced taxes, put a stop to injustice and exploitation, cleared the city of usurers, thieves, and murderers, and took special pains to help the poor, the widow, and the orphan.[18] But like many a reformer of modern days, he seemed to have come too late with too little. In any case, after less than ten years of rule he was overthrown by Lugalzaggesi, the ruler of the neighboring city of Umma, who put much of Lagash to the torch.

Lugalzaggesi claims in his records to have made such extensive conquests east and west of Sumer that fifty princes bowed to his authority.[19] But by this time Semites from the west of Sumer, under one of the more ambitious and capable of their leaders, found it possible to take over the rule of the country and establish a Semitic dynasty. This ruler's name was Sargon, usually referred to as Sargon the Great, because of his extraordinary military and administrative achievements. In the course of his reign of more than half a century, he conquered almost all of western Asia, and perhaps even parts of Ethiopia, Egypt, and Cyprus. He founded a new capital city by the name of Agade,[20] and at least for a time made it the richest and most powerful city in the ancient world. To it, according to later Sumerian historiographers, came the nomadic Martu from the west bringing choice oxen and sheep; to it came the people of Meluhha, "the black land" (probably Ethiopia), with their exotic wares; to it came the Elamite and Subarian from the east and north carrying loads "like load-carrying asses"; to it came all the princes, chieftains, and sheiks of the plains, bringing monthly and yearly gifts.[21]

Upon Sargon's death, two of his sons carried on in his footsteps, and tried with some success to hold on to their father's empire. But his grandson, Naramsin, seemed to have his troubles in Sumer; in any case, for some unknown reason, he destroyed Nippur, Sumer's holy city, and desecrated and plundered Sumer's most sacred shrine, the "House of Enlil." Not long after this he met a crushing defeat at the hands of the Gutians, a semibarbaric people which inhabited the mountains of Iran. Sumer was overrun and laid waste, and all communication by land and sea was made impossible. Agade itself was completely destroyed and never restored; according to Sumerian tradition it was a city forever cursed.[22]

Thus, in less than a century, the mighty empire of Sumer, which held out such brilliant promise in the days of its Semitic ruler Sargon, came to an abrupt and catastrophic end. It took the Sumerians several generations to recover from the blow. Toward the end of the Gutian terror, the city of Lagash once again came to the fore, particularly under an extraordinarily pious governor by the name of Gudea. A score of inscribed statues of this ruler, originally set up in the temples of Lagash and unearthed by the French excavators, have made Gudea's the Sumerian face best known to the modern world. The Gudea "cylinders," about 60 centimeters in height, and covered from beginning to end with two of the longest Sumerian hymns as yet known, provided a new insight into the range and scope of Sumerian religious literature. The source and extent of Gudea's political power are not known, but his inscriptions indicate that he had at least trade contacts in virtually the entire ancient world. He obtained gold from Anatolia and Egypt, silver from the Taurus, cedars from the Amanus, copper from the Zagros ranges, diorite from Ethiopia, and timber from Dilmun (which may turn out to be India).[23]

Not long after Gudea's rule over Lagash, when the Sumerians freed themselves altogether from the Gutian yoke, a struggle for power broke out between Lagash and Ur for the control of Sumer. Victory went to Ur-Nammu, the king of Ur, who founded a dynasty, the so-called Third Dynasty of Ur. Ur-Nammu was not only a successful military man, but a social reformer and lawgiver as well. Only recently part of a law code compiled by his scribes came to light. It tells us that Ur-Nammu removed the "chiselers" and grafters from the land, established and regulated honest weights and measures, and saw to it that "the orphan did not fall a prey to the wealthy," that "the widow did not fall a prey to the powerful," that "the man of one shekel [that is, the poor] did not fall a prey to the man of sixty shekels [that is, the rich]." Three of the laws found in Ur-Nammu's code are of very special importance for the history of man's moral standards. They lay down the rule that in cases where one man has done bodily injury to another, the guilty party is punished by a fine. Thus as early in history as King Ur-Nammu, almost a thousand years before the Hebrew lawgiver Moses, the barbarous law of "eye for eye" and "tooth for tooth" had already given way to the more humane approach in which a money fine was substituted as a punishment.[24]

Ur-Nammu's son Shulgi was a skillful diplomat as well as a successful soldier. Throughout his reign Sumer continued to prosper and dominate at least some of the lands around it. But hordes of Semitic nomads by the name of Amurru, the biblical Amorites, kept streaming in from the Arabian desert to the west and in the course of time made themselves masters of some of the more important cities, such as Isin, Larsa, and Babylon. In Ur itself, Semitic political power and influence seem to have been in the ascendancy; two of Shulgi's successors bore Semitic names though they were the lineal descendants of the Sumerian founder of the dynasty. In any case the Elamites to the east took advantage of the growing Semitic strength, and the political discord and confusion which presumably resulted from it. They attacked and captured Ur, and carried off its last king, Ibbi-Sin, into captivity.[25]

During the two and a half centuries following the fall of Ur, there was a bitter intercity struggle for dominance and control of Sumer and Akkad, first between the cities of Isin and Larsa, and then between Larsa and Babylon. Finally in the year 1720 B.C., or thereabout, Hammurabi of Babylon defeated Rim-Sin, the last king of Larsa, and emerged as the sole ruler of a united Sumer and Akkad. This date may be said to mark the end of ancient Sumer. By this time the Sumerian people, that is, the people who had spoken the Sumerian language, were practically extinct, and the Semites were in complete control. The kings were all Semites and the spoken language was the Semitic Akkadian. To be sure, the culture as a whole, was predominantly Sumerian in form and content. Not only that, the schools and academies of Sumer and Akkad continued to utilize the Sumerian language and the Sumerian literature as the fundamental basis of their entire curriculum. The vast majority of Sumerian literary works are known not from originals going back to the date of their composition, but from copies prepared, presumably by Semites, during the first four centuries of the second millennium B.C.[26]

## *Social, Political, and Economic Features*

Sumerian civilization was essentially urban in character, though it rested on an agricultural rather than an industrial base. Sumer, in the third millennium B.C., consisted of a dozen or so city-states, each having a large and usually walled city, surrounded by suburban villages and hamlets. The outstanding feature of each city was the main temple situated on a high terrace, which gradually developed into a massive stage tower, a ziggurat, Sumer's most characteristic contribution to religious architecture. The temple usually consisted of a rectangular central shrine or cella, surrounded on its long sides by a number of rooms for the use of the priests. In the cella there was a niche for the god's statue, fronted by an offering table made of mud brick. The temple was built largely of mud bricks, and since these are unattractive in texture and color, the Sumerian architects beautified the walls by means of regularly spaced buttresses and recesses. They also introduced the mud-brick column and half-column, and covered them with colored patterns of zigzags, lozenges, and triangles, by inserting thousands of painted clay cones into the thick mud plaster. Sometimes the inner walls of the shrine were painted with frescoes of human and animal figures, as well as a varied assortment of geometrical motifs.[27]

The temple was the largest, highest, and most important building in the city, in accordance with the theory current among the Sumerian religious leaders that the entire city belonged to its main god, to whom it had been assigned on the day the world was created. In practice, however, the temple corporation owned only some of the land, which it rented out to sharecroppers; the remainder was the private property of the individual citizens. Political power lay originally in the hands of these free citizens and a city governor known as *ensi* who was no more than a peer among peers. In case of decisions vital to the city as a whole, these free citizens met in a bicameral assembly consisting of an upper house of "elders" and a lower house of "men." As the struggle between the city-states grew more violent and bitter, and as the pressures from the barbaric peoples to the east and west of Sumer increased, military leadership became a pressing need, and the king, or as he was known in Sumerian, the "big man," came to the fore. At first he was probably selected and appointed by the assembly at a critical moment for a specific military task. But gradually kingship with all its privileges and prerogatives became a hereditary institution, and was considered the very hallmark of civilization. The kings established a regular army, with the chariot, the ancient "tank," as the main offensive weapon, and a heavily armored infantry which attacked in phalanx formation. Sumer's victories and conquests were due largely to this superiority in military weapons, tactics, organization, and leadership. In the course of time, therefore, the palace began to rival the temple in wealth and influence, and by the end of the third millennium the king had become the sole and absolute ruler of the land.

Still, it is worth stressing, a Sumerian sovereign was no arbitrary despot, no cruel and capricious tyrant; a king such as Shulgi, for example, was fully aware that he was only the vicar and representative of the gods, and responsible to them for the well-being and prosperity of the land and its people. The priests and poets constantly reminded him, in their hymns of glorification and celebration, that he was especially selected by the gods, who had transferred to him some of their divine power and understanding, for no other reason than "to give good guidance to Sumer"; "to let the people of Sumer and Akkad refresh themselves under his shade"; "to supply them with abundant food to eat, and sweet water to drink." He was the divinely guided monarch "whose kingship brought joy to man," "whose shepherdship brought happiness," who saw to it "that the people increased and multiplied" and "that all lands lived in peace."[28]

First and foremost, it was the sacred, patriotic duty of the king to defend the land from enemy attacks, and to extend its territory, domination, and influence. This meant, of course, warfare and all that goes with it: the raising and organizing of armies, leadership in battle, a knowledge of military strategy and tactics, as well as an appreciation of the value of diplomatic ploys of one sort or another.[29]

A far more constructive and productive royal activity was the king's duty to maintain, expand, and improve the irrigation system of the country in order to ensure its prosperity and well-being. Virtually all the kings who have left any records of significance boast of digging new canals and enlarging and repairing the old. Years were often identified and named by these works. Canals, large and small, crisscrossed the land, connecting city with city and town with town. Closely related to this system of communication was the building and repairing of roads and highways throughout the country. Kings prided themselves on keeping the roads in good traveling condition, and Shulgi, who was a speed maniac of sorts—he describes himself as "a fast horse with swinging tail" and as "a nimble, swift traveler over the highways of the land"—exults in building landscaped road-houses (the first motels in recorded history), so that the traveler "from above and below" might spend a refreshing night there.[30]

In the sphere of ethics and morals, it was the king's paramount duty to preserve and promote law and justice in his realm: to see to it that the poor and weak were not oppressed by the mighty and the rich, that the widow and orphan were not victimized, and that the citizen did not suffer at the hands of overbearing and corrupt officials. Kings promulgated regulations, edicts, moratoria, and law codes in order to make the people aware of their legal rights, and thus help prevent the miscarriage of justice. Law, and written law in particular,[31] is undoubtedly one of Mesopotamia's supreme contributions to the ethos and character of civilized life.[32]

While temple administrators and palace officials played a large role in the social and economic life of the country, the great majority of its inhabitants were productive citizens: farmers and cattle breeders, boatmen and fishermen, merchants and scribes, doctors and architects, masons and carpenters, smiths, jewelers and potters. There were of course a number of rich and powerful families who owned large estates. But even the poor managed to own farms and gardens, houses and cattle. The more industrious of the artisans and craftsmen sold their handmade products in the free town market, receiving payment either in kind or in "money," which was normally a disk or ring of silver of standard weight. Traveling merchants carried on a thriving trade from city to city and with surrounding states by land and sea, and not a few of these merchants were probably private individuals rather than temple or palace representatives.[33]

While the majority of the inhabitants of Sumer were free citizens, slavery was a recognized institution, and temples, palaces, and rich estates owned slaves and exploited them for their own benefit. Many slaves were prisoners of war and these were not necessarily foreigners, but could be fellow Sumerians from a neighboring city defeated in battle. Sumerian slaves were recruited in other ways. Freemen might be reduced to slavery as a punishment for certain offenses. Parents could sell their children as slaves in time of need, or a man might turn over his entire family to creditors in payment of a debt, although for no longer than three years. The slave was the property of his master, like any other chattel. He could be branded and flogged, and was severely punished if he attempted to escape. On the other hand it was to his master's advantage that his slave stay strong and healthy, and slaves were therefore usually well treated. They even had certain legal rights: they could engage in business, borrow money, and buy their freedom. If a slave, male or female, married a free person, the children were free. The sale price of a slave varied with the market and the individual involved; an average price for a grown man was twenty shekels, which was at times less than the price of an ass.[34]

The basic unit of Sumerian society was, as with us, the family, whose members were knit closely together by love, respect, and mutual obligations. Marriage was arranged by the parents, and the betrothal was legally recognized as soon as the groom presented a bridal gift to the father; it was often consummated with a contract inscribed on a tablet. While marriage was thus reduced to a practical arrangement, there is some evidence that surreptitious premarital lovemaking was not altogether unknown.[35] The woman in Sumer had certain important legal rights: she could hold property, engage in business, and qualify as a witness. But the husband could divorce her on relatively light grounds, and if she had no children, he could marry a second wife. Children were under the absolute authority of their parents, who could disinherit them, or even sell them into slavery. But in the normal course of events they were dearly loved and cherished, and at the parents' death inherited all their property. Adopted children were not uncommon, and these, too, were treated with utmost care and consideration.[36]

There is no way of estimating with exactness the population of Sumerian cities, since there was no official census, or at least no traces of one have as yet been found. Probably the number of people varied anywhere from ten to fifty thousand. The city streets were narrow, winding, and irregular, with high blank house walls on either side. They were unpaved and undrained, and all traffic was either on foot or donkey. The average Sumerian house was a small one-story, mud-brick structure consisting of several rooms grouped around an open court. The well-to-do Sumerian, on the other hand, probably lived in a two-story house of about a dozen rooms, built of brick, plastered and whitewashed inside and out. The ground floor consisted of a reception room, kitchen, lavatory, servants' quarters, and sometimes even a private chapel. For furniture there were low tables, high-backed chairs, and beds with wooden frames. Household vessels were made of clay, stone, copper, and bronze, and baskets and chests were made of reed and wood. Floors and walls were adorned with reed mats, skin rugs, and woolen hangings.[37]

Below the house there was often located the mausoleum where

the family dead were buried, although there were also special cemeteries outside the cities. The Sumerians believed that the souls of the dead traveled to the Nether World, and that there life continued more or less as on earth, though in an emasculated form. They therefore buried with the dead their pots, tools, weapons, and jewels. In the case of kings they sometimes even buried with them some of their courtiers, servants, and attendants, as well as their chariots and the animals which pulled them.[38]

On the technological side, some of Sumer's most far-reaching achievements revolved about irrigation and agriculture. The construction of an intricate system of canals, dykes, weirs, and reservoirs demanded considerable engineering knowledge and skill. Surveys and plans were prepared which involved the use of leveling instruments, measuring rods, drawing, and mapping. For mathematical and arithmetical purposes, a sexagesimal system of numbers was utilized featuring a valuable place notation device not unlike our own decimal system. Measures of length, area, capacity, and weight were standardized. Farming, too, had become a complicated, methodical technique requiring foresight, diligence, and skill. A recently translated Sumerian essay, a veritable "Farmer's Almanac," records a series of instructions and directions for the farmer from the first step to the last, from the watering of the field to the winnowing of the harvested crops. Sumerian craftsmen were skilled in metallurgy; in the processes of fulling, bleaching, and dyeing; and in the preparation of paints, pigments, cosmetics, and perfumes. Pharmacology, too, made no little progress. From a "prescription" tablet recently reinterpreted we learn that the Sumerian physician made use of quite an assortment of botanical, zoological, and mineralogical samples for his materia medica, as well as a number of elaborate chemical operations and procedures.[39]

## *Philosophy, Ethics, and Religion*[40]

On the intellectual and spiritual level the Sumerian thinkers and sages evolved a cosmology and theology which became the basic creed and dogma of the entire Near East. From the fact that the sea and water surround the universe on all sides, they concluded that the primeval sea existed from the beginning of time and was a kind of "first cause" and "prime mover." In this primeval sea was engendered the universe, consisting of a vaulted heaven superimposed over a flat earth and united with it. In between, separating heaven from earth, was the moving and expanding atmosphere. Out of this atmosphere were fashioned the luminous bodies: the moon, planets, and stars. Following the separation of heaven and earth and the creation of the light-giving astral bodies, animal and human life came into existence.

This universe, they believed, was under the charge of a pantheon consisting of a group of living beings, manlike in form but superhuman and immortal, who, though invisible to mortal eye, guide and control the cosmos in accordance with well-laid plans and duly prescribed laws. There were gods in charge of heaven, earth, air, and sea; sun, moon, and planets; wind, storm, and tempest; river, mountain, and plain; city and state; field, farm, and irrigation ditch. The leading deities of this pantheon were the four creating gods, in control of the four major components of the cosmos: heaven, earth, air, and sea; their Sumerian names were An, Ki, Enlil, and Enki. Their creating techniques consisted in the use of the divine word; all the creating deity had to do was to lay his plans, utter the word, and pronounce the name. To keep the cosmic entities and cultural phenomena, once created, operating continuously and harmoniously, without conflict and confusion, they devised the *me,* a set of universal and unchangeable rules and laws which had to be obeyed willy-nilly by everybody and everything.

As for man, the Sumerian thinkers, in line with their world view, had no exaggerated confidence in man and his destiny. They were firmly convinced that man was fashioned of clay and created for one purpose only: to serve the gods by supplying them with food, drink, and shelter, so that they might have full leisure for their divine activities. Life, they believed, is beset with uncertainty and haunted by insecurity, since man does not know beforehand the destiny decreed for him by the unpredictable gods. But in spite of this it was preferable to death by far, since in death the emasculated spirit descends to the dark, dreary Nether World, where "life" is but a dismal and wretched reflection of earthly existence.

On the ethical side, the Sumerians claimed to cherish goodness and truth, law and order, justice and freedom, righteousness and straightforwardness, mercy and compassion, and to abhor their opposites. The gods, too, preferred the ethical and moral to the unethical and immoral. Still, in their inscrutable way they created sin and evil, suffering and misfortune. The proper course for a Sumerian Job to pursue was not to argue and complain but to plead and wail, to lament and confess his inevitable sins and failings to his special personal god, his "good angel" as it were, through whom he would find his salvation.

While private devotion and personal piety were important religious acts, the public rites and rituals played the more prominent role in Sumerian religion. The center of the cult was the temple, its priests, priestesses, singers, musicians, eunuchs, castrates, and hierodules. Here sacrifices consisting of animal and vegetable fats, and libations of water, beer, and wine, were offered daily. In addition there were new-moon feasts and other monthly celebrations. Most important was the prolonged New Year celebration culminating in some cases in the hieros-gamos ceremony, when the reigning monarch married Inanna, the goddess of procreation and fertility, or one of her special devotees as her surrogate. The king thus became symbolically identified with Dumuzi, the biblical Tammuz, an early king who according to Sumerian legend lived as Inanna's husband.[41]

## *The Arts*[42]

The Sumerians were particularly noted for their skill in sculpture. The earliest sculptors were abstract and impressionistic. Their temple statues show great emotional and spiritual intensity, rather than skill in modeling. This came gradually, however, and the later sculptors were technically superior, although their images lost in inspiration and vigor. Sumerian sculptors were quite skillful in carving figures on steles and plaques and even on vases and bowls. From these sculptures we learn a good deal about Sumerian appearance and dress.

Some men were clean shaven; others wore long beards and long hair parted in the middle. The most common form of dress was a kind of flounced skirt, over which long cloaks of felt were sometimes worn. Later the chiton, or long shirt, took the place of the flounced skirt. Covering the shirt was a big, edge-fringed shawl, carried over the left shoulder and leaving the right arm free. Women often wore dresses which looked like long tufted shawls covering them from head to foot, leaving only the right shoulder bare. Hair was usually parted in the middle and braided into a heavy pigtail which was then wound around the head. They often wore elaborate headdresses consisting of hair ribbons, beads, and pendants.

Music, both instrumental and vocal, played a large role in Sumerian life, and some of the musicians were important figures in temple and court. Beautifully constructed harps and lyres were excavated in the royal tombs of Ur. Percussive instruments such as the drum and tambourine were also common, as were pipes of reed and metal. Poetry and song flourished in the Sumerian schools. Most of the recovered works were prepared for use in the temple and palace. But there is every reason to believe that music, song, and dance were a major source of entertainment in the home and market place.[43]

One of the most original art contributions of the Sumerians was the cylinder seal, a small cylinder of stone, engraved with a design which became clear and meaningful when rolled over a clay tablet or the clay sealing of a jar. The cylinder seal became a sort of Mesopotamian trademark, although its use penetrated Anatolia, Egypt, Cyprus, and Greece. The Sumerian artists were highly ingenious in devising suitable designs, especially when the seal was first invented. The earliest cylinder seals are carefully incised gems depicting such scenes as the king on the battlefield, the shepherd defending his cattle against wild beasts; rows of animals, or fairy-tale creatures and monsters. Later the designs became more decorative and formalized. Finally one design became predominant, almost to the exclustion of all others: the "presentation" scene in which a worshiper is presented to a god by his "good angel."[44]

## *Writing, Literature, and Education*

Probably the most important Sumerian contribution to civilization was the development of the cuneiform, or wedge-shaped, system of writing; without it the cultural progress of both the ancient and modern world would have been much slower. The script began as a series of pictographic signs devised by temple administrators and priests for the purpose of keeping track of the temple's resources and activities. At first it was therefore used for the simplest administrative notations only. But in the course of the centuries the Sumerian scribes and teachers so modified and molded the script that it lost its pictographic character and became a purely phonetic system of writing in which each sign stood for one or more syllables. Clay tablets inscribed in cuneiform by means of a reed stylus have been excavated by the tens of thousands in the ancient buried cities of Sumer, and are now found in museums the world over.[45] More than ninety per cent of these tablets are economic, legal, and administrative documents, not unlike the commercial and government records of our own day. But some five thousand tablets and fragments have been found inscribed with Sumerian literature, consisting of myths and epic tales, hymns and lamentations, proverbs, fables, and essays. Quantitatively speaking, the Sumerian literary works surpassed by far other much later compilations such as the Iliad and Odyssey, the Rig-Veda, and the poetic books of the Bible. Most scholars, including myself, would agree that qualitatively they are inferior to the Greek and Hebrew classics in sensibility, perception, profundity, and artistry, although this view might have to be modified in the course of time, as the Sumerian texts come to be better understood and lose some of the strangeness that veils them from the mind and heart of the modern reader. In any case, it is no exaggeration to say that the discovery, restoration, and translation of the Sumerian literary documents have turned out to be a major contribution of modern scholarship to the humanities.[46]

One direct outgrowth of the invention of the cuneiform system of writing was the introduction and development of the Sumerian system of education. The main goal of the Sumerian school was "professional"; it aimed to train scribes, secretaries, and administrative personnel, much like our business schools. But in the course of its growth and development, and particularly as a result of its ever-widening curriculum, the Sumerian school came to be the center of culture and learning. Within its walls flourished the scholar, the "scientist," the writer of poetry and prose. Its head was known as the "school father"; his assistant was "the big brother"; the pupil was the "school-son." Other members of the faculty were, for example, "the man in charge of the whip," "the man in charge of drawing," and "the man in charge of Sumerian." Teachers were poorly paid; although the students all came from well-to-do families, the tuition fee was probably small.

Once the first steps in cuneiform writing had been passed, the curriculum consisted of copying and memorizing "textbooks" containing long lists of words and phrases, including names of trees, animals, birds, insects, countries, cities, villages, stones, and minerals. The Sumerian schoolmen prepared a large and diverse assortment of mathematical tables and problems, as well as some Sumero-Akkadian dictionaries. On the literary side, pupils studied and copied the varied assortment of poetic narratives, hymns, and essays which for one reason or another had met with acceptance and approval throughout the land. School discipline was harsh and severe; there was no sparing of the rod. Most of the graduates probably became scribes in the employ of the palace, temple, and rich estates. But there were those who devoted their lives to teaching and learning, the academicians as it were, who, not unlike their modern counterparts, seem to have been treated with an ambivalent mixture of respect and contempt.[47]

Sumerian education and character, to judge from several essays recently pieced together, was deeply colored by a psychological drive for superiority and preeminence, for prestige and renown. Indeed the Sumerians, not unlike the Hebrews of a later day, considered themselves as a "chosen people," a rather special and hallowed community in more intimate contact with the gods than was the rest of mankind. Nevertheless they had a high regard for humanity as a whole, so much so that the Sumerian word for mankind, like the English counterpart, "humanity," came to mean "humaneness," that is, conduct worthy of humans. They even had a moving vision of man living in peace and security, united by a universal faith and by a universal language. But unlike the Hebrew prophets and modern idealists, they never came to the idea of turning their vision into a starry Utopia. The Sumerian thinking man cherished the past, clung to the present, and longed to be remembered in the future. But he had no vision of human progress and betterment, and the dreams and hopes that go with it.

# 2

# The Poetry of Sumer: Repetition, Parallelism, Epithet, Simile

Sumerian written poetry—and the vast majority of the Sumerian literary works were composed in poetic form—has its roots in the pre-literate and illiterate court minstrel and in the temple singer-musician;[1] it is no wonder, therefore, that repetition, the aesthetic device common to the ballad-monger and folk-singer, was one of its predominant stylistic features.[2] The earliest Sumerian poetic compositions can be dated back to the twenty-fifth century B.C.; one of the outstanding examples is a myth inscribed on a solid clay cylinder inscribed with twenty columns of text.[3] Very little Sumerian literary material has as yet been excavated from the centuries that followed,[4] except for one long magnificent hymn composed about 2100 B.C., which was dedicated to the rebuilding of the temple Eninnu in the city of Lagash. This remarkable document, consisting of at least two parts,[5] is inscribed on two clay cylinders divided into fifty-four columns containing close to fourteen hundred spaces of text; because the protagonist of this hymnal composition is the wise and pious *ensi* of Lagash, Gudea, the two cylinders are commonly known as Gudea Cylinders A and B. Although the literary style of the temple poet who composed it tends to be rather inflated and diffuse, this rich multifaceted hymn is

The Gudea Cylinders (now in the Louvre), inscribed about 2100 B.C. with one of the literary masterpieces of the ancient world.

undoubtedly one of the literary masterpieces of the ancient world; its contents are of prime significance not only for the history of literature, but for various aspects of Sumerian culture: religion, art and architecture, ethics and morals, even for commerce and trade.[6] From the point of view of style, it makes use of virtually all the aesthetic techniques that characterize Sumerian prosody throughout the centuries, and may therefore serve as an instructive and comprehensive example of the Sumerian poetic genius. Here is a translation of approximately the first third of the Gudea Cylinder A:

> When fate was being decreed over heaven and earth,
> He raised the head of Lagash heavenwards in accordance with the great *me,*
> Enlil gazed with a friendly eye upon the lord Ningirsu,
> Brought into being what was vital to the city in accordance with the *me*.[7]
>
> The heart overflowed its banks towards it,
> The heart of Enlil overflowed its banks towards it,
> The heart overflowed its banks towards it,
> The flood-waters shined forth towards it, the majestic,
> The heart of Enlil, the Tigris River, brought sweet water to it.[8]
>
> The temple—its king [Ningirsu]* said:
> "Of the Eninnu, he will make preeminent its *me* on heaven and earth."[9]
>
> The *ensi* [Gudea] being a man of understanding, gives ear,
> Performs great things there,
> Directs thither perfect oxen, perfect rams,
> Lifted head to the blessed brick,
> Braced himself for the building of the house.[10]
>
> His king, that day, in a vision of the night,
> Gudea having beheld him—Ningirsu,
> Of the house, its building he [Ningirsu] commanded him,
> Of the Eninnu, its great *me,* the good, he showed him.[11]

*Words enclosed in brackets are not in the text, but are supplied (and at times restored) to help clarify the meaning.

Gudea—his [Ningirsu's] meaning being distant—
Murmurs at the word:
"Come now, I will tell it to her, I will tell it to her,
May she stand by me in this matter.
On me, the shepherd, a princely command has been directed,
I know not its meaning.
I will bring my dream to my mother,
May my interpretress, knowledgeable in her calling,
My Nanshe, the sister of Sirara-shumta,
Propound its meaning to me.[12]

He set foot in his *magur*-boat,
Directed the boat to his city Nina at the Ninagen Canal,
Sails [ ?] along with the new [ ?] canal in transports of joy.
After he had reached the Bagara, the house stretching along the new
[ ?] canal,
He brought bread-offerings, poured cold water,
Stepped up to the king of the Bagara [Ningirsu], offered a prayer to
him:[13]

"Hero, rampant lion who has no rival,
Ningirsu, mighty in the Abzu,
Who brings security to Nippur,
Hero, you have given me a command,
I would carry it out faithfully,
Ningirsu, I would build you your house,
I would carry out for you the *me* to perfection.
May your sister, the daughter born in Eridu,
Dependable in her calling,
The Lady, the interpretess of the gods,
My Nanshe, the sister of Sirara-shumta,
Show me its path."[14]

His cry was heard,
His king—his offerings and prayers,
The lord Ningirsu accepted of Gudea,
He [Gudea] celebrated the *eshesh*-feast in the house of Bagara,
The *ensi* stepped up to the house of Gatumdug, at her sleeping place,
He brought bread-offerings, poured cold water,
Stepped up to the holy Gatumdug, addressed a prayer to her:[15]

"My Lady, daughter born of An,
Dependable in her calling,
Goddess who lives head high in the land,
Who knows the needs of her city,
You, the Lady, the mother who founded Lagash,
When you have cast your eye upon the land, there is rain and overflow,
When you have cast your eye upon the man, life is long for him.

"I am one who has no mother, you are my mother,
I am one who has no father, you are my father,
You have taken my seed into the womb, have given birth to me in the shrine.

"My Gatumdug, wise and good,
You lay down by me at night,
You are my large sword, clinging to my side,
You are . . .,
You have given me the breath of life,
You who are a broad cover,
Let me refresh myself in your shade,
May you cast upon me, Gatumdug, the noble palm [ ? ] of your lofty hand.

"I am going to the city, may your omen be favorable,
To Nina, the hillock rising out of the water,
May your kindly genie go before me,
May your kindly guardian-angel go behind me.
Come, now, I will tell it to her, I will tell it to her,
May she stand by me in this matter,
I will bring my dream to my mother,
May my interpretress, knowledgeable in her calling,
My Nanshe, the sister of Sirara-shumta,
Propound its meaning to me."[16]

His cry was heard,
His Lady—his offerings and prayers
The holy Gatumdug accepted of Gudea.
He set forth in his *magur*-boat
Moored the boat at his city Nina by the Quay of Nina,
The *ensi* lifted the head heavenward in the courtyard of Sirara-shumta,
He brought bread-offerings, poured cold water,
Stepped up to Nanshe, offered a prayer to her:[17]

"Nanshe, Lordly Lady, Lady of the precious *me,*
Lady who like Enlil decrees the fates,
My Nanshe whose command is enduring, eternal,
You, the interpretress of the gods,
You, the Lady of the lands, the mother of visions [ ?], dreams:

"In [my] dream—a man,
Like heaven his tremendous size, like earth his tremendous size;
He—a god by his head,
An *Imdugud*-bird by his wings,
A Flood-demon by his lower limbs,
To his right and left lions crouch—
Gave me the command to build his house,
I know not his meaning.

"The sun rose for me out of the horizon,
A woman—who is she not! who is she!
She made . . . on the head,
Held a tablet reed of shining silver in the hand,
Placed a star-tablet on the knee,
Takes counsel with it.

"Next, a hero—
He crooked the arm, held a lapis lazuli block,
Of the house, he draws its plan on it.

"Before me a holy basket was planted,
A holy brickmold was set straight,
The brick of fate was placed in the brickmold for me,
In the cultivated *ildag*-bush planted before me,
The *tibu*-birds keep twittering away,
A noble donkey-foal, the 'right hand' of my king, was pawing the ground impatiently."[18]

To the *ensi,* his mother Nanshe gives answer:
"My shepherd, I, your dream I will interpret:
The man tremendous as heaven, tremendous as earth,
A god by his head,
An *Imdugud*-bird by his wings,
A Flood-demon by his lower limbs,
To his right and left lions crouch—
This is surely my brother Ningirsu,
He has commanded you to build his shrine Eninnu.

"The sun that rose for you out of the horizon, is your god Ningishzida,
Like the sun he rose for you out of the horizon.
The maid who made . . . on the head,
Held a tablet reed of shining silver in the hand,
Placed a star-tablet on the knee,
Takes counsel with it—
This is surely my sister Nidaba,
To build the house in accordance with the holy stars,
She has called you.

"Next, a hero—
He crooked the arm, held a lapis lazuli block—
This is Nindub drawing the plan of the house on it.

"The holy basket planted before you,
The holy brickmold set straight,
The brick of fate placed in the brickmold—
This is surely the enduring brickwork of Eninnu.

"In the cultivated *ildag*-bush planted before you,
The *tibu*-birds keep twittering away—
During the building of the house, sweet sleep will not come to your eyes.

"The noble donkey-foal, the right hand of your king, was pawing the ground impatiently,
That is you, like a noble donkey-foal you will paw the ground by the Eninnu."[19]

Having finished the interpretation of the dream, the goddess of her own accord continues with some friendly advice for Gudea: he should bring gifts of weapons to the gift-loving Ningirsu, who was also noted as a god of war; he should bring them into the temple accompanied by the god's famous lyre, *Ushumgal-kalamma;* his heart thus soothed, the god will disclose to him more fully the plan of his house, and bestir himself for him:

"I would instruct you, take my instruction:
Direct your step to Girsu, the forehead of Lagash,
Remove the seal of your storehouse, take out timber,
Fashion a chariot for your king,

Hitch the noble donkey-foal to it,
Adorn that chariot with shining silver and lapis lazuli.
Like the sun, bring forth the arrows from the quiver,
Construct with care the *ankara*-weapon, the might of heroship,
Fashion his beloved standard for him, inscribe your name on it.

"With his beloved lyre, *Ushumgal-kalamma,*
His resonant instrument, far-famed, oracular,
Before the hero who loves gifts,
Your king, the lord Ningirsu,
Enter the Eninnu-imdugud-babbar.
He will accept your lowly word as a noble word,
The lord, his heart distant as heaven,
[The heart] of Ningirsu, the son of Enlil, will be soothed for you,
He will disclose to you all the plans of his house,
The hero whose *me* are great
Will give you a hand with it."[20]

Gudea, according to our poet, carries out Nanshe's instructions item by item to the last detail:

The faithful shepherd, Gudea,
He knows much, brings about much,
Bowed the head to the word that Nanshe spoke to him,
He removed the seal of the storehouse, took out timber. . . .[21]

One of the more poetic passages in the hymn concerns a sign or omen that Gudea requests from Ningirsu, since he still feels that he does not fully understand the god's purpose. It begins with Ningirsu's stepping up to Gudea, who had laid himself down to sleep in order to receive the god's omen in a vision:

Then to the sleeping one, to the sleeping one,
He [Ningirsu] stepped up by [his] hand, touched [his] feet:

"You who will build it for me, you who will build it for me,
*Ensi,* you who will build the house for me,
Gudea, let me give you the sign for the building of my house,
Let me tell you of my rites in accordance with the holy heaven-stars.

"My house, my Eninnu, founded by An,
Whose *me* are great *me,* greater than all *me,*
The house whose king lifts distant eyes,

At whose cry, like the *Imdugud*-bird, the heavens quake,
Whose fierce majesty reaches heaven.
My house, its great terror overwhelms all the lands,
In its name all the lands gather from heaven's bounds,
Magan and Meluhha descend to it from their mountains."[22]

The god then proceeds to expand on his vast powers, on the special names bestowed upon him by the great gods An and Enlil, on his important role as one who "directs the judgment of the city," and closes his address with a promise of prosperity and well-being for the people of Lagash in these ringing words:

"When on my house, the house foremost in all the lands,
The right arm of Lagash,
That roars like the *Imdugud*-bird in the heavenly orb,
The Eninnu, my royal house,
Faithful shepherd, Gudea, you lay a faithful-hand for me—
[Then] will I call to heaven for rain,
Overflow will descend to you from heaven,
The people will thrive in overflow.

"With the founding of my house, overflow will come,
The large fields will grow high for you,
The canals will flood their banks for you,
In the hillocks to which water rose not,
Water will rise up for you,
Sumer will pour out much oil for you,
Will weigh out much wool for you.

"The day you fill up my terrace,
My house—the day you lay a faithful hand on it,
To the mountain where the North Wind dwells,
I, having set my foot,
The man of immense strength, the North Wind,
From the mountain, the pure place,
Will blow the wind straight towards you.

"[Because] I will have given the breath of life to the people,
One man will do the work of more than two men,
During the night, the light of the moon will shine forth for you,
During the day, the bright [?] sun will shine forth for you,
The house will be built for you during the day,
It will be raised high during the night.

"From below, the *hulub*-tree, the refreshing [ ? ],
Will be brought up to you,
From above, the cedar, the cypress, the *zabalum*-tree
Will be brought to you with ease,
From the land of the oak,
Oak will be brought for you,
In the land of the *na*-stone, the large *na*-stone of the mountain,
Will be cut up into slabs for you.

"On that day, fire will have touched your arm,
You will know my sign."[23]

Gudea awakes from his sleep, and now that he has the god's sign, he proceeds to purify the city physically and spiritually, or, as the poet puts it in words that are quite revealing of the breach between the ethical ideals of the ancient Sumerians and their day-to-day practices:

Gudea arose, it was a sleep,
He trembled, it was a vision.
He bowed the head to the word spoken by Ningirsu,
He examines an all-white kid,
The kid he examined—his omen is favorable,
To Gudea, the meaning of Ningirsu,
Came forth like the sun.

He knows much, brings about much,
The *ensi* instructed his city like one man,
Makes one the heart of Lagash like the sons of one mother.
He planted trees, tore out thorns,
Ripped out weeds, turned back complaints,
Turned back evil to its house,
Removed the tongue of whip and cane,
Put in its place the wool of the mother-sheep.

The mother spoke not against her son,
The son contradicted not the mother,
The slave who did wrong,
His master beat him not on the head,
The slave-girl, the captive [ ? ], who worked mischief,
Her mistress struck her not on the face.

To the *ensi* building the house,
To Gudea no one brought any complaints,
The *ensi* purified the city, cleansed it with fire,
The unclean, the bully, the *gian* he sent out of the city.[24]

This remarkable temple hymn was actually inscribed on the Gudea Cylinders as early as 2100 B.C. The century or more that followed is commonly known as the Sumerian Renaissance, an era when, there is every reason to believe, Sumerian literature flourished as never before. Sad to say, it is one of the ironies of archaeological fate that almost no Sumerian literary material from this creative period has as yet been excavated. But fortunately, many of the literary works composed during this era were copied, redacted, studied, and imitated in the schools of Sumer that flourished in the following centuries, and many of these have been excavated in several of the more important Sumerian cities. As a result, there are now available some twenty myths, nine epic tales, over one hundred hymns and hymnal prayers, about twenty lyric songs, and another twenty or so of lamentations—all in all more than twenty thousand lines of Sumerian poetry.[25]

As is clear from the hymn inscribed on the Gudea Cylinders, the Sumerian poets knew nothing of rhyme and meter; their main stylistic devices were repetition, parallelism, epithet, and simile. Myth, hymn, lyric, lament—all exploit them in one way or another. But it is in epic poetry that we find them utilized with superior skill and imagination. Take, for example, the epic tale "Gilgamesh and Agga," concerned with the power struggle between a king of Kish by the name of Agga and the heroic Gilgamesh, the ruler of Erech. The poet sets the scene with a terse, matter-of-fact four-line statement of how the struggle began!

The envoys of Agga, the son of Enmebaraggesi,
Proceeded from Kish to Gilgamesh of Erech,
The lord Gilgamesh before the elders of his city,
Put the matter, seeks out the word.

It is only the rhythmic parallelism of the two halves of the last line that lends a poetic touch to the passage. Contrast this with the passage immediately following, which also consists of four lines:

"To complete the wells, to complete all the wells of the land,
To complete the wells, the small 'bowls' of the land,
To dig the wells, to complete the fastening ropes—
Let us not submit to the house of Kish, let us smite it with weapons."

While the full implications of the first three lines are obscure—it seems to contain an obliquely expressed, capsule-like summation of a demand by Agga that the Erechites perform corveé labor for Kish—the manner in which the author gets his poetic effect is clear enough: the repetition of the two halves of the first line, except for the addition of several words in the second half; the combined repetition-parallelism of the second line as related to the first; the parallelism of the third line with the two preceding. The fourth and closing line, on the other hand, stands by itself and is unrelated to the three preceding ones; it does, however, utilize an inner parallelism of its two halves similar to that of the last line of the first passage.

In spite of Gilgamesh's exhortation to fight for their freedom, the elders of Erech would rather yield to Kish and enjoy peace. To underline the contrasting opinions of Gilgamesh and the elders effectively, the poet has the elders repeat Gilgamesh's words verbatim, except for the last line, where they use the positive for Gilgamesh's negative, and the negative for his positive, thus:

The convened assembly of the elders of his city answer Gilgamesh:
"To complete the wells, to complete all the wells of the land,
To complete the wells, the small 'bowls' of the land,
To dig the wells, to complete the fastening ropes—
Let us submit to the house of Kish, let us not smite it with weapons."

But Gilgamesh is disappointed with the reply of the elders, and so, our poet tells us:

Gilgamesh, the lord of Kullab,
Who put his reliance on Inanna,
Took not the words of the elders of his city to heart.

This brief narrative statement, poetically flavored with an epithet and descriptive phrase, is followed by a passage that repeats once again Agga's harsh demands and Gilgamesh's incitement to war, except that this time he is addressing the young, fighting men of the city who, presumably, would be more responsive to his heroic stance:

Next, Gilgamesh, the lord of Kullab, before the young men of his city,
Put the matter, seeks out the word:
"To complete the wells, to complete all the wells of the land,
To complete the wells, the small 'bowls' of the land,
To dig the wells, to complete the fastening ropes,
Do not submit to the house of Kish, let us smite it with weapons."[26]

The reply of the young men is highly poetic; the poet makes use of the oblique allusive statement, of contrasting and cumulative parallelism, of repetition, epithets, and descriptive phrases, of the exclamatory line:

The convened assembly of the young men of his city answer Gilgamesh:
"Of those who stand, of those who sit,
Of those who have been raised with the sons of kings,
Of those who press the donkey's thigh,
Who of them, has spirit![27]
Do not submit to the house of Kish, let us smite it with weapons.

"Erech, the handiwork of the gods,
Eanna, the house ascending to heaven—
It is the great gods who have fashioned its parts—
Its great walls touching the clouds,
Its lofty dwelling place established by An,
You have cared for, you king and hero.

"Conqueror, prince beloved of An,
Who should fear his [Agga's] coming!
The army is small, its rear totters,
Its men hold not high their eyes."

As expected, Gilgamesh is more than pleased with this response:

Then, Gilgamesh, the lord of Kullab,
At the words of the young men of his city,
His heart rejoiced, his spirit brightened.[28]

Let us turn now to another epic poem, "Gilgamesh and the Land of the Living." Concerned primarily with man's fear of death and its sublimation in an obsessive quest for an immortal name, it is quite different in mood and temper from "Gilgamesh and Agga," though the stylistic devices are essentially the same. The poet begins with a typical two-line repetition in which the second line is identical with the first, except for the introduction of the hero's name:

The lord set his mind toward the Land of the Living,[29]
The lord Gilgamesh set his mind toward the Land of the Living.

His mind made up, Gilgamesh tells his faithful servant Enkidu of his decision in these allusive, touching, and stirring lines:

"Enkidu, brick and stamp have not yet brought forth the fated end,[30]
I would enter the Land, would set up my name,
In its place where names have been raised up, I would raise up my name,[31]
In its places where names have not been raised up, I would raise up the name of the gods."

To this speech, constructed of relatively long, ponderous clauses, Enkidu responds in terse phrases that weave a rather intricate repetition pattern:

"My master, if you would enter the Land, inform Utu,
Inform Utu, the valiant Utu,
The Land, it is Utu's charge,
The land of the felled cedar, it is valiant Utu's charge,
Inform Utu."

Gilgamesh accepts his advice, or as the poet puts it in typical lines of parallelism and repetition:

Gilgamesh laid his hands on an all-white kid,
Pressed to his breast a speckled kid as an offering,
Placed in his hand the silver scepter of his command,
Says to the heavenly Utu:
"Utu, I would enter the Land, be my ally,
I would enter the land of felled cedar, be my ally."

But Utu is rather skeptical and mistrustful of his intentions, and Gilgamesh finds it necessary to be more explicit and persuasive. He therefore addresses the god in a bitter, poignant, forceful speech that exploits several of the more effective devices in the poetic arsenal: two parallel introductory lines, the first of which omits a self-evident verb; five lines of terse, laconic narrative, the first two of which parallel each other very closely; the insertion of a pithy proverb to enhance the force of his argument; the repetition of his moving speech to Enkidu in which he had stated his reasons for journeying to the Land of Living, in enigmatic riddle-like phrases:

"Utu, a word I would speak to you, to my word your ear!
I would have it reach you, give ear to it!
In the city man dies, oppressed is the heart,
Man perishes, heavy is the heart.
I peered over the wall,
Saw the dead bodies floating in the river's waters,
As for me, I too, will be served thus, verily it is so!
Man, the tallest, cannot reach to heaven,
Man, the widest, cannot cover the earth.
Brick and stamp have not yet brought forth the fated end,
I would enter the Land, would set up my name,
In its places where the names have been raised up, I would raise up my name,
In its places where the names have not been raised up, I would raise up the names of the gods."

This time Utu is impressed with Gilgamesh's plea, and "like a man of mercy, he showed him mercy." The hero now proceeds to mobilize his city in order to pick fifty volunteers, unattached men who have neither mother nor family, or, as the poet puts it in a rhythmic weaving of repetition and parallelism, including the striking omission of a verb in four of the lines:

Who felled the cedar, was overjoyed,
The lord Gilgamesh was overjoyed,
Mobilized his city like one man,
Mustered [its men] like twin companions:

"Who has a house, to his house!
Who has a mother, to his mother!
Let single males who would do as I do stand at my side."

Who had a house, to his house!
Who had a mother, to his mother!
Single males who would do as he did, fifty, stood at side.

Gilgamesh now has weapons of bronze and wood prepared for himself and his companions, and they set out for the Land of the Living. They cross seven mountains, and it is not until they have crossed the seventh that Gilgamesh finds "the cedar of his heart." He cuts it down and has his men bundle up the wood to carry back triumphantly to his city Erech. But watching from the distance is the monster Huwawa, the guardian of the cedars, who casts a heavy magic sleep on the hero. The companions, anxious and apprehensive, try to wake him with rhythmic, tender, beseeching phrases, including a rare example of nature imagery:

He touches him, he rises not,[32]
He speaks to him, he answers not,
"Who are asleep, who are asleep,
Gilgamesh, lord, son of Kullab,
How long will you sleep!

"The land has become dark, it is full of shadows,
Dusk has brought forth its [dim] light,
Utu has gone forth with lifted head to his mother Ningal,[33]
Gilgamesh, how long will you sleep!

"Let not the sons of your city who have accompanied you,
Stand waiting for you at the foot of the mountain;
Let not the mother who gave birth to you,
Be driven off to the city's square."

Gilgamesh rouses himself, covers himself "with his wood of heroism like a garment," raises himself "on the great earth like a bull," and swears by his divine father and mother that he will not return to his city until he has vanquished Huwawa, be he man or god. But his servant Enkidu is full of fear, and in a passage noted particularly for its contrasting parallel lines, the poet has him try to stop his master from pursuing his hazardous course:

"My master, you who have not seen that fellow, are not terror-stricken,
I who have seen that fellow, am terror-stricken.
The warrior, his teeth are a dragon's teeth,
His face is a lion's face,
His roar is the onrushing flood-water,
From his canebrake-devouring forehead none escape.

"My master, journey you to the Land,
I will journey to the city,
Will tell your mother of your glory,
Let her squeal with laughter,
Then will tell her of your death,
Let her shed bitter tears."

Gilgamesh's reply is a stirring obliquely worded allusive speech, that could hardly fail to reassure the faltering Enkidu:

"For me another will not die,
The loaded boat will not sink,
The three-ply cloth will not be cut,
On the wall no one will be overwhelmed,
House and hut, fire will not destroy,
Do you but help me, I will help you,
What can happen to us!

"After it had sunk, after it had sunk,
After the *Magan*-boat had sunk,[34]
After the boat 'Might of Magilum' had sunk,
All the living dwell in the 'boat of the living.'

"Come, let us go forward, we will cast eyes upon him!
If when we go forward,
There be fear, there be fear, turn it back!
There be terror, there be terror, turn it back!"[35]

In the three compositions selected to illustrate the Sumerian poetic techniques, the simile was only rarely represented, at least in the parts cited. However, to judge from a recently prepared survey of more than a score of compositions representing virtually every Sumerian literary genre, the Sumerian poets did make considerable use of the simile.[36] And though the comparisons they favored are not especially imaginative or profound, they do reflect a measure of sensitivity and sensibility relative to the natural and animal world as well as to man and his handiwork. In any case, as the following detailed analysis will show, they are revealing for Sumerian culture and character.[37]

The cosmic spheres and entities represented in Sumerian imagery are heaven and earth, moon, sun, and stars. Heaven appealed to the Sumerian poets primarily because of its height and distance: Nippur, Sumer's holy city, is "as lofty as heaven"; the height of the goddess Inanna "is like heaven"; a king who has suffered misfortune complains that "his good omen is as far away as heaven." Heaven's beauty also impressed the poets: Nippur is described as "beautiful within and without like heaven."

Like the height of heaven, the width of the earth lent itself to ready comparison: the goddess Inanna was not only "as high as heaven" but also "as wide as the earth." The earth was also thought of as eternal, hence the rituals of the Ekur, Sumer's holiest temple, were "as everlasting as the earth." The sea, on the other hand, seems to have been used rather sparingly in Sumerian imagery; there was not a single example of sea simile in the texts surveyed.

Height, as expected, is also in the imagery of the moon: mountains, for example, "are as high as the moon in the upper sky." But it was the beauty of its light that appealed most to the poets: the goddess Inanna "shines forth like the moonlight," she is filled with beauty like the "rising moonlight." Light, too, is naturally the most attractive feature of the sun: kings boast of "coming forth like the sun, the light of the land"; temples are adorned with "splendid horns like the sun coming forth from his sleeping chamber." But since the sun is the god in charge of justice, according to the Sumerian theologians, kings boast of making "just decisions like Utu [the sun-god]."

In contrast to the light of the moon and sun, it was the dimness of dusk that served for poetic comparison. The depth of the downfall of the Ekishnugal, the great temple of the moon-god at Ur, is graphically depicted with the help of the two contrasting similes: formerly, in its heyday, it "had filled the land like sunlight," but now "it has become as dim as dusk." On the other hand, since dusk is the time of the golden sunset, it is depicted as "going to its house with blood-filled face." As for the stars, it was their permanence rather than their twinkling that seemed to impress the poets, hence the prayer that Ur "should not come to an end, like a star."

Turning to weather phenomena, it is not surprising to find that the leading place was given to Mesopotamia's major affliction, the flood-storm, the Near East counterpart of our hurricane and tornado. Fierce winds destroy cities "like a flood-storm"; the vengeful Inanna attacks again and again in battle "like the all-attacking storm"; when the gods decreed the destruction of Ur, they sent a deluge that "roared like a great storm over the earth, who could escape it!"

A weaker relative of the storm is the "torrent," the "gushing forth high waters": the fierce winds cannot be restrained, like torrents; the cruel Elamites destroyed Ur and "trampled it like a torrent"; the oldest counterpart of our "torrent of words" is found in an epic tale where it is said "he [the ruler] spoke to his herald from where he sat, like a torrent."

The imagery evoked by rain was that of plenitude and copiousness: kings boast of pouring out libations of strong drink "like rain gushing from heaven," and on a more sombre note, the arrows of the enemy fill the bodies of the people of Ur "like heavy rain." Since rain sinks into the earth and does not return to heaven from which it came, the poet curses the storm that attacked Ur with the words: "it should not return to its place, like rain from heaven." As for water, sad to say, kings boast that their weapons "made flow the blood of the people like water," and when Ur was destroyed "famine filled the city like water, there was no respite from it."

The obvious and widespread image of flashing lightning had its Sumerian counterpart in such royal boasts as "arrows flash before me like lightning," or "I am one who flashes in battle like lightning"; a hero eager to return to his city as speedily as possible says "I would rise like a flame, flash like lightning." The flame not only rises, it also trembles; hence the plea: "On the anguished heart that you have made tremble like a flame, cast a friendly eye."

In the realm of nature, the mountain, high and pure, played a large role in Sumerian imagery: cities are made "pure as a mountain"; temples are built in pure places "like a rising mountain"; city walls reach heaven "like a mountain." But there was also the mined mountain whose cuts and gashes evoked an image of ruin and destruction; hence an evil king is depicted as forging mighty axes in order to turn the Ekur into dust "like a mountain mined for silver," and to cut it to pieces "like a mountain of lapis lazuli." Rivers rarely served as images; in the material surveyed we find only two river similes, and these rather forced and colorless: the gates of a city are said to open their mouths "like the Tigris emptying its waters into the sea"; the rivers of an unfortunate city were without water "like rivers cursed by Enki."

Vegetation, as expected in a basically agricultural country, is well represented in Sumerian imagery. The tree most popular with the poets was the cedar: a king is said to be "a good shade [for the land] like a cedar"; incense is heaped up "like a fragrant cedar forest." The date palm, and especially the date palm of Dilmun, was highly prized; a king is cherished "like a date palm of Dilmun." But since virtually every part of the date palm was broken up and utilized in one way or another, one poet was moved to lament that the "heavenly throne," as well as the temple's choice oxen and sheep, were "cut to pieces like date palms." The boxwood impressed the poets with its luxuriance and height: a temple is said to be "luxuriant like the boxwood", or to wear a crown "like the boxwood." The as yet unidentified *mes*-tree was noted for its fruit: a king is "a wondrous sight like a fertile *mes*-tree adorned with fruit"; the holy storeroom of a temple is piled high with fruit "like a *mes*-tree." The *ildag*-tree on the other hand was remarkable for its strength; a king is depicted "as vigorous as a mature *ildag*-tree planted by the water-course."

Though the reed of Mesopotamia was put to many practical uses, it evoked a sombre, melancholy mood in the poetic imagination: the city Ur in its travail "droops its head like a solitary reed"; a solitary, drooping reed in a dream is interpreted as a "drooping of the head" in anticipation of a death; the reed pipe was the musical instrument played on sad funereal occasions; reed rushes evoked images of tearing and plucking, as did also the easily plucked crunched leek, in spite of its value as a staple food.

The major source of imagery for the Sumerian poets was the animal kingdom. The lion and wolf provided such stereotype similes as the king's inspiring terror "like a lion," or leaping forward "like a lion"; raging waters destroy a boat by "devouring" its bow "like a wolf" and striking at its stern "like a lion"; a herald springing forward on his mission is "like a wolf pursuing a kid."

The wild ox, or mountain bull, was a high favorite with the Sumerian poets: shrines raise their shining horns over Sumer "like a wild ox"; kings are thick of neck "like a wild ox"; the city Ur in its heyday was "a great wild ox that steps forth confidently, secure in its strength." But powerful though he was, there seemed to be Sumerian "cowboys" who had no difficulty in throwing him by means of a nose-rope: Gilgamesh, for example, ties a nose-rope to the monster Huwawa "like a captured wild ox"; statues are hurled to the ground by nose-ropes "like captured wild oxen."

Unlike the wild ox, the wild cow is rarely used in the similes; the only one found in the texts surveyed is the rather ambiguous "he [the herald] turned on his thigh like a wild cow," presumably to deliver his message posthaste. The clumsiness of the elephant is used for comparison in the proverb "you are [the kind of man] who climbs on a sinking boat like an elephant." The gazelle, in spite of its speed, was readily trapped, and therefore evoked an image of utter defeat; hence the vanquished people of Ur "bit the dust like a gazelle caught in a trap"; or a conqueror traps the enemy "like a gazelle in the thicket." The mountain goat rather than the gazelle served as an image for speed; a king boasts that "like a mountain goat hurrying to its shelter," he arrived at his temple at great speed. As for the snake, its imagery relates to such obvious characteristics as crawling, slithering, and spitting forth venom.

Turning to domestic animals, we find the bull, or ox, like his wild ancestor, a great favorite in the imagery of poets: his bellowing roar was suggested by the voices of rulers, the busy bustle of temple life, the utterance of oracles—no wonder that the sound boxes of Sumerian lyres frequently terminate in the head of a bull. The image of the firm-standing bull appears in such similes as "He [Gilgamesh] stood on the great earth like a bull"; "the hero whom I lean on like a bull." But firmness can be carried to the point of obstinacy, hence the Sumerian counterpart of our "bullheaded" in the proverb "You are one who like a bull knows not how to turn back." Angered, the bull becomes violent, hence "to attack like a bull." At the end of the day's work he heads straight for home, hence the poet's plea to the goddess who had abandoned her city to return "like an ox to your stall, like a sheep to your fold." So, too, the fish, for whom a special house, a kind of ancient aquarium, had been built, is urged to enter "like an ox to your stall, like a sheep to your fold."

The ox who is not permitted by a miserly peasant to eat any of the grain he threshed was used as an image for the frustrated man: "He is a man deceived like an ox escaping from the threshing floor." Oxen belonging to important bureaucrats were allowed to wander freely in the streets, hence "You wander about in the street like the ox of a *shabra.*" A Sumerian poet laments that Ur "the city of lordship and kingship, built on pure ground," was doomed "to be thrown in a trice by the nose-rope, to be fastened neck to earth, like a bull." The pathos of the thrown bull is revealed in the bitter words of a deity whose city has been destroyed: "Like a fallen bull, I cannot rise up from your wall."

The cow, unlike the bull, failed to inspire the poetic imagination. Of the two similes found in the texts surveyed, one relates to compassion: a goddess, distressed at the suffering of her city, prostrates herself "like a cow for her calf"; the other characterizes a man given to illusion and fantasy: "Like a barren cow you keep on searching for your non-existing calf." Ewes are images of fecundity, hence the oft repeated simile "as numerous as ewes." Deprived of their lambs, they served as a melancholy image for a city whose people have been led away into captivity by the enemy: "Oh my city like an innocent ewe, your lamb has been torn from you." They were readily scattered: the people of a city in distress are as "scattered ewes."

The image of the heavily loaded donkey, the burden carrier of the ancient world, prompted the obvious simile for peoples bringing to a city "all sorts of goods like a laden donkey." The stubborness of the donkey is alluded to in "Into a plague-stricken city he has to be driven like a rebellious donkey"; its stupidity is envisaged in the proverb: "I will not marry a wife who is [only] three years old, like a donkey." The poets also knew of wild donkeys, "donkeys of the steppe," and pedigreed "noble donkey-foals," all of which evoked images of speed on journeys made by heralds or travel-minded kings.

The dog and his character and way of life evoked a congeries of images that are of no little cultural and psychological significance: a woman suffering in silence is "like a dog imprisoned in a cage"; a bloodthirsty deity devours dead bodies "like a dog"; a man who stands up for his rights is one "who hates to grovel as if he were a dog." On the other hand, there is the fellow who whelps "like a noble dog beaten by a stick," and the one who has to be admonished not to let himself be mauled by a noble dog "like a bone"; there is also the man who acts high-handedly "like the bitch of a scribe."

The large birds of prey naturally evoked images of fearless flight: a king boasts of rising in flight "like a falcon"; the soul fleeing from the body is "like a falcon flying against a bird." As for the smaller birds, they did not inspire images of "sweet song" in the Sumerian poets, but of terror and mourning: a deity flees her destroyed city "like a flying bird"; a pathetic king is led away captive and "will not return to his city, like a sparrow that has fled its house"; an unfortunate high priestess bemoans her fate. "I was forced to flee the cote like a sparrow"; a husband lamenting the death of his wife moans "like a dove in its hole," thrashes about "like a dove in terror"; a king swings his arms "like a dove hysterically fleeing a snake." Bats evoke a similar imagery: the gods flee before the raging Inanna "like fluttering bats to the clefts"; arrows fly in battle "like flying bats." One bird, the as yet unidentified *gamgam,* provides a rare example of an image for tenderness: a sick hero is said to be fed by his sorrowful friends "like a *gamgam*-fledgling, sitting in its nest."

From the insect world, the locust is repeatedly used as an image of devouring and destruction: the possessions of Ur are devoured as by a "heavy swarm of locusts"; the enemy is made to "eat bitter dust like an all-cowering locust," and is cut down with throw-sticks and slingshots "like a locust." The ant, not unlike the sparrow, dove, and bat, served as an image for terrified men and gods seeking refuge, who scurry into crevices "like ants." Fish evoked the tragic image of death: the life of the people of a destroyed city is carried off "like fish caught by hand," or "like fish writhing for want of water"; its little children are "carried off by the waters like fish."

The imagery of inanimate objects, primarily man's artifacts and handiwork, is limited in number and rather nondescript and commonplace. Among the more interesting is milk as an image for the emptying of a city and land of its people; ghee, a kind of liquid butter, is an image for the ease with which goddesses give birth. For some unknown reason, thirty shekels (compare the thirty pieces of silver for which Judas betrayed Christ), was an image of contempt to the Sumerian poets: "Like a runner contemptuous of his body's strength he treated the *giguna*-shrine as if it were thirty shekels"; the mighty hero Gilgamesh is said to handle his armor weighing fifty minas (about fifty pounds) as lightly "as thirty shekels." The storm-tossed boat is an image for the distraught wife who after her husband's death is "set adrift in a tempestuous storm like a boat, with her anchor of no avail." A man of vacillating character is one who "bobs up and down like a boat." The boat provided a cumulative series of tersely phrased comparisons in one of the more extended similes as yet known from Sumerian literature (the *Imdugud*-bird is speaking to the hero Lugalbanda, who is eager to return to his city Kullab after much wandering in strange lands):

"Come, my Lugalbanda,
Like a boat of metal, like a boat of grain,
Like a boat of *balbale*-apples,
Like a boat of shade-giving [?] cucumbers,
Like a boat of luxuriant harvest,
Go head high to the brickwork of Kullab."

# 3

# The Sacred Marriage: Origin and Development

The Sacred Marriage Rite was celebrated joyously and rapturously all over the Ancient Near East for some two thousand years. And no wonder![1] The idea behind it was simple, attractive, and highly persuasive. To make his people happy, prosperous, and teeming in multitude—there was no fear of a "population explosion" in those olden golden days—it was the king's pleasant duty to marry the passionate, desirable goddess of fertility and fecundity, the alluring deity who controlled the productivity of the land and the fruitfulness of the womb of man and beast. But simple, attractive, and persuasive credos do not come ready-made—they are the products of individuals and cultures who for one reason or another have the need, the drive, and the capacity to invent and develop them and to give them enduring institutional form. In the case of the Sacred Marriage Rite there is little doubt that it was the innovating, imaginative, methodical Sumerian thinkers, priests, and poets of the early third millennium B.C. who first conceived and developed it as an essential element of their religious faith and ritual practice. For they had the psychological need—Sumerian culture fostered an obsessive drive for wealth and possessions—that in an agricultural and pastoral economy could be sustained only by fertility of the land, and fecundity of the womb.

The well-nigh obsessive veneration of prosperity and well-being, of the fertile field and the fecund womb, pervades the Sumerian literary compositions, their myths and hymns, their lamentations and disputations. In a composition commonly known as "The Curse of Agade," for example, the poet relates that in order to make Agade the outstanding city of the land, the goddess Inanna permitted herself no sleep in order to see to it:

That everything be gathered in the storehouses,
That their city be a firmly established dwelling,
That its people eat "dependable" food,
That its people drink "dependable" water,
That the bathed "heads" make joyous the courtyards,
That the people beautify the place of festivity . . . .

In those days the dwellings of Agade were filled with gold,
Its bright-shining houses were filled with silver,
Into its granaries were brought copper, tin, and slabs of lapis lazuli,
Its silos bulged [?] at the sides.[2]

Or, to take the other side of the coin, here is a poet's bitter depiction of the desolation of Sumer that came about, he avers, as a result of an inimical decision of the great gods:

That cities be destroyed, that houses be destroyed,
That stalls be destroyed, that sheepfolds be wiped out,
That its [Sumer's] oxen no longer stand in their stalls,
That its sheep no longer spread out in their sheepfolds,
That its rivers flow with bitter water,
That its cultivated fields grow weeds,
That its steppes grow wailing plants,
That the mother care not for her children,
That the father say not "Oh, my wife,"
That the young wife rejoice not in [his] lap,
That the young child grow not sturdy [on their] knee,
That the nursemaid chant not a lullaby . . . ,
That the banks of the Tigris and Euphrates in their entirety, grow sickly plants,
That no one tread the highways, that no one seek out the roads,

That its well-founded cities and hamlets be turned to ruins,
That its teeming blackheaded people be given over to the weapon,
That the cultivated fields be not hoed, that no seeds be implanted in the soil . . . ,
That the stalls provide not cream and cheese, that no dung be implanted in the soil,
That the shepherd twirl not the *shukur*-reed in the holy sheepfold,
That the hum of the turning of churn resound not in the sheepfold,
That on the steppe the cattle large and small become scarce, that all living creatures come to an end,
That the four-legged creatures of Sumugan implant no dung in the soil . . . ,
That in the swamps there grow sick-headed reeds, that they come to [their] end in stench [?],
That in the orchards and gardens, there be no growth, that they just waste away . . . ,
An, Enlil, Enki, and Ninhursag decreed as its fate.[3]

In a hymn to Enlil, Sumer's leading deity, we find this resounding *magnificat:*

Without Enlil, the Great Mountain,
No cities would be built, no settlements founded,
No stalls would be built, no sheepfold erected . . . ,
The rivers—their high floodwaters would not bring overflow [?] . . . ,
The sea would not readily produce its bountiful treasure,
The fish of the sea would lay no eggs in the canebrake,
The birds of heaven would not spread [their] nests over the wide earth,
In heaven the rain-laden clouds would not open their mouths,
The fields and meadows would not be filled with rich grain,
In the steppe grass and herbs, its delight, would not grow,
In the garden, the wide "mountain"-trees would bear no fruit . . . ,
The cow would not "throw" its calf in the stall,
The ewe would not bring forth the . . . lamb in its sheepfold,
Mankind, the teeming multitude, would not lie down in their . . . ,
The beasts, the four-legged, would bring forth no offspring,
Would not want to copulate.

And here is what the poet has to say about Enlil's word, sublime and unchangeable:

It approaches heaven—there is overflow,
From heaven overflow rains down,
It approaches the earth—there is luxuriance,
From the earth luxuriance burgeons forth,
Your word—it is plants, your word—it is grain,
Your word—it is the flood-water, the life of all the lands.[4]

Of Enki, the god of water and wisdom, who organized the universe and its cultural activities, one poet relates:

When Father Enki comes out into the seeded land, it brings forth fecund seed,
When Nudimmud comes out to my fecund ewe, it gives birth to the lamb,
When he comes out to my "seeded" cow, it gives birth to the fecund calf,
When he comes out to my fecund goat, it gives birth to the fecund kid,
When you go to the field, to the cultivated field,
You pile up heaps and mounds [of grain] on the high steppe.

And the god himself boasts, according to the same poet:

"I am the lord, I am one whose command is unquestioned, I am the foremost in all things,
At my command, the stalls have been built, the sheepfolds have been enclosed,
When I approached heaven, a rain of prosperity poured down from heaven,
When I approached the earth, there was a high flood,
When I approached its green meadows,
The heaps and mounds [of grain] were piled high at my word."

But it is not only rain from heaven that Enki brings down to fertilize the land, he also fills the rivers with their sparkling fresh water, the semen of his libido. Or, as the same poet puts it:

After Father Enki had lifted it [his eye] over the Euphrates,
He stood up proudly like a rampant bull,

He lifts [his] penis, ejaculates,
Fills the Tigris with sparkling water,
The wild cow mooing for the young in the pastures, the scorpion [infested] stall,
The Tigris surrendered to him as [to] a rampant bull.
He lifted [his] penis, brought the bridal gift,
Brought joy to the Tigris like a big wild bull on giving birth.
The water he brought is sparkling water, its "wine" tastes sweet,
The grain he brought, its rich grain, the people eat,
He filled the Ekur, the house of Enlil with possessions,
With Enki, Enlil rejoices, Nippur is delighted.

With water aplenty, the fields can now produce their rich harvest, and the flocks their tasty cream and milk. And so our poet continues:

He [Enki] directed the plow and the "yoke,"
The great prince Enki put the "horned" oxen in the . . . ,
Opened the holy furrows,
Made grow the grain in the cultivated field.
The lord who dons the diadem, the ornament of the high steppe,
The robust one, the farmer of Enlil,
Enkimdu, the man of ditch and dike,
Enki placed in charge of them.

The lord called to the cultivated field, put there the rich grain,
Heaped up its . . . grain, the rich grain, the . . . grain, into piles,
Enki multiplied the heaps and mounds [of grain],
Her whose head and sides are dappled, whose face is honey-covered,
The Lady, the procreatress, the vigor of the land, the life of the blackheads,
Ashnan, the nourishing bread, the bread of all,
Enki placed in charge of them. . . .
He built stalls, directed their cleansing,
Erected sheepfolds, placed there the best fat and milk,
Brought joy to the dining halls of the gods,
In the vegetation-like steppe he made prosperity prevail.
The trustworthy provider of Eanna, the friend of An,
The beloved son-in-law of the valiant Sin, the husband of holy Inanna,
The Lady, the Queen of all the *me,*

Who time and again commands the procreation of the. . . of Kullab,
Dumuzi, the divine "*ushumgal* of heaven," the friend of An,
Enki placed in charge of them.[5]

Or take this rather unusual lyrical hymn addressed to Ninurta, who, though primarily the god in charge of the stormy South Wind, a god of war who destroys the rebellious land, is also known as "The Farmer of Enlil":

Life-giving semen, life-giving seed,
King whose name was pronounced by Enlil,
Life-giving semen, life-giving seed,
Ninurta whose name was pronounced by Enlil,
My king, I will utter your name again and again,
Ninurta, I your man, your man,
I will utter your name again and again.
My king, the ewe has given birth to the lamb,
The ewe has given birth to lamb, the ewe has given birth to the good
sheep,
I will utter your name again and again. . . .

As long as he was king . . . ,
In the river flowed fresh water,
In the field grew rich grain,
The sea was filled with carp and . . . fish,
In the canebrake grew old reeds, young reeds,
The forests were filled with deer and wild goats,
The *mashgur*-tree grew in the steppe,
The orchards were filled with honey and wine,
In the palace "grew" long life.[6]

According to one poet, there was a time when:

There was no ewe, no lamb was dropped,
There was no goat, no kid was dropped,
The ewe did not give birth to its two lambs,
The goat did not give birth to its three kids . . . ,
The *shesh*-grain of thirty days did not exist,
The *shesh*-grain of forty days did not exist,
The small grain, the grain of the mountain, the grain of the pure
living creatures did not exist.

But then, the gods Enlil and Enki fashioned the two sisters Lahar and Ashnan, one as the goddess of the sheepfolds, and the other as the goddess of the crops, and sent them down to earth, where, our poet continues:

Lahar standing in her sheepfold,
A shepherdess increasing the bounty of the sheepfold is she.
Ashnan standing among the crops,
A maid kindly and beautiful is she.

Abundance that comes from heaven,
Lahar and Ashnan caused to appear.
In the assembly they brought abundance,
In the land they brought the breath of life,
The *me* of the gods they direct,
The contents of the warehouses they multiply,
The storehouses they fill full,
In the house of the poor, hugging the dust,
They enter and bring abundance,
The pair of them, wherever they stand,
Bring heavy increase into the house,
The place where they stand they sate, the place where they sit they supply,
They make glad the heart of An and Enlil.[7]

According to another composition, Enlil, having decided to bring forth all sorts of trees and grain and to bring abundance and prosperity to the land, created the two brothers Emesh, "Summer," and Enten, "Winter," and assigned to each his special task which they executed, according to the author, as follows:

Enten made the ewe give birth to the lamb, the goat give birth to the kid,
He made cow and calf to multiply, cream and milk to increase,
In the steppe he made rejoice the heart of the wild goat, sheep, and donkey,
The birds of heaven he made set up their nests in the wide earth,
The fish of the sea he made lay their eggs in the canebrake,
In the palm grove and vineyard he made honey and wine abound,
The trees, wherever planted, he caused to bear fruit,

The gardens he decked out in green, made their plants luxuriant,
Made the grain increase in the furrows,
Like Ashnan, the kindly maid, he made it come forth sturdily.

Emesh, too, performed well his task;
Emesh brought into being trees and fields, made wide the stalls and the sheepfolds,
In the farms he multiplied produce, bedecked the earth . . . ,
Had the abundant harvest brought into the houses, heaped high the granaries,
Caused cities and habitations to be founded, houses to be built in the land,
Temples to rise mountain high.[8]

With so much emphasis on the value of material wealth, it is not surprising that the sun-god Utu, the brother of Inanna, wants his sister to marry the shepherd because:

"His cream is good, his milk is good,
The shepherd, whatever he touches, is bright . . . ,
His good cream he will eat with you."

But Inanna turns the shepherd down for the farmer, saying:

"I, the maid, the farmer will I marry,
The farmer who grows many plants,
The farmer who grows much grain."

Which so provokes the shepherd that he cries out angrily:

"The farmer, more than I, the farmer more than I,
The farmer, what has he more than I."

He then proceeds to match his own products, item by item against those of the farmer: black and white ewes against black and white flour, milk against beer, cheese against bread, and ends up by boasting that he has so much cream and cheese that the farmer could live on the leftovers.[9]

But if our Sumerian literary documents underline the obsessive concern of the Sumerians with grain-laden fields, vegetable-rich gardens, bulging stalls and sheepfolds, milk, cream, and cheese in profusion, they also reveal that on the spiritual side, the Sumerians evolved, developed, and systematized a cosmology and theology that carried high intellectual conviction and deep emotional fulfillment; so much so, that they became the fundamental creed and dogma of much of the ancient Near East. From their literary documents we learn that the Sumerians believed that the universe was created and operated by a pantheon functioning as an assembly headed by the four creative deities, the gods of heaven, earth, atmosphere, and sea, that is, the gods who were in charge of the four major components of the cosmos.[10] These were the gods who planned and brought into being everything essential to the cosmos—sun, moon, star, and planet, wind and storm, river, mountain and steppe—and placed one or another of their offspring in charge of it. It is they who created man and the animals and plants to feed and nourish him. Once man came into existence on earth, they were obliged to plan and bring into being cities and states, dikes and ditches for irrigation, fields and farms, stalls and byres, and to appoint specially qualified deities to supervise them.[11]

But what man and beast needed most to insure their procreation, propagation, and proliferation was obviously the passionate love and desire that culminated in sexual union and generated the fertilizing semen of the womb, "the water of the heart." These tender and rapturous emotions were given into the hands of the attractive and alluring, sensuous and voluptuous goddess of love, Inanna, who was especially adored and worshipped in one of Sumer's leading cities, Erech, from about 3000 B.C. or even earlier.[12] And it may have been not long thereafter that some of the more thoughtful and imaginative priests and theologians of Erech conceived the cheering and reassuring idea of having their king become the lover and husband of the goddess and thus share her invaluable fertility power and potency, as well as her divine immortality. Thus, we may assume, the Sacred Marriage Rite involving Dumuzi, who must have been one of the memorable rulers of Erech, and Inanna, its lusty, lustful, and deeply venerated deity, came into being.

Actually, there are indications that a Sacred Marriage Rite involving the goddess Inanna was current in Erech several generations before Dumuzi came on the scene. In an epic tale concerned with Erech's heroic ruler Enmerkar, and his struggle with the ruler of Aratta, we learn of a challenge sent by herald. The gist of the message was that Enmerkar should recognize the ruler of Aratta as his overlord, and that the goddess Inanna should be brought to Aratta. And this is how the poet puts it:

> "Let him [Enmerkar] bend the neck before me, carry the basket before me,
> When he has bent the neck before me, has indeed bent the neck before me,
> Then he and I—
> He will live with Inanna by a wall,
> But I will lie with Inanna in the lapis lazuli house of Aratta;
> He will lie by her side in a fruitful bed,
> But I will lie in sweet slumber on an ornate bed;
> He will gaze upon Inanna only in a dream,
> But I will converse with Inanna by her feet, the all-white."

Now, while not every word in this passage is crystal clear, it does indicate that according to the author of this epic poem, the ritual marriage of Inanna to the ruler of Erech as well as of Aratta was current at least as early as Enmerkar, who, according to Sumerian historical tradition, reigned two generations before Dumuzi.[13]

But it was not the name of Enmerkar that was fated to become linked with Inanna in the Sacred Marriage Rite throughout the centuries, but that of Dumuzi,[14] better known to the Western world as Tammuz, the form of the name found in the book of Ezekiel (8:14). Just why Dumuzi came to be thought of as Inanna's husband par excellence is still unknown. Unlike his predecessors Enmerkar and Lugalbanda, or his far-famed successor Gilgamesh, there are no heroic epic tales in which Dumuzi plays any role. According to one tradition, and probably the one closest to historical fact, he was not a native of Erech, but of the city Kua, in the neighborhood of Eridu (one of Sumer's most hallowed cities in the extreme south of Sumer).[15] Nevertheless, the Sumerian poets relate that it was Inanna of Erech who picked him especially for "the godship of the land,"[16] in accordance with her parents' wishes, or in her own words:

"I cast my eye over all the people,
Called Dumuzi to the godship of the Land,
Dumuzi, the beloved of Enlil,
My mother holds him ever dear,
My father exalts him."

And, continues our poet, she bathes, scours herself with soap, dresses in her special "garments of power," and has Dumuzi brought to her prayer- and song-filled house and shrine to rejoice by her side. His presence fills her with such passion and desire that then and there she composes a song for her vulva in which she compares it to a horn, "the boat of heaven," to the new crescent moon, to fallow land, to a high field, to a hillock, and ends by exclaiming:

"As for me, my vulva,
For me the piled-high hillock,
Me—the maid, who will plow it for me?
My vulva, the watered ground—for me,
Me, the Queen, who will station the ox there?"

To which the answer comes:

"Oh Lordly Lady, the king will plow it for you,
Dumuzi, the king, will plow it for you."

And joyfully she responds:

"Plow my vulva, man of my heart!"

After bathing her holy lap, they cohabit, and not surprisingly vegetation flourishes all about them:

At the king's lap stood the rising cedar,
Plants rose high by his side,
Grains rose high by his side,
. . . [and] gardens flourished luxuriantly by his side.

col. 1
col. ii
10
20
30
10
20
30

Poem celebrating Inanna's selection of Dumuzi to the godship of the land. Hand-copy by the author of a tablet in the Istanbul Museum of the Ancient Orient.

No wonder that, as our poem continues:

> In the house of life, the house of the king,
> His wife dwelt with him in joy,
> In the house of life, the house of the king,
> Inanna dwelt with him in joy.

Once happily settled in his house, she utters a plea and makes a promise. The plea is for cream, milk, and cheese from her shepherd husband:

> "Make yellow the milk for me, my bridegroom, make yellow the milk for me,
> My bridegroom, I will drink fresh [?] milk with you,
> Wild bull, Dumuzi, make yellow the milk for me,
> My bridegroom, I will drink fresh [?] milk with you,
> The milk of the goat, make flow in the sheepfold for me,
> With . . . cheese fill my holy churn . . . ,
> Lord Dumuzi, I will drink fresh milk with you."

And her promise is to preserve his "storehouse," or in Inanna's own words:

> "My husband, the goodly storehouse, the holy stall,
> I, Inanna, will preserve for you,
> I will watch over your 'house of life.'
> The radiant wonder-place of the land,
> The house where the fate of all the lands is decreed,
> Where people and [all] living things are guided,
> I, Inanna will preserve for you,
> I will watch over your 'house of life,'
> The 'house of life,' the storehouse of long life,
> I, Inanna, will preserve it for you."[17]

The author of this hymnal myth probably lived in the days of the Third Dynasty of Ur, roughly about 2000 B.C., when the flourishing schools of Sumer produced mythographers and poets whose works were to endure in one form or another for centuries to come. By that time, almost a millennium after Dumuzi's day, we have clear evidence that the king of Sumer, whoever he may have been, had to become the husband of Inanna, as a kind of Dumuzi incarnate.[18] Just when this transcendental credo and mystic rite, so rich in promise for both the king and his people, began, and who was the first Sumerian ruler to celebrate the Sacred Marriage Rite as a reincarnated Dumuzi, we have no way of knowing at present, although it is not unreasonable to surmise that it took place some time about 2500 B.C., when the Sumerians were becoming ever more nationally minded. In any case it is only with Shulgi, the second ruler of the Third Dynasty of Ur, that we begin to get some significant details about the Sacred Marriage Rite.[19] Thus the recently published "Blessing of Shulgi"[20] begins with the king's journeying from his capital Ur to Inanna's city Erech. There he docks his boat at the quay of Kullab, Erech's most ancient and venerated district, and loaded down with sacrificial animals he proceeds to Inanna's shrine, the Eanna. This is told in straight narrative style by the poet:

Shulgi, the faithful shepherd, set out on the boat,
At the *me* of kingship, the *me* of princeship Sumer and Akkad marvelled,
At the quay of Kullab he docked his boat,
With large mountain bulls led by the arm,
With sheep and goats tied to the hand,
With dappled [ ?] kids and bearded kids pressed to the breast,
To Inanna in the shrine of Eanna he came.

Once there, Shulgi dresses himself in a ritual *me*-garment, covers his head with a crown-like wig, and so impresses the goddess with his wonder-inspiring presence that she breaks spontaneously into a passionate song:

"When for the wild bull, for the lord, I shall have bathed,
When for the shepherd Dumuzi, I shall have bathed,
When with . . . my sides I shall have adorned,
When with amber my mouth I shall have coated,
When with kohl my eyes I shall have painted,
When in his fair hands my loins shall have been shaped,
When the lord, lying by holy Inanna, the shepherd Dumuzi,
With milk and cream the lap shall have smoothed [ ?] . . . ,

When on my vulva his hands he shall have laid,
When like his black boat, he shall have . . . it,
When like his narrow boat, he shall have brought life to it,
When on the bed he shall have caressed me,
Then shall I caress my lord, a sweet fate I shall decree for him,
I shall caress Shulgi, the faithful shepherd, a sweet fate I shall decree for him,
I shall caress his loins, the shepherdship of all the lands,
I shall decree as his fate."

And this, according to our poet, is the glorious fate she decreed for her attractive lover and husband:

"In battle I am your leader, in combat I am your helpmate [?],
In the assembly I am your champion [?],
On the road I am your life.
You, the chosen shepherd of the holy [?] house [?],
You, the sustainer [?] of An's great shrine,
In all ways you are fit:
To hold high your head on the lofty dais, you are fit,
To sit on the lapis lazuli throne, you are fit,
To fix the crown on your head, you are fit,
To wear long garments on your body, you are fit,
To gird yourself in the garment of kingship, you are fit,
To carry the mace and the weapon, you are fit . . . ,
To guide straight the long bow and the arrow, you are fit,
To fasten the throw-stick and the sling at the side, you are fit,
For the holy scepter in your hand, you are fit,
For the holy sandals on your feet, you are fit . . . ,
To prance on my holy bosom like a 'lapis lazuli' calf, you are fit.
May your beloved heart be long of days.
Thus has An determined the fate for you, may it not be altered,
Enlil the decreer of fate—may it not be changed,
Inanna holds you dear, you are the beloved of Ningal."[21]

That Shulgi was not the last king to celebrate the sacred marriage with Inanna as an avatar of Dumuzi, we learn from a hymn to the goddess, the last stanzas of which describe in considerable detail what actually took place during the marriage ceremony. First a bed of cedar and rushes is set up in the palace on New Year's eve, and over it is spread a very special coverlet.[22] Then the goddess is bathed and soaped, fragrant oil is sprinkled on the ground, and the king proceeds to the holy bed, where they unite in sexual bliss. Or as the poet describes the scene:

In the palace, the house which guides the land, the house of the king of all the lands,
In its judgment-hall [?], where the black-headed people gather,
He [the king] erected a dais for the "Queen of the Palace" [Inanna],
The king, the god, lived with her in its midst.
In order to care for the life of all the lands,
To examine closely . . . ,
To carry out to perfection the divine rules on the day of "sleeping,"
On the New Year, the day of rites,
A sleeping place was set up for "my queen."
They [the people] purify it with pots full of rushes, and cedar.
They set them up for "my queen" as their bed,
Over it they spread a coverlet,
A coverlet which rejoices the heart, makes sweet the bed.

"My queen" is bathed at the holy lap,
Is bathed at the lap of the king,
Is bathed at the lap of Iddin-Dagan,
The holy Inanna is scrubbed with soap,
Fragrant cedar oil is sprinkled on the ground.
The king goes with lifted head to the holy lap,
Goes with lifted head to the lap of Inanna,
Amaushumgalanna beds with her,
Fondles lovingly her holy lap.
After the queen had long reposed on the holy lap,
She murmurs. . .
"O Iddin-Dagan, you . . . ."

Then, probably on New Year's day, there is prepared a rich banquet in the larger reception hall of the palace:

For the holy sacrifices, for the well-established rites,
For the fire-seared altar, for the cypress [?]-altar,
For the abundant bread-offerings, for the amply-filled vases,
He entered with her in his lofty palace,
He embraced his beloved wife,

Embraced the holy Inanna,
Led her forth like the light of day to the throne on the great dais,
Installed [ ?] himself at her side like the king Utu,
Paraded abundance, cheer, and plenty before her,
Prepared a goodly feast for her,
Paraded the black-heads before her, [saying]:
"With the drum [ ?] whose speech is louder than the storm,
The sweet-voiced lyre [ ?], the ornament of the palace,
The harp that soothes the spirit of man,
O singers, let us utter songs that rejoice the heart."
The king put a hand to the food and drink,
Amaushumgalanna put a hand to the food and drink,
The palace is in song, the king in joy,
By the people sated with plenty,
Amaushumgalanna stands in lasting joy,
May his days be long on the fruitful throne.

# 4

# The Sacred Marriage: Wooing and Wedlock

Marriage presupposes courting and wooing, and the Sacred Marriage was no exception. We now have six poems concerned in one way or another with the premarital courting of the holy couple, and they present five different versions of the romance—the poets seemed to be fancy-free in inventing and improvising the pertinent details. In this chapter a sketch of the contents of these six poems will be followed by a rather frustrating attempt to reconstruct the ritualistic procedural patterns of the Sacred Marriage Rite in the light of all the literary material now available.

The tender, passionate poem whose contents were sketched in the preceding chapter,[1] where Inanna is depicted as saying

> "I cast my eye over all the people,
> Called Dumuzi to the godship of the land,
> Dumuzi, the beloved of Enlil,
> My mother holds him dear,
> My father exalts him. . . ."

might well give the impression that Dumuzi was Inanna's enthusiastic, and one and only, choice for her husband-to-be, and that she could hardly wait to have him at her side to "plow her vulva."

Yet there is a version of the premarital courtship that tells an entirely different story: Inanna actually at first rejects Dumuzi the shepherd for his rival, Enkimdu[2] the farmer and it took no little argument and suasion on the part of Dumuzi to induce her to change her mind. This account of the episode is told in two playlet-like compositions that are closely related, the one beginning where the other ends.[3]

The first of the two, consisting almost entirely of a question-answer tête-à-tête between the sun-god Utu, Inanna's brother, and the goddess, concerns the making of a cover for her nuptial bed.[4] The dialogue runs as follows:

"Lordly Queen, the cultivated flax, luxuriant,
Inanna, the cultivated flax, luxuriant,
The grain luxuriating [?] in the furrow—
Sister, who have your fill of lofty trees,
Lordly Queen, who have your fill of lofty trees—
I will hoe for you, will give the plant to you,
Sister mine, I will bring you the cultivated flax,
Inanna, I will bring you the cultivated flax."

"Brother, after you have brought me the cultivated flax
Who will comb it for me? Who will comb it for me?
That flax, who will comb it for me?"

"Sister mine, I will bring it to you combed,
Inanna, I will bring it to you combed."

"Brother, after you have brought it to me combed,
Who will spin it for me? Who will spin it for me?
That flax, who will spin it for me?"

"Sister mine, I will bring it to you spun,
Inanna, I will bring it to you spun."

"Brother, after you have brought it to me spun,
Who will braid it for me? Who will braid it for me?
That flax, who will braid it for me?"

"Sister mine, I will bring it to you braided,
Inanna, I will bring it to you braided."

"Brother, after you have brought it to me braided,
Who will warp it for me? Who will warp it for me?
That flax, who will warp it for me?"

"Sister mine, I will bring it to you warped,
Inanna, I will bring it to you warped."

"Brother, after you have brought it to me warped,
Who will weave it for me? Who will weave it for me?
That flax, who will weave it for me?"

"Sister mine, I will bring it to you woven,
Inanna, I will bring it to you woven."

"Brother, after you have brought it to me woven,
Who will dye it for me? Who will dye it for me?
That flax, who will dye it for me?"

"Sister mine, I will bring it to you dyed,
Inanna, I will bring it to you dyed."

It is only now that we learn the purpose of this colloquy, as Inanna puts the question that is really on her mind.

"Brother, after you have brought it to me dyed,
Who will bed with me? Who will bed with me?"

To which Utu replies unhesitatingly that it is Dumuzi, or to use two of his epithets, Ushumgalanna and Kuli-Enlil, who will be her husband:

"With you he will bed, he will bed,
With you your husband will bed,
Ushumgalanna will bed with you,
Kuli-Enlil will bed with you,
He who came forth from the fertile womb, will bed with you,
The seed begotten of a king, will bed with you."

But Inanna demurs, gently but firmly:

"Nay, the man of my heart is he—
The man of my heart is he—
Who has won my heart is he—

Who hoes not, [yet] the granaries are heaped high,
The grain is brought regularly into the storehouses,
The farmer—his grain fills all the granaries."[5]

Here the poem ends. But, continues its sequel, Utu will not take no for an answer; he insists that his sister marry the shepherd, not the farmer:

"Sister mine, marry the shepherd,
Maid Inanna, why are you unwilling?
His cream is good, his milk is good,
The shepherd—whatsoever he touches is bright.
Inanna, marry the shepherd,
Who is bedecked with *unu*-stones, with *shuba*-stones,
Why are you unwilling?
His good cream he will eat with you, he, the king protector,
Why are you unwilling?"[6]

But Inanna is adamant:

"I—the shepherd I will not marry,
I will not wear his coarse garments,
I will not accept his coarse wool,
I, the maid—the farmer I will marry,
The farmer who grows many plants,
The farmer who grows much grain."

This so infuriates Dumuzi, who is presumably on the scene—the text is broken at this point—that he speaks out angrily in his own defense, claiming that he has much more to offer than his rival suitor, the farmer:

"The farmer, more than I, the farmer more than I,
The farmer, what has he more than I?"
If he give me his black flour,
I give him, the farmer, my black ewe,
If he give me his white flour,
I give him, the farmer, my white ewe,
If he pour me his prime beer,
I pour him, the farmer, my yellow milk,
If he pour me his goodly beer,

I pour him, the farmer, my *kisim*-milk,
If he pour me his mellow beer,
I pour him, the farmer, my well-shaken milk,
If he pour me his diluted beer,
I pour him, the farmer, my 'plant'-milk,
If he give me his sweet *habala*-plant,
I give him, the farmer, my *itirda*-milk,
If he give me his goodly bread,
I give him, the farmer, my honey-cheese,
If he give me his small beans,
I give him, the farmer, my small cheeses.
From what I have eaten, I have drunk,
I could leave him the surplus cream,
I could leave him the surplus milk,
More than I, the farmer, what has he more than I?"

This outburst seemed to have its intended effect, and Inanna must have had a change of heart. For the poet now tells us that:

He rejoiced, he rejoiced,
On the "breast" of the river-bank he rejoiced,
On the river-bank, the shepherd, on the river-bank, rejoiced.

But then who should come up to the river-bank? None other than Enkimdu—which puts Dumuzi once again into a fighting mood; or as our poet puts it:

The shepherd pastured his sheep on the river bank,
To the shepherd pasturing his sheep on the river bank,
The farmer approached, the farmer Enkimdu approached,
To Dumuzi, the king of dikes and ditches approached.
In his steppe, the shepherd, in his steppe starts a quarrel,
The shepherd Dumuzi, in his steppe starts a quarrel.

Happily, however, the farmer is a meek fellow who craves peace and friendship; he refuses to quarrel with the shepherd, and even offers him pasturing ground and water for his sheep:

"I with you shepherd, with you shepherd,
I with you why shall I strive?
Let your sheep eat the plants of the river bank,

Let your sheep pasture on my cultivated ground,
Let them eat my grain on the stalk,
Let them eat grain in the bright fields of Erech,
Let your kids and lambs drink the water of my canal, Surugal."

And so the story has a happy ending. Dumuzi invites the farmer to his wedding:

"I, the shepherd, at my marriage,
Farmer, you will be counted as my friend,
Farmer, Enkimdu, as my friend,
Farmer, as my friend, you will be counted as my friend."

The farmer is more than gratified and promises to bring suitable gifts for the bride from the produce of his fields:

"I will bring you wheat, I will bring you beans,
I will bring you lentils [?] . . . ,
Maid, whatever is fit for you,
Maid Inanna . . . grain and . . . beans, I will bring you."

Dumuzi thus finally succeeded in convincing his bride-to-be of the immensity of his wealth and possessions. But she also had some misgivings about his pedigree. Thus there is a recently published poem in which Inanna begins an argument with her lover, claiming that if it were not for her mother Ningal, for her sister "Lady of the Holy Reed," for her father, the moon-god Sin, and for her brother, the sun-god Utu, he—Dumuzi—would be chased about in street and steppe, without a roof on his head. But Dumuzi cools her down:

"Young lady, do not start a quarrel,
Inanna, let us talk it over,
Inanna, do not start a quarrel,
Palace-queen, let us take counsel together.
My father is as good as your father,
Inanna, let us talk it over,
My mother is as good as your mother,
Palace-queen, let us take counsel together.
Geshtinanna is as good as . . . ,[7]

Inanna, let us talk it over,
I am as good as Utu,
Palace-queen, let us take counsel together,
Enki is as good as Sin,
Inanna, let us talk it over,
Sirtur is as good as Ningal,
Palace-queen, let us take counsel together."

Fortunately this quarrel, our poet adds, seems only to arouse the lovers' passion:

The word they had spoken,
It is a word of desire,
With the starting of a quarrel,
Comes the heart's desire.

There follows a loving tête-à-tête between the two, full of obscure allusions and enigmatic metaphors: there are references to Dumuzi filling Inanna's "roof" and wells with water, and to his "plowing" the *shuba*-stones that the goddess seems to wear about her sacred body. But what attracts her most about her lover is his beard of lapis lazuli, or in her own words:

"Who was made for me, who was made for me,
His beard is lapis lazuli,
The wild ox who was made by An for me in accordance with the *me,*
His beard is lapis lazuli,
The king [ ? ]—his beard is lapis lazuli,
His beard is lapis lazuli."[8]

Inanna, as this poem suggests, was the proud daughter of her father, Sin, the great moon-god of Ur, one of Sumer's major metropolises. It is not surprising to find, therefore, that according to another of the courting tales, she felt the need of asking Sin's approval before giving herself to her lover, who was waiting for her longingly in the *gipar* of her temple Eanna in Erech. This is told in a narrative poem that begins with a detailed, itemized account of the goddess's bedecking the various parts of her body with precious stones, jewels, and ornaments. From a treasure

Tablet in the Museum of the University of Pennsylvania inscribed with the pedigree quarrel between the lovers.

brought her by a devotee she selects lapis lazuli stones for her breast, egg-shaped beads for her buttocks and head, *duru*-lazuli stones for her chignon, gold ribbons for her coiffure, gold earrings for her ears, bronze ear drops for her ear lobes, diverse ornaments for her face, nose, and loins, bright alabaster for her navel, willow for her vulva, sandals for her feet. Thus bedecked and bejeweled, Dumuzi "standing at the lapis lazuli door of the *gipar* met her," no doubt burning with passion and desire. But first Inanna sends a message to her father, telling him of the planned union with her lover in these joyous words:

"My house, my house, he will make it 'long' for me,
I the queen—my house, my house, he will make it 'long' for me,
My *gipar*-house, he will make it 'long' for me,
The people will set up my fruitful bed,
They will cover it with plants of *duru*-lapis lazuli,
I will bring there the man of my heart,
I will bring there Amaushumgalanna,
He will put his hand by my hand,
He will put his heart by my heart,
His putting hand to hand—its sleep [ ? ] is so refreshing,
His pressing of heart to heart—its pleasure is so sweet."[9]

Not unexpectedly, however, the goddess was far closer to her mother Ningal than to her father; it is to her "mother's house" that the bridegroom must come to ask for her hand, and it is to her mother that she turns for advice and approval when Dumuzi comes knocking at her door. Thus we find one poet relating how Dumuzi came to the house where Inanna lived with her mother, carrying gifts of milk, cream, and beer, and pleading for admittance. But Inanna seems to hesitate, and it is her mother who urges her to let him in, saying:

"Lo, the youth, he is your father,
Lo, the youth, he is your mother,
His mother cherishes [ ? ] you like your mother,
His father cherishes [ ? ] you like your father,
Open the house, my queen, open the house."

And so Inanna prepares herself to meet her spouse-to-be as befits a Sumerian queen:

Inanna, at her mother's command,
Bathed herself, anointed herself with goodly oil,
Covered her body with the noble *pala*-garment,
Took along the . . , her dowry,
Arranged the lapis lazuli about her neck,
Grasped the seal in her hand.
The Lordly Queen waited expectantly,
Dumuzi pressed open the door,
Came forth into the house like the moonlight,
Gazed at her joyously,
Embraced her, kissed her. . . .[10]

But though Inanna loved her mother and on occasion followed her advice, she was not beyond deceiving her, at her lover's suggestion, in order to tarry with him by the silver light of the moon. At least that is what happened according to one of the more tender and ardent love lyrics, that begins with Inanna, who was also the Venus-goddess, soliloquizing:

"Last night, as I, the queen, was shining bright,
Last night, as I, the queen of heaven, was shining bright,
Was shining bright, was dancing about,
Was uttering a chant at the brightening of the oncoming light,
He met me, he met me,
The lord Kulianna met me,
The lord put his hand into my hand,
Ushumgalanna embraced me."

To be sure, she claims she tried to free herself from his embrace, since she did not know what to tell her mother:

"Come now, wild bull, set me free, I must go home,
Kuli-Enlil, set me free, I must go home,
What can I say to deceive my mother,
What can I say to deceive my mother, Ningal."

But her lover had the answer that Inanna, noted for her frequent deceits, was only too happy to hear from his lips:

"Let me inform you, let me inform you,
Inanna, most deceitful of women, let me inform you,
Say my girl friend took me with her to the public square,
There she entertained me with music and dancing,
Her chant the sweet she sang for me,
In sweet rejoicing I whiled away the time there.
Thus deceitfully stand up to your mother,
While we by the moonlight indulge our passion,
I will prepare for you a bed pure, sweet, and noble,
Will while away sweet time with you in plenty and joy."

But Dumuzi evidently so relished the savor of Inanna's love that he must have promised to make her his rightful spouse. For the poem ends with the goddess singing exaltingly and ecstatically:

"I have come to our mother's gate,
I, in joy I walk,
I have come to Ningal's gate,
I, in joy I walk.
To my mother he will say the word,
He will sprinkle cypress oil on the ground,
To my mother Ningal he will say the word,
He will sprinkle cypress oil on the ground,
He whose dwelling is fragrant,
Whose word brings deep joy.
My lord is seemly for the holy lap,
Amaushumgalanna, the son-in-law of Sin,
The lord Dumuzi is seemly for the holy lap,
Amaushumgalanna, the son-in-law of Sin."[11]

From courting and wooing, we turn to the Sacred Marriage itself, and the manner in which it was celebrated, although as will soon become only too evident, our information on what actually took place during the ceremony is vague and contradictory. All in all we now have five compositions that shed some significant light on the rite. Two of these involve well-known rulers of Sumer, Shulgi of Ur and Iddin-Dagan of Isin, but the accounts presented in the two compositions[12] differ in almost every important detail.

In the case of Shulgi, the rite takes place in the goddess's temple in Erech, whither the king has travelled by boat. As far as the ceremony itself is concerned, all the poet tells us is that the king has changed into a ritual garment and has put on a crown-like wig, and that Inanna is so taken by the wonder of his appearance that she breaks into a passionate song of desire, followed by a precious blessing. We are not even told when the ceremony was performed, whether annually or at more prolonged intervals—one gets the impression that it took place but once, sometime early in the king's reign in the course of a journey to several Sumerian cities to receive the blessings of their tutelary deities.

In case of Iddin-Dagan, on the other hand, the poet tells us that the rite was performed on the eve of New Year's day in the king's palace, presumably located in his capital city Isin, and that step by step this is what took place: first, a bed of rushes and cedar was set up, and over it was spread a specially prepared coverlet;[13] then Inanna was washed and soaped and presumably laid on the bed; the king then "proceeded to the holy lap" with "lifted head," on ground fragrant with cedar oil, and blissfully bedded with the goddess. The following day a rich banquet was prepared in the large reception hall of the palace; there was much eating and drinking, music and song, as the people "paraded" before the divine couple sitting side by side on their thrones.

Even if all this actually took place as recorded by the poet—and some of the description seems to contain more fancy than fact—there are still some important questions left unanswered: Did the ceremony take place annually? Who were "the black-heads"? Who actually participated? It certainly could not have been all the people of the city. And who, finally, played the role of the goddess throughout the ceremony? It must have been some specially selected votary of the goddess, but this is never stated—it is Inanna herself who, according to poets, bedded with the king during the night and sat by his side during the banquet on the day following.[14]

Something of what took place during the Sacred Marriage Rite may be gleaned from the composition recording Inanna's selection of Dumuzi to the "godship of the land," which was sketched in the preceding chapter.[15] According to this text, the ceremony seems to have taken place in the goddess's temple and shrine, and only later did she go to dwell in the king's palace, "the house of life." We also hear of the bathing of the goddess, and her dressing in special garments to meet her husband-to-be, but nothing is said about the preparation of the bed and its coverlet. There is of course music and song; in fact, the goddess herself, inspired by her lover's presence at her side, breaks into song, just as she did upon beholding the ritually garbed and bewigged Shulgi[16]—the two songs are quite different in content, but both are passionate and rapturous.

In 1959 the British Museum published two "Sacred Marriage" texts that had been lying about in its cupboards for well-nigh a century; these provide a number of interesting details and particulars concerning the celebration of the rite. But they also serve to further mystify and confuse with their ambiguities, inconsistencies, and disparities—the priests and poets seem to have been as fancy-free in inventing the ritual procedures for the Sacred Marriage ceremony as they were in depicting the premarital wooing of the holy couple. One of these newly published texts tells us that after a "fruitful bed" has been set up in the goddess's shrine Eanna, ritual priests, designated as "linen-wearers," announce her presence to Dumuzi, before whom food and drink has been placed. In riddle-like phrases they invite him to approach Inanna in the *kiur* of her shrine, where Enlil, the leading deity of the Sumerian pantheon, has been installed. Or, to quote the poet's rather enigmatic words:

In Eanna the "linen-weavers," prepared an altar for him,
Water was placed there for the lord, they speak to him,
Bread was placed there, they speak to him,
In the palace he was refreshed, they speak to him:

"Dumuzi, radiant in the palace, and on earth,
Mother Inanna, mother Inanna, your treasure, your treasure!
Mother Inanna, mother Inanna, your garment, your garment!
Your black garment, your white garment!
My lord, you who have come to the house—approach her,
Approach her with a chant, a heart moving melody,

Approach their seat [ ? ], the seat [ ? ] on which they are sitting,
Approach their place, the place where they are standing,
There they are installing, there they are installing,
They are installing Enlil in the *kiur*."

A brief blessing by the goddess for Dumuzi follows:

"Wild bull, 'eye of the land', I will bring life to its people,
I will fulfill all its needs [ ? ],
Will make its people carry out justice, in the princely house,
Will make its seed utter [ ? ] words of justice in the palace."

The composition closes with a plea to Inanna, probably by Dumuzi, to give him her breast, her "field" that pours out rich vegetation:

"Lordly Queen, your breast is your field,
Inanna, your breast is your field,
Your broad field that pours out plants,
Your broad field that pours out grain,
Water flowing from on high—the lord—bread from on high,
Water flowing, flowing from on high—the lord—bread, bread from on high,
[Pour] it out for the lord, the bespoken one,
I will drink it from you."[17]

The other British Museum "Sacred Marriage" text parallels to some extent the Shulgi and Iddin-Dagan poems sketched earlier in the book,[18] but once again, the details vary greatly. The poet-priest begins with an address to the goddess, informing her that Gibil, the fire-god, had purified her "fruitful bed, bedecked with lapis lazuli," and that the king himself—his name is not mentioned anywhere in the text—had erected an altar for her and carried out her rites of purification:

The house of Eridu—its guidance,
The house of Sin—its radiance,
The Eanna—its habitation [ ? ],
The house—it has been presented to you,[19]
In my enduring house, floating cloudlike,
Whose name is truly a vision sweet,

Where a fruitful bed, bedecked with lapis lazuli,
Gibil has purified for you in the shrine, the great,
For you who are best suited for queenship,
The lord, has erected an altar,
In his reed-filled house that he has purified for you,
He performs your rites.

There then follows a plea to the goddess to bless the king during the night of love:

The sun has gone to sleep, the day is passed,
As in bed you gaze upon him,
As you caress the lord,
Give life unto the lord—
Give the staff and crook to the lord.

The poet then sings ecstatically, if perhaps too repetitively, of the king's craving for the nuptial bed and of his preparing a cover for it, so that his beloved might make it "sweet":

He craves it, he craves it, he craves the bed,
He craves the bed, that rejoices the heart, he craves the bed,
He craves the bed that sweetens the lap, he craves the bed,
He craves the bed of kingship, he craves the bed,
That she make it sweet, that she make it sweet, that she make the bed sweet,
That she make sweet the bed that rejoices the heart, that she make sweet the bed,
That she make sweet the bed that sweetens the lap, that she make sweet the bed,
That she make sweet the bed of kingship, that she make sweet the bed,
That she make sweet the bed of queenship, that she make sweet the bed,
[The lord] covers the bed for her, covers the bed for her,
[The king] covers the bed for her, covers the bed for her. . . .

With the bed prepared and the goddess ready to receive her bridegroom, the poet introduces the deity Ninshubur, Inanna's faithful vizier, who leads the king to the bride's lap with the plea that she bless him with everything essential to make his reign happy and memorable: firm political control over Sumer and the neighboring lands, productivity of the soil and fertility of the womb, plenty and abundance for all. Or, as the poet depicts it in impressive detail:

"May the lord whom you have called to your heart,
The king, your beloved husband, enjoy long days at your holy lap, the sweet.
Give him a reign goodly and glorious,
Give him the throne of kingship on enduring foundation,
Give him the people-directing scepter, the staff and the crook,
Give him an enduring crown, a radiant diadem on his head.
From where the sun rises to where the sun sets,
From south to north,
From the Upper Sea to the Lower Sea,
From [the land of] the *hulub*-tree to [the land] of the cedar,
Over [all] Sumer and Akkad give him the staff and the crook,
May he exercise the shepherdship of the black-heads wherever they dwell,
As the farmer, may he make productive the fields,
As the shepherd, may he multiply the sheepfolds.

Under his reign may there be plants, may there be grain,
At the river may there be overflow,
In the field may there be rich grain,
In the marshland may the fish and birds make much chatter,
In the canebrake may the old reeds and young reeds grow high,
In the steppe may the *mashgur*-tree grow high,
In the forests may the deer and the wild goats multiply,
May the orchards produce honey and wine,
In the garden beds may the lettuce and cress grow high,
In the palace may there be long life,
In the Tigris and Euphrates may there be floodwater,
On their banks may the grass grow high, may it fill the meadows,
May the holy queen of vegetation pile high the grain in heaps and mounds,
My queen, queen of heaven and earth, queen who encompasses heaven and earth,
May he enjoy long days [at your holy] lap."

Following Ninshubur's all-embracing request, the poet continues:

The king goes with lifted head to the holy lap,
He goes with lifted head to the holy lap of Inanna,
The king coming with lifted head,
Coming to my queen with lifted head . . . ,
Embraces the Hierodule [of An]. . . .[20]

This concludes the sketch of the contents of the Sumerian compositions concerned in one way or another with the Sacred Marriage Rite. As noted earlier, the information they provide is vague, elusive, fanciful, and contradictory—after all their authors were rhapsodic poets, not anthropologically oriented scholars. One fact is certain, however: the Sacred Marriage was a jubilant, rapturous occasion celebrated with joyous music and ecstatic love songs. Not a few of these have become known to the scholarly world, some only very recently, and many more are no doubt still buried in the ruined cities of Sumer. We come now to the "Song of Songs," a biblical collection of love lyrics, some of which may have been sung at a Palestinian Sacred Marriage Rite going back to Sumerian roots.

# 5 

# The Sacred Marriage and Solomon's Song of Songs

One of the more perplexing problems of modern biblical scholarship is the puzzling presence of the book commonly known as "Solomon's Song of Songs" in the Old Testament. It is not concerned in any way with the history of the Hebrew people, and contains no revealing prophecies or inspiring preachments—in fact it seems to be nothing more than a loosely organized collection of sensuous love-songs devoid of any religious, theological, moralistic, or didactic content. Even a cursory reading of its voluptuous erotic verses is enough to convince the unprejudiced reader that the book fairly reeks of love and passion, of lust and desire. How then was a book of such profane and mundane contents accepted into the sacred biblical canon, and placed cheek by jowl with the instructive and inspiring Books of Moses, the spiritual, prayer-filled Psalms, the moral thundering Books of the Prophets? How did it ever pass the sharp eyes of the austere, puritanical rabbis, to whom chastity, virginity, and sexual purity were sacrosanct?

To be sure, once the decision was taken and the book was made part of the Old Testament canon, the rabbis found little difficulty in harmonizing its rather libidinous contents with their own attitudes and predilections. In fact they went about doing so with such conviction that to this day the little book has been accepted by the more orthodox Jewish teachers, preachers, and plain folk alike as one of the most inspiring of all biblical works, a veritable "Holy of Holies," to be read and studied, chanted and cherished, hallowed and revered. For the rabbis were fully convinced that the "Song of Songs" was written in its entirety by none other than King Solomon, whom they conceived to be a rare, if rather paradoxical, combination of sage, poet, and lover—just as they believed that Moses was the author of the Torah, and King David of the Psalms. A book composed by so noble and revered a king as Solomon must have deep religious significance and profound spiritual values, in spite of its superficial frivolity and sensuality. All that had to be done was to disregard the ostensible, literal meaning of the text; to look for the "meaning behind the meaning," and thus discover the inspiring, edifying allegories intended by the devout and inspired Solomon. The lover in the "Song of Songs" was not a ruddy, bushy-locked, dove-eyed sweet-mouthed youth, but none other than Jahweh himself. And the beloved was not a fair maid with curly hair, scarlet lips, jewel-like thighs, and goblet-round navel, but the people of Israel—his bride and spouse.

Nor were the rabbis alone in their allegorical interpretation of the book. The Church Fathers, too, troubled by its presence in the sacred canon, sought for its deeper, hidden meaning, and had little difficulty finding it: the two lovers were Christ and the Church; the friends and attendants were the angels in heaven and the believers on earth; the "kisses of the mouth" symbolized the yearning of the Church to touch the lips of Christ. And so it went right up to the end of the eighteenth century, when modern biblical scholarship was born. In the course of the past two centuries the literal interpretation of the "Song of Songs" gradually took over and finally prevailed; there is probably no serious biblical scholar today who sees the book as anything but an assortment of exquisite lyrics of love and passion.[1]

This is not to say that today's exegetes actually understand the book from beginning to end, or that they are fully agreed as to its origin, structure, and date of composition—far from it. The "Song of Songs" is one of the most difficult, obscure, enigmatic, and disconcerting books in the Bible. Though it consists of only eight small chapters and no more than 117 verses, it contains scores of words and expressions of doubtful meaning, not a few of which are unique to this book, occurring nowhere else in the Bible. It has numerous disturbing repetitions and awkward refrains, not to mention misreadings, glosses, and proverbial expressions that crept into the text before it became fixed and inviolate. And to make matters worse, it is replete with what seem to be overbold images and extravagant metaphors whose implications and allusions are often obscure and enigmatic, if not altogether unintelligible.

The entire book is written in the form of speeches, invocations, colloquies, and soliloquies, but there are no directions or notations of any sort to indicate their beginning and end. Nor is it clear just who the speakers, the lyrical protagonists, are. There is of course, the unnamed love-sick maid, usually described as "girl friend," "bride," and "sister." Then there is the lover who seems to be designated as "the king," and even more specifically "King Solomon," but then again he is a lusty, ruddy, strong-limbed shepherd with nothing royal or courtly about him. In addition to these two main characters there are scattered references to "the daughters of Jerusalem," "the daughters of Zion," "the watchmen that go about the city," and to "friends" of the lover—all obviously introduced as literary devices to provide an opportunity for the rhetorical, exclamatory asides by the main characters.

And if all these textual difficulties are not enough, there is the troublesome matter of the literary form and structure of the book, which has proved to be a source of bitter controversy among modern biblical scholars, who, in general, are not noted for their jovial and amiable dispositions. One of the more persistent theories holds that the "Song of Songs" was composed as a drama divided into numerous acts and scenes. Scholars holding this view often let their fertile imagination run riot in their efforts to identify and extend its dramatis personae, to uncover and develop its rather tenuous plot-motifs, and to multiply the number of acts and scenes into which the drama was presumably divided.

There were scholars who argued that the book is an epithalamium, a collection of secular wedding songs chanted by and for a bride and groom during the marriage festivities. This view gained in vogue in the late nineteenth century after the ethnologist J. G. Wetzstein reported his observations of the marriage ceremonies prevailing in modern Syria and Palestine. He found that throughout these festivities, which lasted for seven days, the bride and groom are actually called king and queen by the peasants and villagers, who sing and dance before them as they sit upon a "throne" erected over the threshing floor. Accordingly, the "Songs of Songs," itself a Palestinian creation, was a collection of songs chanted at a Palestinian marriage feast that took place when the bride and groom would be designated as king and queen[2]—Solomon's palanquin mentioned in the book was the threshing floor, the bridesmaids were called "the daughters of Zion," etc. Some scholars even surmised that in spite of its obvious eroticism and accent on sex, the book was really a kind of moral tract to teach the blessedness of wedded love. All this however, is too fanciful and far-fetched for most modern scholars, who generally take the view that the "Song of Songs" is nothing but a collection of independent love lyrics between a man and a maid full of sighs, kisses, and tender embraces.[3]

This theory brings us right back to where we started. If the "Song of Songs" is nothing more than a repertory of secular, sensuous love lyrics without any traditional, hallowed, religious background, how did it ever occur to the circumspect, straight-laced, pious rabbis to include it in the Holy Scripture? And why, in a book of simple, wistful, tender songs of love between a man and a maid, should the lover be pictured both as an alluring, irresistible king living in courtly luxury, and as a lowly shepherd following his flocks alongside those of his fellows? And would a simple maid sighing with love and panting with passion take time out from her tender outpourings to utter refrain-like soliloquies and adjurations to the daughters of Jerusalem, who seem to be ever at her side, prepared to lend a sympathetic ear, and to ask questions that will evoke a moving, passionate response? All this hardly speaks for a simple, artless, idyllic love poetry.

Or take the rich, bold, metaphoric imagery that pervades the book: the maid is swarthy as the tents of Kedar, as the hangings of

Solomon; she is a steed of Pharoah's chariot; her hair is flocks of goats; her teeth are flocks of ewes; her neck is a tower of ivory; her nose is a peak of Lebanon; her navel is a rounded goblet; her belly is a heap of wheat set about with lilies! And as for the lover: he has a head of gold; his locks are the branches of a tree; his cheeks are beds of spices; his lips are myrrh-dripping lilies; his hands are golden rods studded with rubies; his belly is sapphire-studded ivory; his legs are pillars of marble set on golden sockets. All these polished, ornate, rhetorical figures of speech hardly smack of the home-made bard and ballad-monger; rather they seem to flow from the well-stocked repertoire of the professional court poet. Moreover, palace and court are mentioned repeatedly in the book, and one of the lyrics[4] is actually a stirring and impressive wedding song in which King Solomon is depicted as the joyous bridegroom. All of which leaves the impression that the "Song of Songs," repetitive, obscure, and difficult as the text is, goes back, at least in part, to some ancient ritual, to a nuptial ceremony in which the king played the role of groom, and for which the court poets composed appropriate songs and lyrics.

With considerations more or less like these running through his mind, Theophile Meek, a scholar who was at home in cuneiform as well as in biblical research, propounded a theory of the origin of the "Song of Songs" which, in my opinion, is fundamentally sound and constructive, in spite of the fact that a number of his assumptions, inferences, and arguments have turned out to be erroneous, wholly or in part. Here in a nutshell are the main lines of his thesis[5]:

The "Song of Songs," or at least a good part of it, is a modified and conventionalized form of an ancient Hebrew liturgy celebrating the reunion and marriage of the sun-god with the mother-goddess, which had flourished in Mesopotamia from earliest days. This Sacred Marriage had been part of a fertility cult which the nomadic Hebrews took over from their urbanized Canaanite neighbors, who, in turn, had borrowed it from the Tammuz-Ishtar cult of the Akkadians, a modified form of the Dumuzi-Inanna cult of the Sumerians. Nor is this at all surprising. As had been noted repeatedly by biblical scholars, traces of this fertility cult are found in a number of books in the Bible, and though the prophets condemned it severely, it was never fully eradicated. In fact the prophets themselves did not hesitate to draw some of their symbolism from the cult, and the frequent descriptions in the prophetic writings of the relation between Jahweh and Israel as that of husband and wife indicate the existence of a Sacred Marriage between Jahweh and the goddess Astarte, the Canaanite counterpart of the Mesopotamian Ishtar-Inanna. Even as late as the Mishnaic times, that is, roughly the time of the canonization of the Old Testament, the maidens of Jerusalem are reported to have gone out at the close of the Day of Atonement and during the "Festival of Trees" to dance in the vineyard. They were met by youths singing "Go forth and gaze, daughters of Zion, on King Solomon and the crown with which his mother crowned him on his wedding day, on the day his heart was overjoyed" (Song of Songs 3:11). This, too, is but a late, if hardly recognizable, reflection of an ancient Hebrew Sacred Marriage Rite.

This theory of the origin of the book, argues Meek, would resolve not a few of the difficulties that have beset the biblical scholar in the past. It would explain why the lover in the "Song of Songs" is designated both shepherd and king—these are the very epithets of Tammuz-Dumuzi in the cuneiform documents. It would also explain why the beloved is designated as both bride and sister—these are identical with the epithets of Ishtar-Inanna. The Mesopotamian Dumuzi-Inanna cult-liturgies consist largely of dialogues and monologues uttered by the sacred couple, interrupted here and there by chorus-like refrains—this would account for the otherwise inexplicable literary structure of the book. Best of all, it would help to explain its acceptance as part of the Holy Scriptures. For even after later Jahwehism had purged its contents by obliterating almost all traces of its fertility cult elements, it still carried with it a hallowed aura of religious traditions that smoothed its way for admittance into the sacred canon, especially since Solomon's name had in some way become attached to it.[6]

Meek's general thesis that the "Song of Songs," or at least parts of it, had its roots in a Sacred Marriage Rite borrowed by the Canaanites from the Tammuz-Ishtar (Dumuzi-Inanna) cult as practiced in neighboring Mesopotamia introduced a fresh note into the stagnating quest for the book's origin, and in one form or another, it gained the adherence of not a few of the leading biblical scholars.[7]

But there are two erroneous assumptions in Meek's thesis that seriously damaged his case. In the first place, Meek, like most scholars of his day, assumed that Tammuz was a genuine, bona fide, immortal Mesopotamian deity right from the beginning; his marriage with Ishtar-Inanna, therefore, was a marriage between deities.[8] This led him to surmise that the Canaanites and Hebrews, too, believed that it was a *god* who was wed to Astarte, and in case of the Hebrews, this would naturally be Jahweh, or the king representing Jahweh. The introduction of Jahweh into the Sacred Marriage Rite weakened considerably Meek's thesis, since Jahweh is nowhere mentioned in the book, an omission that Meek found difficult to explain away. But now we know that Tammuz was originally not a god at all, but a mortal king who was wed to Ishtar-Inanna primarily to ensure the well-being of his land and people. So, too, among the Hebrews, it was not the god Jahweh who was wed to Astarte, but the king—a Solomon, for example—and presumably for the same reasons. With Jahweh eliminated from the rite, Meek's thesis would have been considerably more acceptable to biblical scholars.

In the second place, because in his day well-nigh all the cuneiform texts concerned with the Tammuz-Ishtar cult were dirges and laments, Meek was impelled to comb the "Song of Songs" for all possible (and impossible) references and allusions to the "god who died" and to the "goddess who descended to the Nether World to save him."[9] This led to a number of far-out interpretations that did little to make his thesis creditable.[10] In fact it is rather ironic that most of the parallels from the Tammuz-Ishtar cult (or rather the Dumuzi-Inanna cult as it should be designated, since nearly all the compositions are in the Sumerian language[11]) that he could cull for the tender, joyous songs of the biblical book came from the desolate laments for a dying god. It is only now, when we have more than a dozen Sumerian Sacred Marriage songs of celebration and rejoicing, that we begin to get a true picture of the parallels between the biblical book and some of its probable cuneiform forerunners.[12] For it is now evident that the similarities and resemblances between them are not confined to the general stylistic features, such as the portrayal of the lover as both shepherd and king, and of the beloved as both bride and sister, or the formal interlacing of soliloquies, colloquies, and refrains; they extend to theme, motif, and occasionally even to phraseology.[13]

Take, for example, the very first four verses of the "Song of Songs," in which the beloved pleads with the king, presumably Solomon, whom the "maidens love," and who "has brought me into his chambers," to "kiss me with the kisses of your mouth, for your love is better than wine"—a plea that is followed with the maidens singing "We will exult and rejoice in you, we will extol your love more than wine." These have their counterpart and prototypes in the ecstatic words of a beloved bride of the king Shu-Sin, who sang:

"Bridegroom, dear to my heart,
Goodly is your pleasure, honey-sweet;
Lion, dear to my heart,
Goodly is your pleasure, honey-sweet.

"You have captivated me, I stand trembling before you.
Bridegroom, I would be carried off by you to the bedchamber;
You have captivated me, I stand trembling before you,
Lion, I would be carried off by you to the bedchamber.

"Bridegroom, let me give you of my caresses,
My precious sweet, I would be laved [?] by honey,
In the bedchamber, honey-filled,
Let us enjoy your goodly beauty;
Lion, let me give you of my caresses,
My precious sweet, I would be laved [?] by honey.

"Bridegroom, you have taken your pleasure of me,
Tell my mother, she will give you delicacies [?]
Tell my father, he will give you gifts.

"Your spirit—I know where to cheer your spirit,
Bridegroom, sleep in our house till dawn,
Your heart—I know where to gladden your heart,
Lion, sleep in our house till dawn.

"You, because you love me,
Lion, give me pray of your caresses,
The lord my god, the lord my good genie,
My Shu-Sin who gladdens the heart of Enlil,
Give me pray of your caresses.

"Your place sweet as honey, pray lay a hand on it,
Like a *gishban*-garment, bring your hand over it,
Like a *gishban-sikin*-garment, cup your hand over it".[14]

As the last lines of the rapturous lyric indicate, this was no common maiden unburdening herself of her love for an ordinary sweetheart. This was a devotee of the goddess of love—the ancient poet actually designates it a *balbale* of Inanna—singing of blissful union with her bridegroom, the king Shu-Sin, who "gladdens the heart of Enlil," a sexual mating that would bring the favors of the god to the land and its people. Shu-Sin, not unlike the Solomon of a much later day, seemed to have been a high favorite with the "ladies of the harem," the hierodules and devotees, that made up the cult personnel of Inanna-Ishtar, and it is not surprising to learn that the excavators of ancient Erech, where Inanna had her most revered temple, dug up a necklace of semiprecious stones, one of which was inscribed with the words "Kubatum, the *lukur*-priestess of Shu-Sin" —*lukur* being a Sumerian word designating an Inanna devotee who evidently played the role of the goddess in the Sacred Marriage Rite.

To judge from another love lyric, Shu-Sin made it a habit to present precious gifts to Inanna's votaries, especially if they cheered him with sweet song. In this poem, the beloved of Shu-Sin begins by exalting his birth:

She gave birth to the holy one, she gave birth to the holy one,
The queen gave birth to the holy one,
Abisimti gave birth to the holy one,
The queen gave birth to the holy one.

Then follows a strophe of four exclamatory lines, whose meaning is obscure, but from them we learn that the attractive Kubatum—the very votary whose four-thousand-year-old necklace had been excavated some forty years ago—had now become a "queen," presumably a concubine:[15]

"O my [queen] who is favored of limb,
O my [queen] who is . . . of head, my queen Kubatum,
O my [lord] who is . . . of hair, my lord Shu-Sin,
O my [lord] who is . . . of word, my son of Shulgi."

Like Kubatum, the votary chanting this song, too, had received precious gifts from Shu-Sin, as we hear in the following strophe:

"Because I uttered it, because I uttered it, the lord gave me a gift,
Because I uttered the *allari*[16]-song, the lord gave me a gift,
A pendant of gold, a seal of lapis lazuli, the lord gave me a gift,
A ring of gold, a ring of silver, the lord gave me a gift.
Lord, your gift is brimful of . . . , lift your face unto me,
Shu-Sin, your gift is brimful of . . . , lift your face unto me."

In the next strophe that is only fragmentarily preserved, we find her exalting Shu-Sin as a great king:

". . . lord . . . lord,
. . . like a weapon . . . ,
The city lifts its head like a dragon, my lord Shu-Sin,
It lies at your feet like a lion cub, son of Shulgi."

But then she returns to her own concern, which is to arouse the passion of the king, her "god," in preparation for their union of love:

"My god, sweet is the drink of the wine -maid,
Like her drink sweet is her vulva, sweet is her drink,
Like her lips sweet is her vulva, sweet is her drink,
Sweet is her mixed drink, her drink."[17]

In the last strophe she extols Shu-Sin as "the beloved of Enlil," and "the god of his land," that is, as Dumuzi incarnate, whom Inanna had chosen "to godship":[18]

"My Shu-Sin who favored me,
My [Shu-Sin] who favored me, who fondled me,

My Shu-Sin who favored me,
My beloved of Enlil, Shu-Sin,
My king, the god of his land."[19]

Shu-Sin is also the lover in another lyric chanted by a devotee who may well have been chosen for a night of love with the king, and who had therefore prepared a very special hairdo to make herself attractive in his eyes. For we find her singing:

"Lettuce is my hair by the water planted,
*Gakkul*-lettuce is my hair by the water planted,
Combed [ ?] smooth are its tangled coils [ ?],
My nurse has heaped [ ?] them high.
Of my hair luxuriant in water [ ?],
She has piled thick its small locks,
She puts to rights my 'allure',[20]
The 'allure'—my hair that is lettuce, the fairest of plants.

"The brother has brought me into his life-giving gaze,
Shu-Sin has chosen me, the . . . , the fair. . . ."

Here there is a break of about seven lines in the text. When it begins again, it is not the "bride" who is speaking, but her companions:

"You are our lord, you are our lord,
Silver and lapis lazuli, you are our lord,[21]
Our farmer who makes stand high the grain, you are our lord."

But it is the "bride" who "solos" the last lines:

"For him who is the honey of my eyes, who is the lettuce of my heart,
May the day of life come forth, for my Shu-Sin."[22]

Lettuce was a favorite plant of the Sumerians—not only was the lofty hairdo of the beloved likened to it, the lover, too, is "lettuce by the water planted." He is also a well-stocked garden, grain in the furrow, and a fruit-laden apple tree, according to the exuberant words of his ecstatic beloved:

"He has sprouted, he has burgeoned, he is lettuce by the water planted,

My well-stocked garden of the . . . -steppe, my favorite of his mother,
My grain luxuriating in the furrow, he is lettuce by the water planted,
My apple tree that bears fruit up to its crown,[23] he is lettuce by the water planted."

But most of all she loves him because he is a "honey-man" dripping with sweetness:

"The honey-man, the honey-man sweetens me ever,
My lord, the honey-man of the gods, my favorite of his mother,
Whose hand is honey, whose foot is honey, sweetens me ever,
My sweetener of the . . . navel [?], my favorite of his mother,
My . . . of the fairest thighs, he is lettuce by the water planted."[24]

By wedding Inanna, who according to the theologians was the daughter of the moon-god Nanna-Sin and his wife Ningal, Dumuzi, or the king who was his avatar, became their son-in-law. As such he was to some extent the provider and bread-giver of the "house." This is the theme of a rather short *balbale* of Inanna, most of which was chanted by the companions of the beloved, her confidants and associates in the entourage of the goddess. Following the first two lines, which are fragmentary and unintelligible, we hear them chanting:

"You are our brother, you are our brother,
You are the versatile [?] brother of the palace,
You are the captain of the *magur*-boat,
You are the overseer of the chariot,[25]
You are the city father, the judge,
Brother, you are our father's son-in-law,
You are the noblest of the sons-in-law,
You provide our mother with all this good."

But at the end, it is the beloved who takes over, greeting her lover with these joyous words:

"Life is your coming,
Your coming into the house is abundance,
Lying by [your] side is my greatest joy . . . ."[26]

Another and considerably longer poem is in the form of a playlet, and if I understand it correctly,[27] the scenario goes as follows: The lover is standing outside the beloved's house and asks:

"My sister, why have you shut yourself in the house?
My little one, why have you shut yourself in the house?"

To which she answers:

"I washed myself, soaped myself,
Washed myself in the holy kettle,
Soaped myself in the white basin,
Dressed myself in the garments of queenship, of the queenship of heaven,
That is why I shut myself in the house.
I painted my eyes with kohl,
I fixed my hairdo, the . . . ,
Loosened my tangled hair,
Tested the weapon that will make triumphant his reign,[28]
Set straight my twisted lips,
Piled up my loosened locks,
Let them fall to the 'border' of my nape,
Put a silver bracelet on my hand,
Fastened small beads about my neck,
Fixed their . . . about my neck-sinews."

But though she is now fully dressed, bejeweled, and "made-up," she still has not opened the door. To induce her to let him in, the lover reminds her that it is he who had brought gifts of honey and bread to her:

"Sister, before your heart I brought honey,
[Before] your heart, the beloved heart, I brought it,
Your bread and offerings [?], all [?] I have given you,
Sister, starlight, honey of the mother who bore her,
My sister to whom I have brought five breads,
My sister to whom I have brought ten breads,
I carried out for you your . . . to perfection."

Upon hearing this, the goddess turns graciously to her attendants, saying:

"[As] my brother enters from the palace,
Let the musicians [play] for him,
And I will [pour] wine [?] from [my] mouth for [him],
Thus will his heart rejoice,
Thus will his heart be pleased—
Let him come, let him come, . . . pray [?] let him come!"

The lover—and as will soon become evident, it was the shepherd, Dumuzi, though his name is not mentioned anywhere in the poem—must have heard the welcome invitation of his beloved, for we next find him saying:

"My sister, I will bring them with me into the house,
Lambs as lovely as ewes,
Kids as lovely as goats,
Lambs as goodly as ewes,
Kids as fair as goats,
Sister, I will bring them with me into the house."

From here on, the text becomes obscure, primarily because there is a shift of speakers but no indication of their identity. Thus the next three lines seem to be chanted by the companions of the goddess:

"Lo, high [?] is our bosom,
Lo, hair has grown on our vulva,
At the lap of the bridegroom let us rejoice. . . ."

And the goddess seems to encourage them:

"Dance ye, dance ye,
O Bau,[29] let us rejoice because of my vulva,
Dance ye, dance ye,
Thus [?] will he be pleased, will he be pleased."

Following the rubric designating this song as a *balbale* of Inanna, the poet repeats as a refrain, the line:

"Let him come, let him come, . . . pray [?] let him come."[30]

In this poem there is little that is reminiscent of the "Song of Songs," at least as we have it in our undoubtedly expurgated form, except for such stylistic features as the brother-sister designation of the lovers and the presence of a chorus of maidens.

Nor is there much resemblance to the biblical book in another poem that begins with what seems to be an address to their son-in-law by the bride's parents, that reads in part:

"Our son-in-law, when the day has passed,
Our son-in-law, when night has come,
When moonlight has entered this house,
When moonlight has dimmed [ ?] [the light] in this house,
We [ ?] will remove for you the lock from the door."

There follows a passage of about sixteen lines that are only partially preserved and largely unintelligible; we then find the beloved, in transports over her love's mane of hair, pleading with him to press it close to her bosom:

"My [beloved] fit for [his] mane, my [beloved], fit for [his] mane,
My sweet, my [beloved] fit for [his] mane,
Like the palm tree, my [beloved] fit for [his] mane,
Like the tamarisk, my [beloved] fit for [his] mane,
My bridegroom, fit for [his] six-layer mane,
My sweet, press it to our bosom,[31]
My lion heavy with [his] four-layer mane,
My brother of fairest face, press it close to our bosom."

There follows another fragmentary and obscure passage in which the bridegroom seems to exalt his "lapis lazuli" beard and (perhaps) his rich possessions. In any case, the couple unite in bliss, and the poem ends with this blessing of the goddess for her lover:

"May you be a reign that brings forth happy days,
May you be a feast that brightens the countenance,
May you be bronze that brightens the hands,
Beloved of Enlil, may the heart of your god find comfort in you.[32]
Come in the night, stay in the night,
Come with the sun, stay with the sun,

May your god prepare the way for you,
May the basket carriers and axe carriers level it smooth for you."[33]

A favorite motif of the "Song of Songs" is the "going down" of the lovers to garden, orchard, and field;[34] this is also the theme central to several Sumerian poems of the kind that might have been chanted during the Sacred Marriage celebration. One of these is a rather poorly preserved composition that purports to be a dialogue between King Shulgi and his "fair sister" Inanna. It opens with the goddess complaining of a scarcity of vegetation: no one is bringing her the date clusters due her, and there is no grain in the silos. Whereupon Shulgi invites her to his fields in these words:

"My sister, I would go with you to my field,
My fair sister, I would go with you to my field,
I would go with you to my large field,
I would go with you to my small field,
To my 'early' grain irrigated with its 'early' water,
To my 'late' grain irrigated with its 'late' water,
Do you [fructify ?] its grain,
Do you [fructify ?] its sheaves."

Following a break of some lines, we come to a passage ending with a command by the goddess to a farmer to plow Shulgi's barren fields. Shulgi next invites her to his garden and orchard:

"My sister, I would go with you to my garden,
My fair sister, I would go with you to my garden,
My sister, I would go with you to my garden,
My sister, do you [fructify ?] my garden,
Do you [fructify ?] the *ildag*-tree.
I would go with you to my orchard [ ?],
My sister I would go with you to my apple tree,
May the . . . of the apple tree be in my hand.
My sister, I would go with you to my pomegranate tree,
I would plant there the sweet [ ?] honey-covered [ ?] . . .
My sister, I would go with you to my garden,
Fair sister, I would go with you to my garden,
Like the plants of the orchard [ ?]. . . .[35]

Closer in content and mood to the biblical book is a passage in an Inanna composition inscribed on a still unpublished tablet in the British Museum,[36] in which the goddess sings:

"He has brought me into it, he has brought me into it.
My brother has brought me into the garden.
Dumuzi has brought me into the garden,
I strolled [ ?] with him among the standing trees.
I stood with him by its lying trees,
By an apple tree I kneeled as is proper.

"Before my brother coming in song,
Before the lord Dumuzi who came toward me,
Who from the . . . of the tamarisk, came toward me,
Who from the . . . of the date clusters, came toward me,
I poured out plants from my womb,
I placed plants before him, I poured out plants before him,
I placed grain before him, I poured out grain before him. . . ."

In a like vein, there is a passage in a fragmentary poem in which the goddess chants that after her lover had placed "his hand in mine," "his foot by mine," "had pressed her lips to his mouth," and had taken his pleasure of her, he brought her into his garden, where there were "standing trees," and "lying trees" and where she seems to heap up the fruit of the palm tree and apple tree for her lover, whom she addresses repeatedly as "my precious sweet."[37]

It is not only the garden that Inanna blesses with her presence, but the stall and sheepfold as well. There is a poem in which the goddess is depicted as coming into the stall, where, says the poet:

"The faithful shepherd, he of the sweet chant,
Will utter a resounding [ ?] chant for you,
Lordly Queen, you who sweeten all things,
Inanna, it will bring joy to your heart.

Lordly Queen, when you enter the stall,
Inanna, the stall rejoices with you,
Hierodule, when you enter the sheepfold,
The stall rejoices with you. . . .

The holy sheepfold is filled with cream because of you,
In the sheepfold there is rejoicing,
Ishme-Dagan is long of days."[38]

But not everything in the stall and sheepfold is simple, innocent joy. In a poem inscribed on a tablet in the British Museum which was published more than fifty years ago, but whose contents have been repeatedly misunderstood and misinterpreted,[39] Dumuzi is found amusing Geshtinanna by showing her the incestuous practices that went on in the animal world. The poem begins on a happy note:

Those were days of plenty, those were nights of abundance,
Those were months of pleasure, those were years of rejoicing—
In those days, the shepherd, to make the heart rejoice,
To go to the stall, to brighten its spirit,
To light up the holy sheepfold like the sun,
The shepherd Dumuzi took it into his holy heart.

First, however, he informs his wife, the goddess Inanna, of his projected journey:

"My spouse, I would go to the desert land,
Would look after my holy stall,
Would learn the ways of my holy sheepfold,
Would provide food for my sheep,
Would find for them fresh water to drink."

Inanna's answer is ambiguous and obscure; it is not impossible that she gives him counsel on how to proceed. In any case, we next find Dumuzi in his holy stall accompanied by his sister Geshtinanna. After a rich meal in the well-stocked stall, Dumuzi decides to entertain his sister; or as the poet puts it:

The stall is filled with plenty,
The sheepfold flows with abundance,
They eat—holy food they eat,
They pour honey and butter,
They drink beer and wine,

Dumuzi, to bring joy to his sister,
The shepherd Dumuzi takes it into [his] heart.

The passage depicting this entertainment is very difficult—some of the key words are missing, and the meaning of others it uncertain; the translation that follows is the best that can be done with it at the moment:

He lined up [?] [sheep], brought them into the stall,
The lamb, having jumped [on the back] of its mother,
Mounted her . . . , copulated with her.

The shepherd says to his sister:
"My sister, look! What is the lamb doing to its mother?"

His sister answers him:
"He having [jumped] on his mother's back, she [?] let out [?] a shout of joy."

"If, he having jumped on his mother's back, she [?] let out [?] a shout of joy,
Come now [?], this is because . . . he has filled her with his semen."

The kid having jumped [on the back] of his sister,
Mounted her . . . , copulated with her.

The shepherd says to his sister:
"My sister, look! What is the kid doing to his sister?"

His sister answers him innocently [?]:
"He having jumped on his sister's back, she [?] let out [?] a shout of joy."

"If, he having jumped on his sister's back, she [?] let out [?] a shout of joy,
Come here now [?], [this is because] he has flooded her with his fecundating semen. . . ."[40]

But there can be much too much of a good thing, even if it is love,[41] at least according to one *balbale* of Inanna, where the beloved seems to reproach her lover for being all too eager to leave the "fragrant honey-bed," and return to the palace. Only the last half of this poem is preserved, and there we find the goddess relating sadly:

> My beloved met me,
> Took his pleasure of me, rejoiced as one with me,
> The brother brought me into his house,[42]
> Laid me down on a fragrant honey-bed.
> My precious sweet, lying by my "heart,"
> One by one "tongue-making," one by one,
> My brother of fairest face, did so fifty times. . . .
> My brother, with staying [ ?] [his] hand on his hips [ ?],[43]
> My precious sweet is sated:
> "Set me free, my sister, set me free,
> Come, my beloved sister, I would go to the palace. . . ."[44]

"For love is strong as death, jealousy as cruel as the grave," broods the poet of the "Song of Songs" in one of his more melancholy moods.[45] In some ways this echoes the bitter end of the Dumuzi-Inanna love romance, which began in joyous bliss and ended in tragic death. Just how this came about is related in one of Sumer's more intricate and imaginative myths, whose contents will be sketched in the next chapter. But the grim, inexorable fate that awaited her lover was foreseen and foretold by the goddess in a poem that links love and death by an inseparable bond. It starts with the lover, seemingly quite unaware of his inevitable doom, singing joyously of the delight of his beloved's eyes, mouth, lips, and tasty luxuriance:

> "O my *lubi,* my *lubi,* my *lubi,*[46]
> O my *labi,* my *labi,* my *labi,* my honey of the mother who bore her,
> My . . . wine [ ?], my . . . honey, my comfort [ ?] of her mother,
> Your eyes—their gaze delights me, come now my beloved sister,
> Your mouth—its words of welcome delight me, my comfort [ ?] of her mother,
> Your lips—their bosom-touch delights me, come now my beloved sister.[47]
> My sister, your grain—its beer is tasty, my comfort [ ?] of her mother,
> Your herbs—their juice [ ?] is tasty, come my beloved sister,
> In your house, your luxuriance delights me, my comfort [ ?] of her mother,

My sister, your riches delight me, come now my beloved sister,
Your house is a steadfast house . . . , my comfort [ ? ] of her mother."

But the beloved's response is sombre and sorrowful: because he had dared love the goddess, sacred and tabu to mortals, he has been doomed to die:

"You, royal son, my brother of fairest face,
You will come to an end, you will come to an end, you have been decreed an evil fate,
Brother, on the outskirts of the city you will come to an end, you have been decreed an evil fate,
You upon whom the enemy had not put a hand, you have been decreed an evil fate,
You against whom the enemy had not . . . , you have been decreed an evil fate.

"My . . . ,
My beloved, my man of the heart,
You, I have brought about an evil fate for you, my brother of fairest face,
My brother, I have brought about an evil fate for you, my brother of fairest face.

"Your right hand you have placed on my vulva,
Your left, stroked my head,[48]
You have touched your mouth to mine,
You have pressed my lips to your head,
That is why you have been decreed an evil fate,
Thus is treated the 'dragon'[49] of the women, my brother of fairest face."

Evidently, Dumuzi had been altogether too tempting and alluring for his own good, at least as the goddess recalls it in these lines that end the poem:

"My blossom bearer, my blossom bearer, sweet was your allure,
My blossom bearer in the apple garden, sweet was your allure,
My bearer of fruit in the apple garden, sweet was your allure,
Dumuzi-abzu, my well qualified one, sweet was your allure,

My holy provider [?], my holy provider [?], sweet was your allure,
[My] provider [?], outfitted with sword and lapis lazuli diadem,
sweet was your allure."

But fortunately for mankind, Dumuzi's death was only temporary; he was saved from death eternal by the tender love of his sacrificing sister. This annual drama of Dumuzi's death and resurrection is the theme of the following chapter.

6

# The Sacred Marriage: Death and Resurrection

It was not just whimsical caprice that prompted the Sumerian theologians and mythographers to doom Dumuzi to death, temporary though it proved to be, and thus leave much of the promise of the Sacred Marriage unfulfilled. Rather it was the inevitable consequence of their realistic observation of the "facts of life." For Sacred Marriage or not, the grim truth was that for half the year, during the long, dry scorching Mesopotamian summer, all vegetation withered and drooped, while life in stall and fold was barren and sterile, and this could mean only that the god in charge of these essential activities had died and gone to the Nether World and could no longer function.[1] But then how could this be reconciled with the reassuring credo that Dumuzi had wed the all-powerful goddess Inanna, who loved him so dearly that she raised him to godhood over the land, and this presumably had made him immortal?[2] To resolve this dilemma the Sumerian poets and mythmakers put their imagination to work and created an intricate tale of frustrated ambition, divine cunning, ungrateful infidelity, morbid jealousy, and tender sisterly love. The text of this myth of some four hundred lines has been pieced together over the years from more than twenty tablets and fragments, several of which were published more than fifty years ago; it is now nearly complete, and the following sketch of its contents is beyond reasonable doubt.[3]

The poem begins with Inanna's decision to descend to the Nether World, the dark, dread home of the dead. For it would seem that not satisfied with being queen of the "Great Above" only, she aspires to be queen of the "Great Below" as well.[4] She therefore abandons heaven and earth, "lordship" and "ladyship," and all her most renowned cities and temples; decks herself out in all her rich finery and tempting jewels; and holding on tightly to the sacred emblems of her powers and prerogatives, she is all set to descend to the ghastly, ghostly "Land of No Return." Or, as the poet puts it in his repetitious narrative style:

From the Great Above she set her mind to the Great Below,
The goddess, from the Great Above she set her mind to the Great Below,
Inanna, from the Great Above she set her mind to the Great Below.

My lady abandoned heaven, abandoned earth—to the Nether World she descended,
Inanna abandoned heaven, abandoned earth—to the Nether World she descended,
Abandoned lordship, abandoned ladyship—to the Nether World she descended,
In Erech she abandoned Eanna—to the Nether World she descended,
In Badtibira she abandoned Emushkalamma—to the Nether World she descended,
In Zabalam she abandoned Giguna—to the Nether World she descended,
In Adab she abandoned Esharra—to the Nether World she descended,
In Nippur she abandoned Baradurgarra—to the Nether World she descended,
In Kish she abandoned Hursagkalamma, to the Nether World she descended,
In Agade she abandoned Eulmash—to the Nether World she descended.[5]

The seven *me* she fastened at the side,
Gathered all the *me,* placed them in her hand,

Set up the goodly *me* at her waiting foot,
The *shugurra,* the crown of the steppe, she put upon her head,
Locks of hair she fixed upon her forehead,
The measuring rod and line of lapis lazuli she gripped in her hand,
Small lapis lazuli stones she tied about her neck,
Twin egg-stones she fastened to her breast,
A gold bracelet she gripped in her hand,
The breast-plate "Come, man, come" she bound about her breast,
With the *pala*-garment, the garment of ladyship she covered her body,
The ointment "Let him come, let him come" she daubed on her eyes.[6]

But the queen of the Nether World is her older sister and bitter enemy, Ereshkigal,[7] who would certainly not tolerate her presence in the lower regions, and would no doubt try to put her to death for daring to usurp her dominion. She therefore, summons her vizier and messenger, Ninshubur, who is ever at her beck and call, and says to her:

"You who are my constant support,
My vizier of favorable words,
My courier of true words,
I am now descending to the Nether World.
When I shall have come to the Nether World,
Set up a lament for me by the ruins,
In the assembly shrine beat the drums for me,
Rend your eyes for me, rend your mouth for me . . . ,
Like a pauper in a single garment dress for me,
To the Ekur, the house of Enlil, all alone direct your step.

"Upon entering the Ekur, the house of Enlil, weep before Enlil:
'Father Enlil, let not your daughter be put to death in the Nether World,
Let not your good metal be covered with the dust of the Nether World,
Let not your good lapis lazuli be broken up into the stone of the stoneworker,
Let not your boxwood be cut up into the wood of the woodworker,
Let not the maid Inanna be put to death in the Nether World.'
If Enlil stands not by you in this matter, go to Ur.

First half of the poem "Inanna's Descent to the Nether World. Tablet in the Hilprect Sammlung of University of Jena.

"In Ur, upon entering the house that is the terror of the land,
The Ekishnugal, the house of Nanna, weep before Nanna:
'Father Nanna, let not your daughter be put to death in the Nether World,
Let not your good metal be covered with the dust of the Nether World,
Let not your good lapis lazuli be broken up into the stone of the stoneworker,
Let not your boxwood be cut up into the wood of the woodworker,
Let not the maid Inanna be put to death in the Nether World.'
If Nanna stands not by you in this matter, go to Eridu.

"In Eridu, upon entering the house of Enki, weep before Enki:
'Father Enki, let not your daughter be put to death in the Nether World,
Let not your good metal be covered with dust in the Nether World,
Let not your good lapis lazuli be broken up into stone of the stoneworker,
Let not your boxwood be cut up into the wood of the woodworker,
Let not the maid Inanna be put to death in the Nether World.'
Father Enki, the lord of wisdom,
Who knows the 'food of life,' who knows the 'water of life,'
Will surely bring me back to life."

Thus reassured of revival and survival even if the worst befalls her, she proceeds to the world below. Arrived at the "palace" of the Nether World, she speaks up boldly at the door:

"Open the house, gatekeeper, open the house,
Open the house, Neti, open the house, all alone I would enter."

And when the gatekeeper asks: "Who, pray, are you?" she answers proudly, "I am the queen of heaven, of the place where the sun rises."

But the gatekeeper is suspicious:

"If you are the queen of heaven, of the place where the sun rises,
Why, pray, have you come to the 'Land of No Return,'
On the road whose traveler returns never, how has your heart led you?"

Inanna there and then concocts a false excuse:

"My elder sister Ereshkigal,
Because her husband, the lord Gugalanna had been killed,
To witness the funeral rites. . . , so be it."

But this does not allay Neti's suspicions, and he orders her to wait while he speaks to his mistress Ereshkigal. He "enters the house of his queen" and describes her apparel and appearance just as it was depicted above: the *me,* the *shugurra,* the locks of hair, the measuring rod and line, the small lapis lazuli stones, the egg-stones, the gold bracelet, the breast plate, the *pala*-garment, the alluring ointment. Hearing this description, Ereshkigal realizes at once who it was that was trying to "crash the gate" of her dominion and why, and she became so enraged that she "smote her thigh and bit it." There is only one way out: Inanna must be put to death. But nothing can be done to her until her garments, jewels, ornaments, and emblems are removed. She therefore says to the gatekeeper:

"Come, Neti, my chief gatekeeper of the Nether World,
The word that I command you, neglect not,
Of the seven gates of the Nether World, lift their bolts,
Of its one palace *Ganzir,* the 'face' of the Nether World, lift their bolts,
Upon her entering, having removed all her princely garments, make her bow low."

Neti, the chief gatekeeper of the Nether World, heeded the word of his queen,
Of the seven gates of the Nether World, he lifted their bolts,
Of its one palace, *Ganzir,* the 'face' of the Nether World, he pressed open its door,
To the holy Inanna he says: "Come, Inanna, enter."

Upon her entering the first gate,
The *shugurra,* the crown of the steppe, was removed.
"What, pray, is this?"
"Be silent, Inanna, the *me* of the Nether World are perfect,
Inanna, do not deprecate the rites of the Nether World."

Upon her entering the first gate,
The measuring rod and line of lapis lazuli was removed.
"What, pray, is this?"
"Be silent, Inanna, the *me* of the Nether World are perfect,
Inanna, do not deprecate the rites of the Nether World."

In virtually identical five-line passages, the poet depicts the removal of the small lapis lazuli stones, the egg-stones, the gold bracelet, and the breastplate, and ends with the line "Bowed low, she was brought naked before her." Now that Inanna is stark naked, the moment is ripe for punishing her for her violation of the divine laws:

The holy Ereshkigal seated herself upon her throne,
The Anunna, the seven judges, pronounced judgment before her,
She fastened her eyes upon her, the eyes of death,
Spoke the word against her, the word of wrath,
Uttered the cry against her, the cry of guilt,
Struck her, turned her into a corpse,
The corpse was hung from a nail.

In the meantime, Inanna's vizier Ninshubur is awaiting impatiently the return of her mistress from the world below. And when after three days and three nights[8] she fails to do so, Ninshubur goes about carrying out the instructions of her mistress step by step. She wanders about lamenting in "the house of the Gods," with lacerated body and dressed like a pauper, then goes to the Ekur temple of Nippur and weeps before Enlil:

"Father Enlil, let not your daughter be put to death in the Nether World,
Let not your good metal be covered with dust in the Nether World,
Let not your good lapis lazuli be broken up into the stone of the stoneworker,
Let not your boxwood be cut up into the wood of the wood worker.
Let not the maid Inanna be put to death in the Nether World."

But Enlil refuses; he has no sympathy for the ambitious Inanna, who defied the *me* of the gods, and wanted to rule not only the "Great Above," but the "Great Below" as well. Ninshubur then goes to the Ekishnugal temple of Ur, and repeats her plea before the moon-god Nanna, Inanna's father; but he too refuses, and for the same reason. Ninshubur then proceeds to Enki's temple in Eridu, where she finds a sympathetic response:

> Father Enki answers Ninshubur:
> "What now has happened to my daughter! I am troubled,
> What now has happened to Inanna! I am troubled,
> What now has happened to the queen of all the lands! I am troubled,
> What now has happened to the hierodule of heaven! I am troubled."

Now Enki has in his charge the "food of life" and the "water of life" that could revive the goddess. The trouble is that she is down in the Nether World, and even if she could be reached there, Ereshkigal would hardly permit any one to sprinkle them upon her corpse and bring her back to life. But Enki is a god renowned for cleverness and cunning, and he devises a rather intricate plan to compel the unwilling Ereshkigal to deliver Inanna's corpse for resuscitation. His approach is essentially psychological, and his bait is flattery. First, from the dirt of his finger nails, he creates two sexless beings designated as *kalatur* and *kurgarra*—evidently only such creatures could gain admittance to the Nether World unnoticed. There, he informs them, they will find the goddess Ereshkigal lying naked, ill, and groaning.[9] Their instructions are to respond sympathetically, and to sigh and groan with her as if they were deeply touched by her suffering. Flattered by their comforting commiseration, she will reward them by promising to fulfill whatever they may request. But they must not take her word for it—they must make her swear by heaven and earth. They will then be offered as gifts water and grain, but they must not accept them. Instead, they must demand Inanna's corpse as their reward. Once it is delivered to them, they are to sprinkle the food and water of life upon it, and the goddess will revive. All this is related by the poet in a straightforward, laconic narrative style:

> He brought forth dirt from his fingernail and fashioned the *kurgarra,*
> He brought forth dirt from the red-painted fingernail and fashioned the *kalatur,*

To the *kurgarra* he gave the food of life,
To the *kalatur,* he gave the water of life,
Father Enki says to the *kalatur* and *kurgarra:*

"Go, 'lay' the feet towards the Nether World,
Fly about the door like flies,
Circle about the door—pivot like."
The birth-giving mother, because of her children,
Ereshkigal lies there ill,
Over her holy body no cloth is spread,
Her holy chest like a *shagan*-vessel is not. . . ,
Her hair like leeches she wears upon her head.[10]

"When she cries 'Woe! Oh my inside!'
Say to her 'You who sigh, our queen, Oh your inside!'
When she cries 'Woe! Oh my outside!'
Say to her 'You who sigh, our queen, Oh your outside!'
[She will then say to you]: 'Whoever you are,
[Because] you have said: From my inside to your inside,
From my outside to your outside,
If you are gods, I shall pronounce a [kindly] word for you,
If you are men, I shall decree a [kindly] fate for you,'
Make her swear by heaven and earth.

"Of the river they [Ereshkigal's minions] will present you its water, do not accept it,
Of the field, they will present you its grain, do not accept it,
'Give us the corpse hung from the nail,' say to her,
One [of you] sprinkle upon her the food of life, the other, the water of life,
Inanna will arise."

The two creatures carry out Enki's instruction to the last detail,[11] and Inanna, brought back to life, is all set to reascend to earth and reenter her cities and temples. But there is still one serious snag, seemingly unforeseen by the wise Enki: a divine rule was laid down from most ancient days that no one, not even a deity, can leave the Nether World unharmed unless a substitute is provided to take his (or her) place. And so, the poet records:

Inanna was about to ascend from the Nether World,
The Anunnaki seized her [saying]:
"Who of those descending to the Nether World, ever ascends unharmed from the Nether World!
If Inanna would ascend from the Nether World, let her provide someone as her substitute."

Inanna, prepared to fulfill this condition, is permitted to leave. But to make sure that this goddess, whose reputation for deceitfulness is well-known,[12] actually produces her surrogate, she is followed by the *galla,* the small, pitiless, inhuman "constables of the Land of No Return," who are to bring her back by force if she fails to keep her pledge. Or, as the poet tells it:

Inanna ascends from the Nether World,
The small *galla,* like lance-sized reeds,
The large *galla,* like hedge-sized reeds,
Held fast to her side.
Who was in front of her, though not a vizier,
Held a scepter in his hand,
Who was at her side, though not a courier,
Held a mace fastened to his loins,
They who accompanied her,
They who accompanied Inanna,
Were creatures who know not food, know not drink,
Eat not sprinkled flour, drink not libated wine,
Snatch the wife from the man's lap,
Snatch the child from the nursemaid's breast.

And so Inanna, accompanied by the ghoulish *galla,* ascends to earth, where her first task is to find a deity in her entourage for whom she has so little use that she could hand him over without regrets to the little devils to carry off to the Nether World, as her substitute. The very first deity to meet her is the faithful Ninshubur, who, upon seeing her mistress come up from the world below with the monstrous *galla* at her side, dresses herself in sackcloth and prostrates herself at her feet in the dust. When, therefore, the devils, eager to "get their man" and have it over with, seize her in order to carry her off as Inanna's substitute, Inanna stops them, saying:

> "This is my vizier of favorable words,
> My courier of true words,
> Who failed not my instructions,
> Neglected not the word I uttered"

and further reminds them that it was Ninshubur who wandered tearfully from temple to temple pleading with the gods to save Inanna from Ereshkigal's clutches, until finally Enki gave heed to her plea.

Frustrated in their first attempt, the *galla* accompany her to the Sigkurshagga temple in Umma, where Inanna's son, the god Shara, is venerated. Upon seeing his mother pushed about by the cruel demons, he too dresses himself in sackcloth and falls at her feet in the dust. And so, when the cruel harpies lay hands on him, she stops them, saying:

> "This is my Shara who sings hymns to me,
> Who cuts my nails, smooths my hair,
> Him I shall not give to you at any price."

Frustrated a second time, the *galla* accompany her to the temple Emushkalamma in Badtibira, where her son Lulal is worshipped. He, too, upon seeing his mother jostled by the little fiends, dresses himself in sackcloth and throws himself at her feet. And so when the restless, eager *galla* lay a hand on him, she stops them for the third time, saying:

> "This is my Lulal, the leader,
> Who stands at my right and left."

At last they arrive at Inanna's own city Erech, in its sacred district Kullab. There she finds her beloved husband, Dumuzi, "dressed in noble garments," and "sitting on a lofty throne"—not for him the weeping, lamenting, and grovelling in the dust at the heartbreaking sight of his wife surrounded by demons and ghouls. This so incenses Inanna that:

> She fastened her eye upon him, the eye of death,
> Spoke the word against him, the word of wrath,
> Uttered the cry against him, the cry of guilt,

and with no more ado, hands him over to the *galla* waiting impatiently for their victim. Once he is in their hands, they begin to bind, beat, and torture Dumuzi mercilessly in preparation for the descent to the world of the dead.[13] But by this time Dumuzi has realized his wretched plight, and he tries to save himself by pleading with his brother-in-law, the sun-god Utu:

> "Utu, I am your friend, me the young man, you know,
> I took your sister to wife,
> She descended to the Nether World,
> Because she descended to the Nether World,
> She has turned me over to the Nether World as her substitute.
> Utu, you are a just judge, do not let me be carried off,
> Change my hand, alter my form,
> Let me escape the hands of my demons, let them not catch me,
> Like a *sagkal*-snake I will traverse the highland meadows,
> I will carry off my soul to the home of sister Geshtinanna."[14]

There is now a ray of hope for Dumuzi since, as the poet informs us:

> Utu accepted his tears,
> Changed his hands, altered his form,
> Like a *sagkal*-snake, he traversed the highland meadows,
> Dumuzi—his soul left him like a hawk flying against a bird,
> He carried off his soul to the house of Geshtinanna.

Upon seeing her tortured brother, who presumably had resumed his human shape upon arrival at his sister's house:

> Geshtinanna stared at her brother,
> Rent her cheeks, rent her mouth,

Looked to her side, ripped her garments,
Uttered a bitter lament for the suffering lord:
"Oh my brother, oh my brother, the lad whose days [?] were not long [?],
Oh my brother, Amaushumgalanna, the lad whose days [?] and years [?] were not long [?],
Oh my brother, the lad who has no wife, has no child,
Oh my brother, the lad who has no friend, has no companion,
Oh my brother, the lad who brings no comfort to his mother!"

And she has good reason to mourn him, for his miraculous escape from the fiendish ghouls is short-lived. Thwarted for the moment by Dumuzi's getaway, they are determined to pursue him to the bitter end. Taking counsel on what to do next, the little *galla* says to the big *galla:*

"You *galla* who have no mother, have no father, sister, brother, wife, son,
Who ever flutter about over heaven and earth as chief constables,
You *galla* who cling to a man's side,
Who show not kind favor, who know not good and bad—
Who has ever seen the soul of a man panicked by fear, live in peace!
Let us not go to the home of his friend, let us not go to the home of his brother-in-law,
Let us proceed [in search of] the shepherd to the home of Geshtinanna."

Pleased by their decision, they arrive at Geshtinanna's home, but find that their victim has once again flown—evidently he has sensed his danger and was left his sister's house. They torture Geshtinanna mercilessly to force her to tell them his hiding place, but to no avail:

The *galla* clapped their hands, went searching for him,
With cries that ceased not from their mouths,
The *galla* proceeded to the home of Geshtinanna.
"Show us where your brother is," they said to her, but she told them not,
Heaven was brought close, Earth was put in her lap, but she told them not,

Earth was brought close . . . was lacerated, but she told them not,
. . . was brought close, . . . was scattered over her garments, but she told them not,
Pitch was poured on her lap, but she told them not,
They found not Dumuzi in Geshtinanna's house.

But there is no escape from the little fiends. Since Dumuzi was not in his sister's house, they conclude rightly that he must have gone to the desert steppe and hidden in his "holy stall." There they catch up with him, seize and torture him, and are all set to carry him to the Nether World to death everlasting. But this time his doting sister tries to save him by making the supreme sacrifice—she offers to take Dumuzi's place in the Land of No Return, as a substitute for the substitute. Inanna can hardly refuse this generous gesture. But since she does not want to see the ungrateful, unfaithful Dumuzi go unpunished, she decides Solomon-like that he should stay in the Nether World half the year, and his sister should take his place the other half.[15]

Just as the love of the young Dumuzi for Inanna inspired the Sumerian poets to compose songs of joy and delight, so his death and his tragic humiliating descent to the Nether World moved them to write poems filled with bitterness and grief. In one version of the death of Dumuzi there is no mention of his resurrection, although in this poem, too, the sister Geshtinanna plays a major role, and does everything she can to save him. The poet sets the melancholy mood in the very first lines, which depict Dumuzi, who senses his approaching doom, addressing the dreary lifeless steppe and beseeching it to set up a lament for him:

His heart was filled with tears, he went forth to the steppe,
The shepherd—his heart was filled with tears, he went forth to the steppe,
He fastened his flute [ ? ] about his neck, uttered a lament:
"Set up a lament, set up a lament, O steppe, set up a lament,
O steppe, set up a lament, set up a wail,
Among the crabs of the river, set up a lament,
Among the frogs of the river, set up a lament,
Let my mother utter a cry,
Let my mother Sirtur utter a cry,

Let my mother who has not five breads, utter a cry,[16]
Let my mother who has not ten breads, utter a cry,
On the day I die, she will have none to care for her,
On the steppe, like my mother my eyes shed tears,
Like my little sister, my eyes shed tears."

There is good reason for Dumuzi's premonition of doom. For as the poet next tells, Dumuzi had a terrible depressing dream:

Among the buds he lay, among the buds he lay,
The shepherd—among the buds he lay,
As the shepherd lay among the buds, he dreamt a dream:
He awoke—it was a dream,
He trembled, it was a vision,
He rubbed his eyes, he was dazed.

The divine interpreter of dreams was none other than his sister Geshtinanna, who was also an expert scribe, as well as a chanteuse. And so Dumuzi exclaims (the poet does not say to whom):

"Bring her, bring my sister,
Bring my Geshtinanna, bring my sister,
Bring my tablet-knowing scribe, bring my sister,
Bring my little sister, who knows the meaning of words, bring my sister,
Bring my expert who knows the meaning of dreams, bring my sister,
I would tell her my dream."

We next find Dumuzi telling his dream to his sister, who, presumably, had been brought to him (although the poet fails to mention this), and there is little wonder that he is terrified:

"Of the dream, my sister, of the dream, . . . this is the heart of the dream:
Rushes rise all about me, rushes grow thick all about me,
A single-growing reed bows its head for me,
Of a double-growing reed, one is removed
In the wooded grove, the terror of tall [ ?] trees rises all about me,
Over my holy hearth no water is poured,

Of my holy churn, its stand [ ?] is removed,
The holy cup hung on a peg, from the peg has fallen,
My shepherd's crook has disappeared,
My owl takes. . . ,
A falcon holds a lamb in its claws,
My young kids drag their 'lapis lazuli' beards in the dust,
My sheep of the fold, paw the ground with their limbs bent,
The churn lies shattered, no milk is poured,
The cup lies shattered, Dumuzi lives no more,
The sheepfold is given over to the wind."[17]

Geshtinanna then proceeds to interpret this foreboding dream item by item:

"My brother, unfavorable is your dream, tell it not to me;
Dumuzi, unfavorable is your dream, tell it not to me.
Rushes rise all about you, rushes grow thick all about you,
Cutthroats will rise in attack against you.
A single-growing reed bows its head for you—
The mother who bore you will bow her head for you.

"Of a double-growing reed, one is removed—
I and you, one of us will be removed.[18]

"In the wooded grove, the terror of tall [ ?] trees rises all about you—
The evil ones will terrorize you. . . .

"Over your holy hearth no water is poured—
The sheepfold will be turned into a house of desolation.

"Of your holy churn, its stand [ ?] is removed—
The evil ones will put a restraining hand on you.

"The holy cup hung on a peg, from the peg has fallen—
You will fall from the gracious knee of the mother who bore you.

"Your shepherd's crook has disappeared—
The evil one makes everything languish away.

"Your owl takes. . . —
The evil ones will take. . .

"The falcon holds a lamb in his claws—
The big *galla* will drive you from the . . . house,

"Your young kids drag their 'lapis lazuli' beards in the dust—
My . . . will whirl about in heaven like [ ?] a cyclone.

"Your sheep of the fold, paw the ground with their limbs bent—
My . . . will . . . the . . . for you,

"The churn lies shattered, no milk is poured,
The cup lies shattered, Dumuzi lives no more,
The sheepfold is given over to the wind."

There follows a fragmentary passage of about fifteen lines, part of which may have contained Geshtinanna's advice to the panicked Dumuzi to hide and thus escape the *galla,* who, as the dream forebode, would soon catch up with him to carry him off to the Nether World. When the text begins again we find Dumuzi saying to Geshtinanna, whom he here addresses as "friend," rather than "sister":

"My friend, I will hide among the plants, tell not where I am,
I will hide among the small plants, tell not where I am,
I will hide among the large plants, tell not where I am,
I will hide among the ditches of Arali, tell not where I am."

Geshtinanna promises and swears:

"If I tell your hiding place, may your dogs devour me,
The black dogs, your dogs of shepherdship,
The wild dogs, your dogs of lordship,
May your dogs devour me."

But soon, too soon, the *galla* appear on the scene, those inhuman creatures who:

Eat no food, drink no water,
Drink not libated water,
Accept not mollifying gifts,
Sate not with pleasure the lap of the wife,
Kiss not children, the sweet.

They follow Geshtinanna about from city to city, to Adab, Erech, Ur, and Nippur, and everywhere there is death and desolation in their wake. Finally they catch up with her at the "sheepfold and stall," and try to extract from her the whereabouts of her brother. They try to bribe her, but in vain:

Of the river, they present her its water, she accepts it not,
Of the field, they present her its grain, she accepts it not:
"My friend has hidden among the plants, I know not where he is."
They search for Dumuzi among the plants, they catch him not.

"He has hidden among the small plants, I know not where he is."
They search for Dumuzi among the small plants, they catch him not.

"He has hidden among the large plants, I know not where he is."
They search for Dumuzi among the large plants, they catch him not.

"He has hidden among the ditches of Arali, I know not where he is."
They search for Dumuzi among the ditches of Arali, they catch him not.

But Dumuzi has a guilt feeling about the suffering he is causing to his sister and "friend":

Dumuzi wept, turned exceeding pale:
"In the cities I shall have brought an end to my sister,
I shall have killed my friend."

And so, in some way (the passage involved is largely unintelligible),[19] he lets his presence be betrayed to the *galla,* who immediately begin to torture their victim:

They surrounded the prisoner, whirl round and round about him,
They twist a cord for him, splice a string for him,
They twist a *ziptum*-cord for him, scrape a stick for him,
Who went in front of him, beat him,
Who went behind him, plucked him like a plant,
His hands are bound in fetters,
His arms are held fast by pinions.

As in the myth "Inanna's Descent to the Nether World," we

find Dumuzi pleading with the sun-god Utu to transform him into an animal, except that this time it is a gazelle rather than a snake:

> The lad lifted his hands heavenward to Utu:
> "Utu, you are my wife's brother, I am your sister's husband,
> I am he who carried food to the Eanna,
> Who brought the wedding gifts to Eanna,
> Who kissed the holy lips,
> Who danced on the holy knee, the knee of Inanna.
> Turn my hands into the hands of a gazelle,
> Turn my feet into the feet of a gazelle,
> Let me escape my demons,
> Let me carry off my soul to. . . ."[20]
>
> Utu accepted his tears as an offering,
> Like a man of mercy, he showed him mercy.
> He turned his hands into the hands of a gazelle,
> He turned his feet into the feet of a gazelle,
> He escaped his demons,
> He carried off his soul to. . . .

But the *galla* catch up with him there and once again begin to torture him. Again Dumuzi pleads with Utu to turn him into a gazelle, so that he may escape his demons and carry off his soul, this time to the house of Old-Belili.[21] Utu does so, and he arrives at the Belili's home, where he asks the goddess for food and drink:

> "Old one, I am not a [mortal] man, I am the husband of a goddess,
> Pour water so that I may drink,
> Sprinkle flour, so that I may eat."
>
> She poured out water, sprinkled flour,
> He was seized in its midst.

And so for the third time the *galla* begin to torture him. This time he pleads with Utu to turn him into a gazelle so that he may carry off his soul to the holy sheepfold, the sheepfold of his sister. Utu once again heeds his plea and Dumuzi arrives at his sister's sheepfold. But Geshtinanna senses the tragic truth that this is the end for Dumuzi, that the *galla* will catch up with him at the sheepfold and put him to death. Or as the poet puts it (the passage is only partially intelligible):

He arrived at the holy sheepfold, the sheepfold of his sister,
Geshtinanna brought her mouth close to heaven, her mouth close to earth,
Covered the horizon like a garment . . . ,
Wrapped it about like a cloth,
Rent her eyes for him, rent her mouth for him,
Rent her ears for him, the awe-inspiring. . . .

Soon enough the *galla* arrive at the sheepfold and the stall, and then:

The first *galla,* on entering the sheepfold and stall,
Struck him on the cheek with a piercing nail,
The second, on entering the sheepfold and stall,
Struck him on the cheek with the shepherd's crook.
The third, on entering the sheepfold and stall,
Removed the stand from the holy churn.
The fourth, on entering the sheepfold and stall,
Threw down from the peg the cup hung on the peg.
The fifth, on entering the sheepfold and stall,
Shattered the churn, no milk was poured.
Shattered the cup, Dumuzi lives no more,
The sheepfold is given over to the wind, Dumuzi is dead.[22]

The pursuit of Dumuzi by the *galla* of the Nether World was a favorite motif of the Sumerian mythographers, who felt free to elaborate the details as their fancy dictated. There is a version, for example, in which seven *galla,* not five, pursue Dumuzi, and behave towards him in a manner that is not quite as vicious and sadistic as might have been expected. This text is part of a composition that consists of two parts, a brief, bitter lament by Inanna for her dead husband, followed by the story of his death, or rather its closing episode. The death of her husband, which was primarily her own doing, filled the goddess with woe and remorse, not only for her own loss, but for the fate of her city, Erech, and her temple, Eanna. As the poet saw it in his own imagination:

The Lady weeps bitterly[23] for her husband,
Inanna weeps bitterly for her husband,
The queen of Eanna weeps bitterly for her husband,
The queen of Erech weeps bitterly for her husband,
The queen of Zabalam weeps bitterly for her husband,
Woe for her husband, woe for her son,[24]
Woe for her house, woe for her city,
For her husband taken captive, for her son taken captive,
For her husband killed, for her son killed,
For her husband taken captive at Erech,
Killed at Erech, at Kullab,
Who no longer bathes in Eridu,[25]
Who no longer rubs himself with soap in Enun,
Who no longer treats the mother of Inanna as his mother,[26]
Who no longer performs his sweet task among the maidens of his city,[27]
Who no longer competes among the lads of his city,
Who no longer wields his sword among the *kurgarra* of his city,[28]
The noble one who is no longer held dear by his followers.

Inanna laments for her young bridegroom,
"Gone has my husband, sweet husband,
Gone has my son, sweet son,
My husband has gone among the 'head' plants,[29]
My husband has gone among the 'rear' plants,
My husband who has gone to seek food,[30] has been turned over to the plants,
My son who has gone to seek water, has been given over to the water.
My bridegroom, like a hand crushed. . . , has departed from the city,
The noble one, like a hand-crushed 'head' plant, has departed from the city."

Here ends the introductory lament of the composition, and the tale of the pursuit of Dumuzi by the *galla* and his capture begins. "Once upon a time," relates the poet, the seven *galla* in pursuit of Dumuzi surrounded his holy sheepfold. The first six entered, and each in turn wrought such havoc in it that in the end it was nothing but a heap of dust, and utterly desolate. But when the seventh entered:

The noble one who was lying asleep he aroused with an *a-u-a* [cry],
The husband of Inanna who was lying asleep he aroused with an *a-u-a* [cry]:
"My king, we are all about you! Rise, come with me!
Dumuzi, we are all about you! Rise, come with me!
Husband of Inanna, son of Sirtur! Rise, come with me!
Brother of Gestinanna, you who [sleep] a false sleep! Rise, come with me![31]
Your ewes have been seized, your lambs have been carried off! Rise, come with me.
Your goats have been seized, your kids have been carried off! Rise, come with me.
Take off the holy crown from your head, go bareheaded!
Take off the *me*-garment from your body, go naked!
Take off the holy scepter from your hand, go bareheaded.
Take off the sandals from your feet, go barefoot!"

And so Dumuzi left his demolished sheepfold in panic and, as expected, prayed to Utu to change him into a gazelle so that he might escape the *galla.* Utu just as expectedly heeded his prayers, and Dumuzi sped over ditch and dike in terror.[32] Whereupon the thwarted *galla* took counsel among themselves:

*Galla* lifted eyes to *galla,*
The little *galla* speaks to the big *galla,*
The *galla* speaks to his companion:

"The lad who has escaped us— . . . ,
Dumuzi who has esacped us— . . . ,
Let us follow him among the dikes of the steppe,
The man of the dikes of the steppe will seize him with us.
Let us follow him among the ditches of the steppe,
The man of the ditches of the steppe will seize him with us.
Let us follow him among the 'head' sheep,
Let us be with him by the 'head' sheep of his friend.
Let us follow him among the 'rear' sheep,
Let us be with him among the 'mounting' sheep of his friend.
Let us follow him among the . . . sheep,

Let us be with him among the . . . sheep of his friend.
Let us go, let us stay close to him,
Let us hold on to him at the lap of his mother Sirtur,
Sirtur the merciful mother, will speak to him of mercy,
At the lap of his sister, his merciful sister—she will speak to him of mercy,
Let us hold on to him at the lap of his spouse, Inanna.
Inanna, the storm whose roar is shattering, will rage against him,
Heaven [is shattered] by the storm, Erech is shattered by the storm."[33]

We next find Dumuzi in Erech by the goddess, where:

By the big apple-tree, by the offering table of the Emush—
On its earth the lad poured the boat-destroying waters of the Nether World,
The husband of Inanna poured the boat-destroying waters of the Nether World,
There was no cream, the cream that was libated,
There was no milk, the milk that was drunk,
There was no stall, the stall that was built,
There were no sheep, they had been bundled off,
The *galla* seized by the shoulders him who had not [even] a reed to lead him.[34]

According to another myth, Inanna shows her great love for the dead Dumuzi by a rather extraordinary feat. In order to "sweeten the place where her husband lies," presumably the desert-like steppe that was his grave, she goes to the trouble of killing another deity and transforming the corpse into a waterskin so that the lad who travels in the steppe will have cold fresh water to drink there. The poet begins this remarkable tale by relating that Dumuzi's holy sheepfold is in ruins and someone is bitterly lamenting its destruction. Inanna, his wife, therefore pleads with her mother Ningal to let her go to her husband's sheepfold, probably to see for herself what has happened. Permission granted, Inanna, whom the poet describes as "very knowing" and "very apt," proceeds to the sheepfold, only to find Dumuzi gone and his sheep dispersed in the steppe.[35] And so Inanna, relates the poet, "though she was not a shepherd, reassembled the sheep of my king." Furthermore, she is so moved by Dumuzi's death that "she gave birth to a song for her husband, fashioned a song for him":

"You, who are lying, shepherd, you who are lying, stood watch over it,
Dumuzi, you are lying, stood watch over it,
By day, standing up, you stood watch over my well-being,[36]
By night, lying down, you stood watch over my well-being."

We are now introduced to three minor, but rather remarkable, deities: an old matron who "knew her business," her son Girgire, a robber-baron and capitalist of sorts, and his son Sirru-Edinlilla ("Sirru of the Desolate Steppe"), a friendless fellow who spent his time sitting in conversation with his father. To quote the poet's graphic, thumbnail portrayal:

In those days, Old Bilulu,
A matron, a lady of endowment—
Her son Girgire, a lonesome man,
Quick-witted, a man of experience,
Filled his stall and fold with the cattle he had rustled,
Heaped high his piles and mounds [of grain],
Hastily dispersed his slaughtered victims,
[While] his son, the friendless Sirru-Edinlilla,
Sat before him, conversing with him.

But then, the poet continues:

The Lady, what did her heart prompt her [to do]!
Holy Inanna, what did her heart prompt her [to do]!
To kill Old Bilulu, her heart prompted her,
For her beloved husband Dumuzi, Amaushumgalanna,
To gladden [his] lying-place, her heart prompted her.

My lady [seized ?] Bilulu in the desolate steppe,
[Gave ?] her son Girgire over to the wind,
His son, the friendless Sirru-Edinlilla,
The holy Inanna made enter [her] *eshdam,*
She stood in judgment, decreed [their] fate:
"Come now, I have killed you [Bilulu]—so it is! I will wipe out your name,

You will become a water-skin[37] for fresh water, a 'thing' of the steppe,
Her son Girgire together with her,[38]
Will become the *Udug* of the steppe, and the *Lamma* of the Steppe,
His son, the friendless Sirru-Edinlilla
Will go about in the steppe, will keep track there of the flour.[39]
The lad[40] going about in the steppe, having libated water, having sprinkled flour,
The *Udug* of the steppe, the *Lamma* of the steppe,
He will let speak there . . . , he will let speak there. . . ,
He will [thus] have set up two places of rest [ ?],
Old Bilulu will rejoice."[41]

Lo! By Utu! On that very day, it was so![42]
She [Bilulu] became a water-skin for fresh water, a "thing" of the steppe,
Her son Girgire together with her,
Became the *Udug* of the steppe, the *Lamma* of the steppe,
His son, the friendless Sirru-Edinlilla,
Went about in the steppe, kept track of the flour,
The lad going about in the steppe, having libated water, having sprinkled flour,
The *Udug* of the steppe, the *Lamma* of the steppe,
He let speak there . . . , he let speak there. . . ,
He [thus] set up two places of rest [ ?],
Old Bilulu rejoiced.

The remainder of the poem is fragmentary and obscure. It is certain, however, that much of its contents centered about Dumuzi's sister Geshtinanna, who is described as "the lordly Lady born in Kua," the "marvel and acclaim of the black-heads," "who utters prayers for the king."[43]

Dumuzi's death was not commemorated in myth and song only; there were no doubt special days of mourning set aside in the various cities of Sumer, during which solemn rites and rituals centering about his demise were perfomed.[44] Nor was Dumuzi of Erech the only deity whom the Sumerian theologians doomed to death and the Nether World; the same fate overtook, for example, Ningishzida of Gishbanda in southern Sumer, Sataran of Der in northern Sumer, and Damu, the healing god of Isin in central Sumer.[45] Just how and why these gods met their death, and whether they, too, were resurrected after a half-year sojourn in the lower regions is unknown—no myths about them comparable to Dumuzi-Inanna tales have been uncovered to date. But since in the extant liturgies[46] these gods are identified with Dumuzi, it is not unreasonable to surmise that the priestly bards who composed and redacted them in the early second millennium B.C. ascribed at least part of the Dumuzi mythologies to them also.[47]

From Mesopotamia, the theme of the dead Dumuzi and his resurrection spread to Palestine,[48] and it is not surprising to find the women of Jerusalem bewailing Tammuz in one of the gates of the Jerusalem temple.[49] Nor is it at all improbable that the myth of Dumuzi's death and his resurrection left its mark on the Christ story, in spite of the profound spiritual gulf between them. Several motifs in the Christ story that may go back to Sumerian prototypes have been known for some time: the resurrection of a deity after three days and three nights in the Nether World;[50] the notion of thirty shekels, the sum received by Judas for betraying his master, as a term of contempt and disdain;[51] the epithets "shepherd," "anointed," and perhaps even "carpenter";[52] the not unimportant fact that one of the gods with whom Dumuzi came to be identified was Damu, "the physician," to whom his mother Ninisinna, "the great physician of the black-heads," entrusted the art of healing by exorcising demons.[53] To all these can now be added the torturing suffered by Dumuzi at the hands of the cruel *galla,* reminiscent to some extent of the agony of Christ: he was bound and pinioned; was forced to undress and run naked; was scourged and beaten. Above all, as we now know, Dumuzi, not unlike Christ, played the role of vicarious substitute for mankind; had he not taken the place of Inanna, the goddess of love, procreation, and fertility, in the Nether World, all life on earth would have come to an end.[54] Admittedly the differences between the two were more marked and significant than the resemblances—Dumuzi was no Messiah preaching the Kingdom of God on earth. But the Christ story certainly did not originate and evolve in a vacuum; it must have had its forerunners and prototypes, and one of the most venerable and influential of these was no doubt the mournful tale of the shepherd-god Dumuzi and his melancholy fate, a myth that had been current throughout the ancient Near East for over two millennia.

# *Notes*

Abbreviations:

*ANET* *Ancient Near Eastern Texts*
*PAPS* *Proceedings of the American Philosophical Society*

## 1. The Sumerians: History, Culture, and Literature

1. For a sketch of the archaeological "resurrection" of the Sumerians, and of the decipherment of their script and language, cf. S. N. Kramer, *The Sumerians* (Chicago, 1963), pp. 5-31.

2. For a sketch of the evidence justifying the designation of Sumer, rather than any other region, as the "cradle of civilization," cf. Chapter 8 of S. N. Kramer, *Cradle of Civilization* (New York, 1967).

3. For an analysis of the relevant source material, tenuous, elusive, and meager as it is, cf. *The Sumerians*, pp. 33-39.

4. The name Sumer is first found in archaeological documents dating from about 2400 B.C., but there is no reason to doubt that it was current as far back as the beginning of the third millennium, or even earlier. For an explanation of the chronology used throughout this book, cf. *The Sumerians*, pp. 31-32.

5. At least this was the consensus of Near Eastern archaeologists until quite recently. The figure 4500 B.C. was obtained by starting with 2500 B.C. as the date that marks the beginning of the Sumerian historic period. To this were added some 2,000 years, a time-span large enough to account for the stratigraphic accumulation of all the prehistoric cultural remains right down to virgin soil, that is, right down to the beginning of human habitation in Sumer. At that time, it was generally assumed, Sumer was a vast swampy marsh broken up here and there by low islands of alluvial land built up by the gradual deposit of silt carried by the Tigris, Euphrates, and Karun rivers. Before that, it was thought, most of Sumer was covered altogether by the waters of the Persian Gulf, which presumably extended much farther inland

than it does today, and human habitation was therefore impossible. In 1952, however, the two geologists Lees and Falcon published a paper that carried revolutionary implications for the date of the first settlements in Sumer. In this study (cf. *Geographical Journal,* vol. 118, 1952, pp. 24-39), they adduced geological evidence to show that Sumer had been above water long before 4500 B..C, and it is not impossible, therefore, that man had settled there considerably earlier than had hitherto been assumed. The reason that no traces of these earliest settlements have as yet been unearthed, it is claimed, may be that the land has been sinking slowly while at the same time the water table has been rising. The very lowest levels of cultural remains are therefore now under water, and the archaeologists, misled by the higher water level into believing they had touched virgin soil, never reached them (cf. also the relevant comment by Joan Oates, *Iraq,* vol. 22, 1960, pp. 47-50).

6. The pertinent evidence derives not, as might have been expected, from archaeological or anthropological sources—these are ambiguous and inconclusive on this mattter—but from linguistics. The name of Sumer's two life-giving rivers, the Tigris and Euphrates, or *idiglat* and *buranun* as they read in cuneiform, are not Sumerian words. Nor are the names of Sumer's most important urban centers; Ur, Eridu, Larsa, Isin, Adab, Kullab, Lagash, Nippur, Kish, are all words that have no satisfactory Sumerian etymology. Both the rivers and the cities, or rather the villages that later became cities, must have been named by a people that did not speak the Sumerian language, just as, for example, such names as Mississippi, Connecticut, Massachusetts, and Dakota indicate that the earlier inhabitants of the United States did not speak the English language. The name of the pre-Sumerian "Ubaidians" is of course unknown, and likely to remain so, since they lived long before writing was invented, and they therefore left no tell-tale records.

7. For more details concerning these excavations, cf. *The Sumerians,* p. 29.

8. For the pertinent evidence, inconclusive though it is, cf. *The Sumerians,* p. 42.

9. The document referred to is the Sumerian King List (cf. *The Sumerians,* pp. 328-331). That Etana was a notable and outstanding early ruler in Sumer is also indicated by the fact that he became a figure of legend in later days; cf. *The Sumerians,* pp. 43-44.

10. For the location of Aratta, cf. my "Sumerian Epic Literature," to be published by the Accademia Nazionale dei Lincei as part of its symposium *La poesia epica e la sua formazione.*

11. For details, cf. *The Sumerians,* pp. 269-275.

12. For a description of these graves, cf. Chapter 3 of Leonard Woolley, *Excavations at Ur* (London, 1954), and especially his magnificent *The Royal Cemetery* (*Ur Excavations,* vol. II, London and Philadelphia, 1934).

13. Between Lugalbanda and Gilgamesh, the Sumerian King List (cf. note 9) inserts the name of Dumuzi and designates him as "the fisherman

whose city was Kua." This is the king who, for some as yet unknown reason, became the major protagonist in the Sacred Marriage Rite treated in this book. He must evidently have been a remarkable figure in his day who had deeply impressed the theologians, but as yet no historical texts concerned with him or his reign have been uncovered. In fact the place given him in the King List between Lugalbanda and Gilgamesh seems rather suspect; in the epic tales, for example, Gilgamesh refers to Lugalbanda as his "father," which seems to imply that Gilgamesh followed immediately after Lugalbanda and that they were not separated by the reign of Dumuzi. Moreover, the King List itself lists a Dumuzi "the shepherd" as an antediluvian king in Badtibira. It is clear, therefore, that there was some confusion in the minds of the Sumerian schoolmen as to both the origin and the date of the king known as Dumuzi, although there is little doubt that he was a historical personage of outstanding importance.

14. For the three-cornered struggle for power between the cities Kish, Erech, and Ur, cf. *The Sumerians,* pp. 45-49.

15. This information is derived not from a contemporary historical inscription, but from a literary document dated long after his reign, but whose contents seem to me to be quite genuine and trustworthy (cf. *The Sumerians,* pp. 50-52 for full details).

16. For a translation of the document relating this event, cf. *The Sumerians,* pp. 313-315.

17. For fuller details concerning this rather extraordinary dynasty, cf. *The Sumerians,* pp. 52-58; for translation of some of the more important documents written by these ancient "historiographers," cf. *The Sumerians,* pp. 308-317.

18. For a translation of this invaluable sociological document, cf. *The Sumerians,* pp. 317-323.

19. For a translation of Lugalzaggesi's most important inscription, cf. *The Sumerians,* pp. 323-324.

20. Agade is written as "Akkad" in the Bible (cf. Genesis 10:10); hence the word "Akkadian" that is gradually coming into use as the name of the Semitic language spoken throughout ancient Mesopotamia, of which the two main dialects are Assyrian and Babylonian. (Note, however that the comprehensive dictionary now being compiled in Chicago is still called the *Assyrian Dictionary;* its less comprehensive German counterpart, on the other hand, is called *Akkadisches Handwörterbuch.*)

21. For more details concerning the reign of Sargon, cf. *The Sumerians,* pp. 59-61.

22. The document depicting this event is a Sumerian poem of 279 lines now generally known as "The Curse of Agade: The Ekur Avenged." For a sketch of its contents cf. *The Sumerians,* pp. 62-66; for a translation of the entire document, and full bibliographical references, cf. the forthcoming Supplement to *ANET* (*Ancient Near Eastern Texts,* James Pritchard, editor,

2nd Edition, Princeton, 1955). Following the reign of the Sargon Dynasty, Sumer came to be known by the compound name "Sumer and Akkad."

23. The late great Sumerologist, Adam Falkenstein, has devoted much time and labor to the Gudea inscriptions, and his scholarly translation of these texts is now in press in the Pontifical Biblical Institute in Rome; cf. for the present his preliminary translations in Falkenstein and Von Soden, *Sumerische und Akkadische Hymnen und Gebete* (Zürich-Stuttgart, 1953), pp. 137-182. For an analysis of the contents and stylistic features of the Gudea Cylinders, cf. pp. 23-34 of this book.

24. For fuller details about Ur-Nammu and his reign, cf. *The Sumerians,* pp. 67-68. An up-to-date translation of the available text of the Ur-Nammu law-code has been prepared by J. J. Finkelstein for the forthcoming *Supplement to ANET;* my edition of a remarkable literary document concerned with the death of Ur-Nammu will appear in the forthcoming number of the *Journal of Cuneiform Studies* in honor of Albrecht Goetze, the dean of American cuneiformists.

25. For fuller details about Shulgi and his successors, cf. *The Sumerians,* pp. 69-71; for a translation of four letters from the royal correspondence of this period, cf. ibid., pp. 331-336; for a translation of two lamentations over the destruction of Ur, cf. *ANET* pp. 455-463, and the forthcoming *Supplement to ANET.*

26. For fuller details, cf. *Cradle of Civilization,* pp. 52-53. An excellent survey of the history and culture of Sumer will be found in Vol. I, Chapters XIII, XIX, XXII, and Vol. II, Chapter V of the *Revised Cambridge Ancient History* now in press, all prepared by the eminent Orientalist C. J. Gadd. (These chapters have already appeared as Fascicles 9 [1962], 17 [1963], 28 [1965], and 35 [1965] under the titles: "The Cities of Babylonia," "The Dynasty of Agade, and the Gutian Invasion," "Babylonia," and "Hammurabi"; note that the word "Babylonia" in these titles might better have read "Sumer".)

27. For the origin and development of Sumerian temple architecture, including its most prominent feature, the ziggurat, cf. *Crade of Civilization* pp. 139-142.

28. All these quotations are from the royal hymns; cf. especially W. H. Römer, *Sumerische königshymnen der Isin Zeit* (Leiden, 1965).

29. Warfare, sad to say, was rampant in Sumer throughout its history. It began with the internecine struggle for power between the burgeoning cities, leading to bitter civil wars that raged intermittently throughout the millennia. When from time to time one city or another succeeded in extending its hegemony over the land as a whole, the king would turn his weapons against the neighboring lands. It was this persistent, perpetual, ever-expanding and intensifying warfare that brought an end to the "cradle of civilization." These struggles only serve to underline the melancholy irony of man and his destiny. For these destructive conflicts were triggered primarily by aggressive ambition, the drive for preeminence and prestige, for victory and

success, the very same motives and incentives that were responsible in large part for the economic, social, educational, and technological advances which made Sumer the home of a high civilzation in the first place.

30. A translation of this Shulgi hymn together with pertinent bibliographical references will be found in the forthcoming *Supplement to ANET*. There is another and very important Shulgi hymn that provides us with a picture of the ideal king as the Sumerians envisioned him, a rare combination of scholar, soldier, sportsman, diviner, diplomat, patron of learning, and provider of all good things for his land and people (cf. my "Shulgi of Ur: A Royal Hymn and a Divine Blessing" in the Seventy-Fifth Anniversary Volume of the *Jewish Quarterly Review*, 1967, pp. 369-380).

31. The Sumerians began writing down some of their legal transactions as early as 2700 B.C. or thereabouts, not long after cuneiform had been developed into a reasonably flexible tool; they had thus unknowingly and unwittingly become the fathers of written law. And only three centuries later, in the days of Urukagina, we find a Sumerian archivist recording a social reform, including a case of tax reduction, that is of outstanding significance for the history of man's perennial struggle for his legal rights and for relief from beaureaucratic injustice and oppression (cf. page 8 above, and note 18). Some two centuries later the first law code known to date was promulgated by Ur-Nammu (cf. pages 9-10 above, and note 24). We also have a Sumerian law code from Lipit-Ishtar (cf. *ANET*, pp. 159-161). And while the justly famous Hammurabi law code (cf. *ANET*, pp. 164-180) is written in Semitic Akkadian, there is little doubt that most of it goes back to Sumerian sources.

32. Not that Sumer's passion for law and justice necessarily had its origins in lofty ideals and sublime ethics; more likely it stemmed from the Sumerian's competitive, aggressive, and individualistic temperament, and to such related characteristics as his love of possessions and high regard for private property. Even the earliest settlers in Sumer, the "Ubaidians," must have brought with them a hatred of oppression and a dread of victimization —otherwise they would hardly have left their homes to "wander in the wilderness" (cf. *Cradle of Civilization*, pp. 16 and 33ff.). Some of these early pioneers were no doubt ambitious and contentious by nature, psychological traits that were nurtured and fostered by the bickering and dickering over water and property rights that were prevalent throughout Sumer's history.

33. For the evidence that Sumerian economy was relatively free, and that private property was the rule rather than the exception—a view that runs counter to the long-current conclusion that Sumer was a totalitarian theocracy dominated by the temple which owned all the land and was in absolute control of the entire economy—cf. *The Sumerians*, pp. 75-78; cf. also *The Cradle of Civilization*, pp. 79-85, and note especially the importance of the merchant for Sumerian city life.

34. For the role of slavery in Sumerian society, cf. Isaac Mendelson, *Slavery in the Near East* (New York, 1948); B. J. Siegel, "Slavery During the Third Dynasty of Ur", *American Anthropologist,* New Series, vol, 2, No. 1, part 2, (1947); Adam Falkenstein, *Die neusumerischen Gerichtsurkunden* (Munich, 1956), pp. 81-95.

35. Cf. especially *The Sumerians,* pp. 250-257.

36. Cf. *The Sumerians,* pp. 257-258. For an excellent summary of the Sumerian marriage and family laws, cf. Falkenstein, pp. 98-116.

37. For the physical appearance of one Sumerian metropolis, cf. Leonard Woolley, *Excavations at Ur,* pp. 175-194; for the house furniture, cf. Hollis S. Baker, *Furniture in the Ancient World* (New York, 1967), pp. 157-178, and Armas Salonen, *Die Möbel des Alten Mesopotamien* (Helsinki, 1963), pp. 9-16; for household vessels, cf. Armas Salonen, "The Household Utensils of the Sumerians and Babylonians" in the *Proceedings* of the Finnish Academy of Science and Letters (1965), pp. 127-137.

38. For the Sumerian notions about death and the Nether World, cf. *The Sumerians,* pp. 129-134.

39. An excellent up-to-date summary of Sumerian agriculture will be found in Armas Salonen, *Agricultura Mesopotamica* (Helsinki, 1968), pp. 11-36; for Mesopotamian medicine and craftsmanship, cf. especially Leo Oppenheim, *Ancient Mesopotamia* (Chicago, 1964), pp. 288-331; for Mesopotamian mathematics and astronomy, cf. Otto Neugebauer, *The Exact Sciences in Antiquity* (Providence, 1957), Chapters 2 and 5; for a very brief sketch of the Sumerian craftsmanship, cf. *Cradle of Civilization,* pp. 145-146.

40. For a comprehensive sketch of the religious ideas and practices of the Sumerians, their theology, rites, and myths, cf. Chapter 4 of *The Sumerians;* for a detailed analysis and interpretation of some of the Sumerian religious ideas and their origin, cf. my review article, "The Intellectual Adventure of Ancient Man," H. Frankfort, editor, *Journal of Cuneiform Studies,* vol. 2 (1948), pp. 39-70.

41. It is this Sacred Marriage Rite that is the theme of Chapters 3-6 of this book.

42. For a comprehensive treatment of Sumerian art cf. especially H. Frankfort, *The Art and Architecture of the Ancient Orient* (Baltimore, 1954), pp. 1-61; cf. also Leonard Woolley, "The Art of the Middle East" (New York, 1961), pp. 43-100, and Seton Lloyd, *The Art of the Ancient Near East* (London, 1961), pp. 79-114. A number of stimulating ideas on the art and architecture of Sumer will be found in S. Gideion, *The Beginnings of Architecture* (New York, 1964), pp. 1-241.

43. For a detailed study of Sumerian music, cf. Henrike Hartmann, *Die Musik der sumerischen Kultur* (Fraukfurt am Main, 1960); for the existence of a musical scale and a coherent musical system in later Babylonia that may go back to Sumerian days, cf. M. Duchesne-Guillemin, "Découverte d'une gamme Babylonienne," *Revue de Musicologie,* vol. 49 (1963), pp.

3-17; and Anne Draffkorn Kilmer, "The Strings of Musical Instruments: Their Names, and Significance," *Assyriological Studies,* No. 16, of the Oriental Institute of the University of Chicago (1965), pp. 261-272.

44. The most comprehensive book on the subject is H. Frankfort, *Cylinder Seals* (London, 1939).

45. For fuller details, cf. my "Cultural Anthropology and the Cuneiform Documents," *Ethnology,* vol. 1 (1962), pp. 299-314.

46. For fuller details, cf. Chapter 5 of *The Sumerians,* and my "Sumerian Similes" in a forthcoming number of the *Journal of the American Oriental Society.*

47. Cf. Chapter 6 of *The Sumerians* and pp. 123-126 of the *Cradle of Civilization* for fuller details.

## 2. The Poetry of Sumer: Parallelism, Epithet, Simile

1. These court minstrels and singer-musicians were found by the hundreds in every important city in Sumer; we actually know by name hundreds of those employed in the various temples from the administrative documents current in Sumer during the second half of the third millennium B.C. For full details about Sumerian musicians, cf. Henrike Hartmann, *Die Musik der Sumerischen Kultur.* (Note especially that what has been written about Sumerian music by F. W. Galpin in his *The Music of the Sumerians and their Immediate Successors, the Babylonians, and Assyrians,* 2nd Edition, Strasbourg, 1955, is quite outdated and erroneous in large part.)

2. In the case of the Sumerians, however, the repetition technique may have been furthered by a characteristic psychological trait. The Sumerian language, for example, is noted for the fact that the verbal form recapitulates by means of infixed elements the various relationships of the nominal complexes that precede it; the cylinder seals show a tendency to repeat a given scene indefinitely; narrative plots often repeat motifs and incidents in a manner that seems redundant to the modern reader (cf. *The Sumerians,* pp. 170-171).

3. Cf. *The Sumerians,* pp. 168; J. Van Dijk, *Acta Orientalia,* vol. 18, 1964, pp. 35-59.

4. There is very little doubt, however, that future excavations will turn up numerous literary works from these centuries, though certainly not as much as from the period of the Third Dynasty of Ur (cf. page 34).

5. The ancient scribe himself designates Cylinder A as "The Middle Hymn of the Building of the House of Ningirsu," and Cylinder B as "The Final Hymn of the Building of the House of Ningirsu," which seems to indicate that there may have been an initial hymn on a cylinder not yet excavated or destroyed in large part (note that there actually exist in the

Louvre a number of unplaceable fragments that do not belong to Cylinder A or B). The texts of the Gudea Cylinders have been carefully copied and published by the eminent French cuneiformist F. Thureau-Dangin, *Les Cylindres de Goudéa* (Paris, 1925). The most recent translation of their text is by Adam Falkenstein in *Sumerische und akkadische Hymnen und Gebete* (Zurich, 1935), pp. 137-182. The translations of the passages here presented were prepared by me with the help of an unpublished manuscript of my late teacher and colleague, Arno Poebel (cf. *The Sumerians,* pp. 24-25).

6. For full details, cf. *The Sumerians,* pp. 137-140.

7. This passage (col. I, spaces 1-4) describes the very beginning of time after the creation of the universe. The gods, under the leadership of Enlil, sat down to decree the destiny of the cities in accordance with the divine laws and regulations. Enlil showed special favor to Lagash and its tutelary deity Ningirsu, particularly in the vital area of water supply. It is written in straight narrative style, except for the suspenseful use of the pronoun "he" in the second line; "he" refers to Enlil, who is not mentioned by name until the line following. Note, too, that the action recorded in line 3 really precedes that of line 2, and that lines 2 and 4 actually belong together; this is a linguistic feature that is rather typical of Sumerian (cf. e.g. notes 11, 14).

8. In this highly poetic passage (Col. II, spaces 5-9) the author depicts the divine act of prime value to any Sumerian city, the overflow of the river that enriched the soil with the help of irrigation and was the basic source of its prosperity and well-being. He obtained his poetic effect by repeating lines 1 to 3, except for the addition of "of Enlil" in line 2; the (probably) metaphorical use of the verb "shine forth" in connection with flood-waters; the unusual position of the adjectival phrase, "the majestic"; the metaphorical identification of "the heart of Enlil" with the Tigris River.

9. Note that these two rather brusque, laconic, prosaic lines (Col. I, spaces 10-11), contrast rather effectively with the preceding high-sounding, circuitous, poetic lines.

10. In this, on the whole straightforward narrative passage (Col. I, spaces 12-16) note that the name of the *ensi* is not mentioned; it does not appear until the following passage—a suspense technique that is a feature of Sumerian poetry in general.

11. To be noted in this passage (Col. I, spaces 18-21) is the unusual position of Ningirsu (the "his king" of line 1) in line 2; the parallelism of lines 3 and 4. Interesting too, is the "illogical," interchanged position of lines 3 and 4, since the action recorded in line 4 no doubt preceded that of line 3 (cf. note 7).

12. The first two lines of this passage (Col. I, space 22-Col. II, space 3) express laconically and elliptically Gudea's perplexity: he had received a vision in the form of a rather complex dream, as we learn later, whose meaning he cannot fathom. In the remaining lines, the author has him solilo-

quizing poetically about his course of action; note especially the cadent repetition in line 3, and the suspenseful position of "it" and "her"; the use of static, stylized epithets in lines 5, 8, and 9.

13. The only poetic devices used in this passage (Col. II, spaces 4-9) are the repetition of "boat" in line 2, and the rhythmic parallelism of the two parts of line 5.

14. In contrast to the preceding one, this passage (Col. II, spaces 10-19) is highly poetic in form; note especially the clustering together of numerous epithets and descriptive clauses (lines 1-3, 8-12), and the metaphorical "its path" (line 12) for a more prosaic expression, such as "how to go about it." Note, too, that lines 6 and 7 seem to be inverted, logically speaking; cf. notes 7, 11.

15. The only poetic devices in this passage (Col. II, spaces 20-27) are the unusual phrasing of line 2-3, and the rhythmic parallelism of the two parts of line 6. Note, too, that the last two lines of this passage are almost identical in phrasing with the last two lines of the preceding passage but one; this type of repetition generates a rhythmic pattern characteristic of Sumerian poetry.

16. This remarkable hymnal prayer, put in the mouth of Gudea by a religious poet of strong faith may be divided into five sections. In the first (Col. II, space 28-Col. III, space 5), observe the clustering of epithets and descriptive clauses in lines 1-5 and the parallelism of lines 6-7. In the second section (Col. III, spaces 6-8) the effect of the parallelism of the first two lines is enhanced by the contrasting parallelism within each of the two lines. Note, too, the rather mystic conception of Gudea as the lineal son of the goddess Gatumdug, who conceived him in her womb impregnated by his divine father Ningishzida (who is not mentioned here, but it known as Gudea's personal god from other sources). On the other hand, the epithet "mother," used by Gudea to describe the goddess Nanshe, is an honorific title only. In the third section of this hymnal prayer (Col. III, spaces 9-17), note especially the metaphorical comparison of the goddess to "a large sword" and "a broad cover." In the fourth section (Col. III, spaces 18-21), note the calculated omission of the verb "I am going" in the second line, the poetic image of the city Nina as "the hillock rising out of the water," and the partially contrasting parallelism of lines 3 and 4. Finally, much of the last section (Col. III, spaces 22-28), is virtually a repeat of an earlier passage in the text (cf. page 27), and is another example of the rhythmic repetition patterns found throughout the Sumerian compositions (cf. preceding note).

17. Note that most of the lines of this passage (Col. III, space 29-Col. IV, space 7) are virtually cliché repeats of lines in earlier passages.

18. Gudea's dream is obviously an imaginative *tour de force* on the part of the poet, an *ad hoc* invention to fit the preconceived interpretation; it is hardly likely that Gudea really experienced this synthetic, contrived,

segmental vision, and later repeated it to the author, who remembered to put it down verbatim when composing his hymn of glorification. The passage may be divided into five sections. The first (Col. IV, spaces 8-13) consists of an epithet-laden hymnal address to the goddess. The dream itself (Col. IV, space 14-Col. V, space 10) is in narrative form with relatively few and not overly impressive poetic devices: the contrasting parallelism in line 2 of the second section; the terse, rhythmic description in the three lines that follow; the turn of phrase in "who is she not! who is she!" for a prosaic "I know not who she is" (note the inverted order of the clauses, at least from our point of view).

19. The long passage (Col. V, space 11-Col. VI, space 13) repeats virtually verbatim the dream as told by Gudea in the preceding passage, but breaks it up into its various segments in order to insert the relevant interpretation.

20. This passage (Col. VI, space 14-Col. VII, space 8) begins with a cliché line used to introduce the giving of instructions or advice. The instructions themselves are on the whole prosaic in style with here and there a metaphorical phrase, a simile, a cluster of epithets.

21. The text (Col. VII, spaces 9-29) goes on to repeat virtually verbatim in the third person indicative the instructions that have been given in the second person in an imperative-like form—a repetition device typical of narrative poetry the world over.

22. In this passage (Col. IX, spaces 5-19), note especially the varied use of repetition and parallelism, epithets and descriptive phrases, and one simile.

23. In this passage (Col. XI, space 1-Col. XII, space 11) replete with epithets, descriptive phrases, and parallel lines, note especially the effective use of parallel introductory lines in sections 1, 2, and 3, and the "night, day—day, night" inversion in section 4.

24. Judging by this passage (Col. XII, space 12-Col XIII, space 15) life in Sumer was far from ideal and tranquil; there was conflict and division among the citizens; thorns and reeds despoiled the streets; evil-doers were lashed with the piercing "tongue" of whip and cane; mothers and sons were contentious and belligerent; slaves were beaten for all sorts of infractions. No wonder that there was a powerful, if unfilled, longing for unity, kindliness, and peace, or as the poet puts it in words reminiscent of the much later Isaiah (Gudea B, Col. IV, spaces 18-22): "The beasts, the creatures of the steppe,/Together kneel,/The lion, the leopard [?], the dragon of the steppe,/Together lie in sweet sleep."

25. And this is but a fraction of the poetic works still lying underground; for fuller details, cf. Chapter V of *The Sumerians,* and my "Sumerian Similes" in a forthcoming number of the *Journal of the American Oriental Society.*

26. "Do not submit" for "Let us not submit" in the earlier passage is probably an insignificant variant.

27. These lines contain a denigrating comment on the elders of the city, who are identified indirectly by some of their activities and prerogatives (note that the translation of the fifth line of the passage differs from that found on page 188 of *The Sumerians*).

28. For the full text of the poem, cf. *The Sumerians,* pages 187-190.

29. Perhaps the Sumerian equivalent of Mt. Olympus, the home of the gods; in any case, it was noted for its cedar, and was under the charge of the sun-god Utu.

30. That is, presumably, the time of his death had not yet been officially decided in the assembly of the gods.

31. The "names" of the first half of the line probably refers to the names of the gods.

32. The first "he" in this line and the next probably refers to Enkidu, who talks for the entire troop.

33. The image seems to be of the sun going down to sleep on his mother's lap.

34. This line and the next two refer to some obscure historical incidents.

35. For the complete poem, cf. *The Sumerians,* pages 192-197. A definitive edition of the composition based on all available tablets and fragments, most of which were identified by the writer, is now being prepared by Aaron Shaffer, a former student at the University of Pennsylvania, who is now Senior Lecturer at the University of Jerusalem.

36. The metaphor, on the other hand, is relatively rare, and is limited largely to the designation of deities and kings by such grandiose epithets as "rampant lion," "fierce-eyed lion," "noble bull," "princely donkey," "life-giving wild cow," etc. There is one epithet, "Great Mountain," that, for some unknown reason, is reserved for Sumer's leading deity, Enlil.

37. For fuller details, cf. my "Sumerian Similes" in a forthcoming number of the *Journal of the American Oriental Society.*

## 3. The Sacred Marriage: Origin and Development

1. The "Sacred Marriage" that is the subject of this study is that of the goddess Inanna of Erech,and Dumuzi, or some later Sumerian ruler who was deemed to be an incarnation of Dumuzi. There were also "Sacred Marriage" rites between deities, of which, however, we know very little (for details, see e.g. J. Van Dijk, in *Bibliotheca Orientalis,* vol. 11, 1954, p. 83; Raymond Jestin, in *Archiv Orientalni,* vol. 17, 1949, pp. 333-339.

2. For a translation of the composition and bibliographical details, cf. the forthcoming *Supplement* to *ANET.*

3. These are the initial lines of the "Lamentation Over the Destruction

of Sumer and Ur"; for a translation of this composition and bibliographical details, cf. the forthcoming *Supplement to ANET.*

4. For a translation of this Enlil hymn and bibliographical details, cf. the forthcoming *Supplement to ANET.*

5. All these passages are from "Enki and the World Order: The Organization of the Earth and Its Cultural Processes"; cf. *The Sumerians* pp. 171-183. A revised edition of the composition is now being prepared by Carlos Benito as part of his doctoral dissertation for the Department of Oriental Studies of the University of Pennsylvania.

6. For the translation of this hymn and bibliographical details, cf. the forthcoming *Supplement to ANET.*

7. These two passages are part of the "Disputation Between Cattle and Grain"; cf. for the present, *The Sumerians,* pp. 220-222. A text edition and translation of the Sumerian disputations including this one, have been prepared by M. Civil, of the Oriental Institute of the University of Chicago, and are about to go to press.

8. This passage is part of the "Disputations between Summer and Winter"; cf. for the present, *The Sumerians,* pp. 218-220, and the preceding note.

9. This passage is part of "Dumuzi and Enkimdu: The Wooing of Inanna"; for a translation of the composition and bibliographical details, cf. *ANET* pp. 41-42.

10. The head of the pantheon in the early third millennium B.C. was probably the heaven-god An, who at that time was the sole tutelary deity of Erech. About 2500 B.C., the air-god Enlil of Nippur took over as head of the pantheon, probably as the result of a political struggle in which Erech lost its supremacy over the surrounding city-states of Sumer. The water-god Enki of Eridu, there is reason to believe, tried to take over Enlil's place and power in the pantheon, but failed (cf. my "Enki and His Inferiority Complex," a paper to be read before one of the forthcoming sessions of the Recontre Assyriologique Internationale).

11. A vivid example of the manner in which this was achieved according to the rather superficial views of the Sumerian sages and poets is provided by "Enki and the World Order: The Organization of the Earth and Its Cultural Processes" (cf. note 5). According to the author of this composition, Enki sets up and blesses several important states, including Sumer with Ur as its capital; and then proceeds to appoint by name the deities in charge of the Tigris and Euphrates canals, of the marshland and the birds and fish that have their homes in it, of the deep sea, of the life-giving rain, of ditch and dike, of the cultivated field, and even of the pickax and brickmold.

12. At that early time, the pantheon, as far as can be judged from the meager available data, was not as thoroughly systematized as in later days, and it is not known just how Inanna came to be venerated in Erech as its

most important deity. Originally, it was no doubt the heaven-god An who was Erech's supreme deity; its famous temple Eanna means literally "the House of An." In one way or another, however, as we may surmise from the Sumerian documents current about 2000 B.C., she gradually superseded An, whose "hierodule" she had become (one of her frequent epithets is "Hierodule of An"), and who now took a back seat, as it were, in his own city and temple (cf. notes 25 and 26 of "Enki and Inferiority Complex," the paper referred to in note 10). In the course of the systematization of the pantheon that began about 2500 B.C., Inanna, in addition to being the goddess of love, became also a goddess of war (cf. e.g. the "Prayer to Enheduanna: The Adoration of Inanna in Ur" in the forthcoming *Supplement to ANET*), and the goddess of the Venus star (cf. e.g. the "Sacred Marriage" hymn to the goddess, edited in Chapter IV of W. H. Römer, *Sumerische Königshymen der Isin-Zeit,* Leyden, 1965). As the latter, she was naturally conceived by the theologians to be the daughter of the moon-god Nanna-Sin and his wife Ningal, and the sister of the sun-god Utu, who was the son of Nanna-Sin (cf. Kramer, *Sumerian Mythology,* revised edition, New York, 1961, pp. 74-75).

13. This historical information comes from the Sumerian King List (cf. *The Sumerians,* pp. 328-331), which is actually a mixture of fact and fancy, especially in its recording of the reigns of the early dynasties, such as the First Dynasty of Erech, to which Enmerkar and Dumuzi belong. But at present this is all we have to go by. Similarly, the epic tale "Enmerkar and Ensukushsiranna," the poem from which the Sacred Marriage passage had been cited (for a sketch of its contents, cf. S. N. Kramer, *History Begins at Sumer* [New York, 1959], pp. 204-207; a comprehensive edition of the text is now being prepared by Adele Feigenbaum as part of her doctoral dissertation for the Department of Oriental Studies of the University of Pennsylvania) can be said to contain only a kernel of truth, since it was written down centuries later than the events that it relates (for the problems involved, cf. *The Sumerians,* pp. 33-39).

14. The name Dumuzi means literally "True Son," a phrase whose full implications are unkown. In the early period he is often called Dumuzi-Abzu, "Dumuzi of the Sea," (Abzu, "Sea," referring to the home of the water-god Enki); it is not impossible, therefore, that the name was given him by the Sumerian theologians after he had been deified and, for some unknown reason, been duly recognized and acknowledged as the son of Enki. For a comprehensive and trustworthy summary sketch of the references to Dumuzi, in the lexical, economic, and historical texts from earliest times to the days of Hammurabi, cf. Adam Falkenstein, *Compte Rendu de la Troisième Rencontre Assyriologique Internationale* (1954), pp. 41-65 (the one serious error on his part is the assumption that Dumuzi-Abzu was a female deity not to be identified with Dumuzi of Erech).

15. The cities of Erech and Eridu seem to have been in close alliance

from at least as early as the days of Enmerkar (cf. the Introduction to S. N. Kramer, *Enmerkar and the Lord of Aratta: A Sumerian Epic Tale of Iraq and Iran,* Philadelphia, 1952). That Erech and Eridu were closely linked is also evident from the close and friendly relations between their two deities Enki and Inanna, cf. "Inanna and Enki: The Transfer of the Arts of Civilization from Eridu to Erech" (*Sumerian Mythology,* pp. 64-68); "Inanna's Descent to the Nether World" (cf. Chapter 6); "Enki and the World Order" (cf. *The Sumerians,* pp. 174-183). Finally, there is the rather curious fact that, as noted earlier in this chapter (page 58), Dumuzi, the ruler of Erech was, according to one historical tradition, originally a native of Kua, in the neighborhood of Eridu.

16. Note, however, that according to the passage from "Enki and the World Order" cited on page 00 above, it was Enki who appointed Dumuzi as the shepherd-god. The Sumerian mythographers, as will be noted repeatedly throughout this book, were not always consistent in their tales of the gods.

17. All these passages are from "Dumuzi and Inanna: Prosperity in the Palace"; cf. *PAPS* (*Proceedings of the American Philosophical Society*), vol. 107, pp. 507-508, and the forthcoming *Supplement to ANET.*

18. Note that this resembles to some extent the Egyptian belief that the Pharaoh was Osiris incarnate, although in Sumer, it never became an all-pervading dogma.

19. There is at least one historical text that may point to a marriage between Inanna and a king of Sumer who lived several centuries before Shulgi. It is said of Eannatum of Lagash, after he had conquered his enemies inside and outside Sumer, that Inanna "*because she loved him,* gave him the kingship of Kish in addition to the *ensi*-ship of Lagash," and it is not impossible that this is a cryptic reference to a ritual marriage between the goddess and Eannatum (cf. *The Sumerians,* p. 310).

20. Cf. pp. 370-380 of the Seventy-Fifth Anniversary Volume of the *Jewish Quarterly Review* (1967).

21. The poem then goes on to describe Shulgi's journey to two other shrines in Sumer and his triumphant return to Ur, where he is blessed by its tutelary deity Nanna-Sin.

22. The fashioning of this coverlet is the theme of the first playlet-like love song treated in the following chapter (cf. pp. 68-69).

## 4. The Sacred Marriage: Wooing and Wedlock

1. See page 59.

2. Enkimdu is the divine farmer (cf. pp. 53-54); he is not to be confused with Enkidu of the Gilgamesh Tales (cf. *The Sumerians,* pp. 186-205).

3. Cf. Falkenstein in *Compte Rendu de la Troisième Rencontre Assyriologique,* pp. 51-52; and Van Dijk, *Le Sagesse Sumero-accadienne* (Leiden, 1953) pp. 73 ff. It is not certain that the two poems were actually intended to follow each other, but in any case their contents dovetail harmoniously.

4. This is one of the rare examples of a literary text that is of some significance for the history of technology; it provides a step-by-step account of the process of weaving as practiced by the Sumerians (cf. my "Sumerian Literature and the History of Technology", *Ithaca,* 26 VIII, 2 IX (1962), pp. 377-380.

5. There is one more line (it speaks of the shepherd as "the man of her heart"), that seems out of place in the context.

6. For the revised rendering of the last four lines of this passage, cf. "CT XLII: A Review Article", *Journal of Cuneiform Studies,* vol. 18 (1964), p. 45, note 76.

7. Since Geshtinanna is Dumuzi's sister, one might have expected here the name of Inanna's sister "Lady of the Holy Reed," but the text is broken, and the traces do not point to this expected restoration.

8. For the text edition of this poem, cf. *PAPS,* vol. 107, pp. 495-497; for a translation, cf. the forthcoming *Supplement to ANET.*

9. For the text edition of this poem, cf. *PAPS,* vol. 107, pp. 495-497; for a translation, cf. the forthcoming *Supplement to ANET.*

10. This is not the end of the poem; it continues with what might be characterized as the honeymoon of the newly married couple. Dumuzi, the mortal king, now himself partially divine, invited his wife to accompany him to his god's house—for like all Sumerian kings, and indeed all other important mortals, he had a personal god to intercede for him with the other gods in time of trouble (cf. *The Sumerians,* pp. 126-129)—where she would be treated with high honor. What follows then is unknown, since the remainder of the text is largely destroyed. For the text edition of this poem, cf. *PAPS,* vol. 107, pp. 497-499; for a translation, cf. the forthcoming *Supplement to ANET* (these are some minor changes in the translation and interpretation here presented).

11. For the text edition of this poem, cf. *PAPS,* vol. 107, pp. 499-501; for a translation, cf. the forthcoming *Supplement to ANET.*

12. Cf. pp. 100-102 for a sketch of their contents.

13. This is the coverlet whose preparation was the theme of the tête-à-tête between Inanna and her brother Utu in the poem treated above on pp. 68-69.

14. For the suggestion that this votary was a hierodule designated as a *lukur*-priestess, cf. the following chapter, page 93.

15. Cf. pp. 58-59.

16. Cf. the preceding chapter, pp. 63-64.

17. All these passages are from the second half of the composition; the first half seems to be unrelated to the Sacred Marriage Rite. For the

text edition of the entire composition, cf. *PAPS,* vol. 107, pp. 503-505, where the difficulties and uncertainties of translating and interpreting this poem, are noted; for a translation, cf. the forthcoming *Supplement to ANET.*

18. Cf. pp. 63-66.

19. Inanna's temple Eanna is in the city of Erech; to judge from this text, however, there may have been a second Eanna in Eridu.

20. This is not the end of the composition, but the remaining text is fragmentary and obscure. For the text edition of this composition, cf. *PAPS,* vol. 107, pp. 501-503; for a translation, cf. the forthcoming *Supplement to ANET.* (There are, however, a number of changes in the translation and interpretation here presented.)

## 5. The Sacred Marriage and Solomon's Song of Songs

1. For an illuminating summary of the various interpretations of the "Song of Songs," cf. Morris Jastrow, *The Song of Songs,* (Philadelphia, 1921).

2. Note, however, that in the "Song of Songs," the bride is never designated as queen.

3. For a complete, up-to-date bibliography of the scholarly books and articles concerned in one way or another with the "Song of Songs," cf. Otto Eissfeldt, *The Old Testament: An Introduction* (Oxford, 1966).

4. Chapter 3, verse 6 ff.

5. The first sketch of his thesis appeared in 1922-23 in vol. 39 of the *American Journal of Semitic Languages and Literature,* pp. 1-14. In 1924 he summarized and enlarged this study in a symposium on the "Song of Songs" held before the Oriental Club; cf. *The Song of Songs: A Symposium* Wilfred H. Schoff, ed. (Philadelphia, 1924), pp. 48-79. For his latest summation, cf. the Introduction to his translation of the book in the Westminster Bible.

6. Solomon was probably the king in whose reign the Canaanite-Hebrew Sacred Marriage Rite flourished, since Astarte was one of his favorite deities (cf. I Kings 11:5).

7. In fact, as is often the case, some of these "disciples" carried the theory far beyond the bounds of its originator, losing themselves in a labyrinthine maze of fanciful inferences and ingenious surmises no less belabored and extravagant than those of their allegory-prone or drama-minded predecessors.

8. That is, it was assumed that Dumuzi of Erech was originally no different from such gods as Enlil of Nippur, Enki of Eridu, Nanna of Ur, Ningirsu of Lagash, who over and above their cosmic duties and powers were the tutelary deities of their respective cities. The cuneiformist who did most to foster this view was Stephen Langdon in his book *Tammuz*

*and Ishtar* (London, 1914), in which mistranslations and misinterpretations of the cuneiform documents abound on virtually every page.

9. This erroneous notion was current until quite recently in scholarly works concerned with the religion of ancient Mesopotamia; cf. note 4 of the following chapter.

10. Cf. especially his interpretation of 2:4-6, 3:3, 5:6, 6:1-3, 8:1.

11. To this day virtually no Akkadian compositions relating to the Dumuzi-Inanna cult have been uncovered. This is not to say that they did not exist; in fact Meek's thesis was inspired to some extent by the publication of a cuneiform catalogue listing the *incipits* of scores of Akkadian songs which, to judge from their initial phrases, must have been part of the repertoire of the Tammuz-Ishtar cult personnel (cf. *Song of Songs: A Symposium,* Philadelphia, pp. 70-79); the songs themselves, however, have not yet been unearthed, and it may be many a year before the accident of excavation brings them to light.

12. A summary sketch of the available source material was presented in a paper read before the 26th International Congress of Orientalists held in New Delhi in 1964 (cf. p. 10 of the *Proceedings of the 26th International Congress*).

13. The parallels between the Mesopotamian and Hebrew Sacred Marriage songs will undoubtedly multiply and become more apparent and recognizable as more and more of the cuneiform literary tablets are dug up from the city ruins of Mesopotamia. And while there is little hope that any of the Hebrew Sacred Marriage compositions like those represented in the "Song of Songs" will ever be recovered, it is not impossible that some of their Canaanite prototypes might turn up on tablets written in the alphabetic cuneiform script such as those uncovered in Palestinian Ugarit. Nor is it at all surprising that the Hebrew and Canaanite literary works should bear some resemblance to those of Mesopotamia; after all, written literature had flourished there many a century before the cuneiform script came to Palestine, and not a few of the Sumero-Akkadian literary themes, motifs, and stylistic features had permeated the entire ancient Near East long before even the earliest parts of the Bible had been written and redacted. All this in no way detracts from the inspired and inspiring genius of the Hebrew poets who transformed the rather static, conventionalized Mesopotamian motifs and formal stylistic patterns, and quickened them with the breath of life. There is, for example, little of the delight in nature, or the touching human tenderness that pervades the biblical book (cf. especially 1:5-7, 2:8-17, 5:1-8, 7:7-13) in the rather aloof, highly stylized Sumerian compositions, whose authors never seem to be able to free themselves of the rigidities of temple ritualism and palace protocol.

14. The meaning of the last three lines, which seem to depict in some way the actual sex act, is obscure. For the text and edition, cf. Cig and Kramer, *Belleten* of the Turkish Historical Commission, vol. 16, pp. 345 ff: for the latest translation, cf. *The Sumerians,* p. 254.

15. Cf. The "Song of Songs" 6:8: "There were queens and eighty concubines and maidens without number." This seems to depict a similar, though perhaps highly exaggerated, female entourage in the court of Solomon.

16. Nothing is known of the nature of this song, which was so great a favorite of the king.

17. Cf. The "Song of Songs" 4:10 and 4:16-5:1, where it is not impossible that the "garden" is a euphemism for the vulva.

18. Cf. page 63 of Chapter 3.

19. For the text edition, cf. Falkenstein in *Die Welt des Orients* I, 1947, pp. 43-50.

20. Literally perhaps "my 'let him come.' "

21. Cf. perhaps 5:14-15 of the "Song of Songs."

22. For the text edition of the poem designated by its author as a "*balbale* of Inanna," cf. *PAPS,* vol. 107, p. 508; for a translation, cf. the forthcoming *Supplement to ANET* (note, however, that there are a number of changes in the translation here presented).

23. Cf. 2:3 of the "Song of Songs."

24. Cf. perhaps the portrayal of the lover in 5:10-16 of the "Song of Songs." For the text edition of this poem designated by its author as a *balbale* of Inanna, cf. *PAPS,* vol. 107:508-509; for a translation, cf. the forthcoming *Supplement to ANET* (note, however, that there are a number of changes in the translation here presented).

25. Cf. perhaps 6:12 of the "Songs of Songs."

26. For the text edition of this poem, cf. *PAPS,* vol. 107, p. 510; for a translation, cf. the forthcoming *Supplement to ANET* (note, however, that there are a number of changes in the translation here presented).

27. There are, of course, no stage directions in this playlet, and this, added to the usual difficulties of translating a Sumerian text, makes the interpretation highly problematical.

28. "His" probably refers to Dumuzi, who as king of his city had to be a brave warrior, whom Inanna, as the goddess of war as well as love, supplied with the invincible weapons.

29. Bau is a goddess of the city of Lagash, whose devotees presumably were part of Inanna's entourage (nevertheless, the mention of Bau is rather strange in this context).

30. For the text edition, cf. Falkenstein, *Zeitschrift für Assyriologie,* 50, pp. 60-63. The translation and interpretation here presented differs considerably from that proposed by Falkenstein.

31. It is not clear why the plural pronoun is used here and in the last line of the passage that is parallel to this line.

32. This no doubt refers to Dumuzi's personal god (cf. note 10 of Chapter 4).

33. The tablet was published in Stephen Langdon, *Sumerian Grammatical Texts* (Philadelphia, 1917), No. 52; the translation and interpretation here presented, based on a careful collation of the text in the University Museum, are the first to appear to date.

34. Cf. 6:2, 6:11, 7:11-13 of the "Song of Songs."

35. The poem continues for another eight fragmentary lines, which mention plants and date clusters in an obscure context. For a text edition and translation, cf. my "Inanna and Shulgi: A Sumerian Fertility Song" in the forthcoming number of *Iraq.*

36. The tablet is catalogued as No. 88318 in the British Museum Tablet Collection; a text edition and translation is planned for the near future.

37. The text is part of a tablet in the Museum of the Ancient Orient in Istanbul catalogued as Ni. 4569, copied by Muazzez Cig. The obverse was published in *PAPS,* vol. 107, p. 525; the entire text will be published in a volume of close to six hundred Sumerian literary tablets and fragments, for which I prepared an introduction and catalogue, by Muazzez Cig and Hatice Kixilyay of the Museum of the Ancient Orient. A text edition and translation is planned for the near future.

38. Cf. Henri de Genouillac, *Textes religieux sumériens du Louvre,* 1930, No. 97, lines 11-24; a text edition and translation of this composition is planned for the near future.

39. The copy of the text was published by L. W. King in *Cuneiform Texts in the British Museum,* CT XV, 1902, plates 28-29; for the erroneous translations and interpretations, cf. e. g. Stephen Langdon, *Tammuz and Ishtar,* pp. 51-53, and M. Witzel, *Tammuz Liturgien und Verwandtes,* pp. 460-465.

40. The text continues with several more obscure lines, and ends with a line reading: "His sister says to him"; the composition must have continued on one or more additional tablets that hopefully will be excavated one day.

41. Cf. "Song of Songs" 2:4.

42. Cf. "Songs of Songs" 6:5.

43. That is perhaps, with idling away the time.

44. The poem continues with two more lines of obscure meaning. For a text edition and translation, cf. *PAPS,* vol. 107, pp. 509-510 (but note that the translation here presented differs in some details).

45. "Song of Songs" 8:6.

46. The words *lubi* and *labi* seem to be onomatopoetic terms of endearment.

47. Cf. "Song of Songs" 2:14-15.

48. Cf. "Songs of Songs" 8:3.

49. The Sumerian word for "dragon" is *ushum,* and its use here may be a play on Dumuzi's most frequent appelative Ama-ushum-gal-anna.

## 6. The Sacred Marriage: Death and Resurrection

1. Dumuzi was primarily the shepherd-god, and strictly speaking, his death should therefore affect only the life in sheepfold and cattle stall. In charge of vegetation and plant life was Enkimdu, Dumuzi's rival for the hand of Inanna, and the one she preferred and would have married had it not been for the persistent prodding of her brother Utu (cf. pp. 68-72). It would not be surprising, therefore, in the course of future excavations, to find a Sumerian myth involving the death of Enkimdu to account for the withering away of vegetation during the hot summer. Perhaps, however, over the centuries, Dumuzi had gained such predominance in the minds and hearts of the Sumerians—after all he was identified with the king, who was the "farmer" as well as the "shepherd" of his people—that the languishing of all life, plant and animal, was attributed to him.

2. Not that the theologians were overly consistent about the immortality of the gods. In theory the gods possessed eternal life; this was one of their main advantages over mortal man. Nevertheless we find quite a number of deities in the Nether World, including the mightiest of the gods, Enlil (cf. *The Sumerians,* p. 133).

3. For full details of the gradual process of the piecing together of the text of the myth, cf. Kramer, *Sumerian Mythology,* revised edition (New York, 1961) pp. 84-86; *ANET,* pp. 52-57; *Journal of Cuneiform Studies,* vol. 4 (1950), pp. 199-211, and vol. 5 (1951) pp. 1-17; *PAPS,* vol. 107, pp. 490-493. There is also an Akkadian version commonly known as "Ishtar's Descent to the Nether World," a highly condensed, incomplete paraphrase of its Sumerian prototype, that became known to the scholarly world some decades before any of the Sumerian material was published, cf. E. A. Speiser's translation in *ANET,* pp. 84-85, where full bibliographical material will be found.

4. The reason for Inanna's descent to the world of the dead is not stated explicitly anywhere in the text. That she was driven by her unbounded ambition may be surmised from the reproachful response of Enlil and Nanna to Ninshubur in explanation of their refusal to help Inanna, as well as from the role she plays in several myths, cf. e.g., "Enki and the World Order: The Organization of the Earth and its Cultural Processes" (*The Sumerians,* pp. 171-183); "Inanna and Enki: The Transfer of the Arts of Civilization from Eridu to Erech" (*Sumerian Mythology,* pp. 64-68); "Inanna and the Subjugation of Mt. Ebih" (*Sumerian Mythology,* pp. 82-83). There is also the rather unlikely possibility that her "revolutionary" and "subversive" invasion of the Nether World was motivated by her desire to raise the dead and thus eliminate death altogether. In the Akkadian

version (cf. preceding note), too, no reason is given for the goddess's descent, but because Dumuzi is mentioned in a rather obscure context at the very end of the text, virtually all translators had assumed that her purpose was to rescue Dumuzi, who, for some unknown reason, was being held captive in the Nether World. This conclusion, still current in almost all writings concerned with the mythology of the ancient world, proved to be entirely erroneous; as the Sumerian myth shows, Dumuzi was not in the Nether World at all when Inanna arrived there—in fact, it was the goddess herself who sent him to "hell" after she had reascended to earth. As for Dumuzi's resurrection, this was nothing more than a surmise on the part of scholars, and it is only now, as a result of the recently discovered end of the Sumerian myth (coupled with a brilliant insight by the late lamented Adam Falkenstein) that we actually have textual evidence for Dumuzi's annual return to life after a six-month sojourn in the land of the dead (cf. my "Dumuzi's Annual Resurrection: An Important Correction to Inanna's Descent," *Bulletin of the American School of Oriental Research,* No. 183, 1966).

5. These seven temples are among the most important of her shrines. But she had many more temples, and one variant version lists thirteen of them.

6. There are several variant versions of these lines, but the differences are of little significance.

7. Inanna's designation "older sister" for Ereshkigal is not to be taken literally, since they did not have the same parents.

8. According to another version she was in the Nether World seven years, seven months, and seven days; while a third version has her stay there seven months. As these artificial numbers show, the mythographers at times embellished the details of their tales according to their fancy.

9. This seems to be inconsistent with the description of Ereshkigal in the earlier part of the poem, when the enraged goddess is depicted seated on her throne surrounded by the Anunnaki while imposing the death sentence on Inanna.

10. Ereshkigal, before she came to the Nether World, was none other than Ninlil, the wife of Sumer's leading deity, Enlil. According to the myth "Enlil and Ninlil: The Birth of the Moongod" (cf. *Sumerian Mythology,* pp. 47-49, and *The Sumerians,* pp. 145-146), Ninlil follows Enlil to the Nether World (whither he had been banished by the gods from Nippur because he had raped the young goddess) and there gives birth to three underworld deities, evidently suffering severe pains in doing so.

11. The poet simply repeats the entire passage in virtually identical form, substituting the indicative of the verb for the imperative where relevant.

12. Cf., e.g., the poem cited on pp. 77-78, and Gilgamesh's insulting address to the goddess in the Akkadian Version of the Epic of Gilgamesh (cf. E. A. Speiser's translation in *ANET,* p. 84).

13. According to the newly discovered version treated in *PAPS,* vol. 107, pp. 402-403. In the earlier known version, there is no detailed description of the torturing; the *galla,* according to that text, merely "seized him by the anus," poured out the milk from his seven churns, and attacked him seven times.

14. This is the wording of Dumuzi's prayer to Utu in the new version (cf. preceding note). In the earlier known version the prayer reads somewhat differently: " 'Utu, you are my wife's brother, I am your sister's husband,/ It is I who carried fat to your mother's house,/ It is I who carried milk to Ningal's house,/ Turn my hands into the hands of a snake,/ Turn my feet into the feet of a snake,/ Let me escape my demons, let them not seize me,/ Like a *sagkal*-snake I will traverse the meadows,/ I will carry off my soul to the home of sister Geshtinanna.' "

15. The passage containing Geshtinanna's offer of self-sacrifice is largely broken from the text, but its contents can be surmised from Inanna's pronouncement of her decision to Dumuzi toward the very end of the myth. As a result of Adam Falkenstein's illuminating reading (cf. note 4 above) the line is to be rendered "You—half the year, your brother—half the year."

16. The "five breads" and "ten breads" probably refer to Dumuzi as a provider for his mother (cf. also the "five breads" and "ten breads" in the poem sketched on page 97).

17. The poet seems unconscious of the fact that in the last line he gives away the essential meaning of the dream.

18. As Falkenstein suggested (cf. note 4 above) this refers to their separation as a consequence of Inanna's decision that each stay in the Nether World half the year.

19. The passage seems to read literally: "Let the son . . . by the sister, let him come, let him be kissed,/ The son . . . by the friend, let him come, let him be kissed." Note that there may be some reference to betrayal by a "kiss of death."

20. The name of the place to which he wants to carry off his soul is uncertain.

21. Not much is known about this goddess; it is certain, however, that she is not identical with Dumuzi's sister Geshtinanna as is usually assumed (cf., e.g., *Journal of Near Eastern Studies,* vol. 12, 1953, p. 188).

22. The text of this poem has been pieced together from some thirty tablets and fragments, and is now being prepared for publication.

23. The words "weeps" and "weeps bitterly" (in the following line) are not in the text but are no doubt to be understood.

24. The word "son" here and in the lines following is not to be taken literally; Dumuzi was not Inanna's son, but her husband, whom she loved dearly as a mother loves her son.

25. This may have been a baptismal ritual performed by Dumuzi (and later kings) in Eridu, the seat of the water-god Enki, Dumuzi's father.

26. The translation and meaning of this line are uncertain.

27. Taken literally it seems to imply that Dumuzi had ready access to intercourse with the maidens of his city.

28. The *kurgarra* were part of the Inanna cult personnel who entertained the goddess by duelling with knives and swords; cf. especially lines 74 ff. of the Inanna hymn edited by W. H. Römer in chapter IV of his *Sumerische Königshymnen der Isin-Zeit* (Leiden, 1965).

29. The implication of this line and the lines following is not clear.

30. In Sumerian the words for "food" and "plant" are identical; there is therefore a play of words here that is missed in the translation.

31. "Who sleeps a false sleep" is a recurring epithet for Dumuzi; perhaps it refers to his false sense of security even as the *galla* were about to seize him.

32. The text of the passage is obscure, but that Dumuzi tries to escape by speeding over dike and ditch is evident from the conversation of the *galla* that follows.

33. The meaning of this passage is obscure, and the rendering of the two last crucial lines is uncertain, but that is all that can be done with the text at present.

34. The literal translation of this passage is not difficult, but its real meaning in the context is obscure. The text of this composition was published more than fifty years ago (for details, cf. M. Witzel, *Tammuz-Liturgien und Verwandtes,* pp. 88 ff., but note that his translation and interpretation of the text are quite untrusworthy); an excellent translation of the beginning of the composition was published by Jacobsen in "Toward the Image of Tammuz," *Journal of the History of Religions,* vol. 1 (1961), pp. 193-194; the interpretation here presented is the result of much time and study, and by and large offers a reliable sketch of the contents of the composition, though much of it still remains uncertain and obscure.

35. More than twenty lines of text are destroyed at this point, and so we have no way of knowing what happened between the time Inanna started for the sheepfold and the time of her reassembling Dumuzi's scattered sheep; it is not unreasonable to surmise, however, that part of the passage told of Dumuzi's seizure by the *galla.*

36. "Well-being" presumably is an allusion to the sheep as the source of Inanna's support and sustenance.

37. Literally, the Sumerian word means "a skin filled with water for the steppe."

38. Since Inanna is still addressing Bilulu, this line should have read: "Your son Girgire together with you"; the shift of person is probably due to the carelessness of the poet.

39. The Sumerian can be translated "will knead" as well as "will keep track"; perhaps the former will turn out to be correct in this context.

40. "Lad" here probably refers to Sirru-Edinlilla.

41. The literal translation of the passage as given here is reasonably assured, but its interpretation and real meaning in the context are uncertain.

42. This line is a cliché frequently used in Sumerian narrative poetry to introduce a passage that repeats virtually verbatim the execution of a command recorded in a passage immediately preceding it.

43. For the text edition and translation, cf. Jacobsen and Kramer, "The Myth of Inanna and Bilulu," *Journal of Near Eastern Studies,* vol. 12 (1953), pp. 160-191, but note that the interpretation here presented differs in numerous details.

44. As yet this is largely surmise; cf. Falkenstein, *Compte Rendu de la Troisième Rencontre Assyriologique Internationale,* p. 47, and Jacobsen, *PAPS,* vol. 107, p. 478, note 6.

45. The assertion that the Damu of the Dumuzi liturgies is not the healing-god Damu of Isin, but a god of the city of Girsu (cf., e.g., Jacobsen, *PAPS,* vol. 107, pp. 476-477, note 8) is quite unjustified; cf. Landsberger *apud* Kraus, *Journal of Cuneiform Studies,* vol. 3 (1951), p. 61, note 51; and especially the Damu liturgy in the *Babylonian Expedition of the University of Pennsylvania,* vol. 30 (cf. following note), No. 2, where Damu, the "physician," is depicted as going to the Nether World, "the distant," and is mourned by his mother Ninisinna of Isin. Damu was thus originally venerated in Isin as a healing deity who, for some as yet unknown reason, was believed by the Sumerian theologians to have died and gone to the Nether World like Dumuzi (just as Sataran of the city of Der, for example, originally a god of judgment, was also believed to have suffered death for some unknown reason). Once Damu was identified with Dumuzi because of their common fate, laments and liturgies concerned with Damu tended to follow the Dumuzi pattern.

46. Much of the contents of these liturgies is enigmatic, ambiguous, obscure, and problematical. Many of the texts are fragmentary, and written in a phonetic spelling that at times makes even the word division uncertain, while those that are well preserved and written in the customary historical spelling are so cryptic and allusive that much of their meaning eludes us. Nevertheless, over the decades, considerable progress has been achieved in their translation and interpretation, and some of them are now available to the scholarly world. The outstanding pioneer in this area was Heinrich Zimmern, whose two monographs, *Sumerisch-babylonische Tammuzlieder* (Leipzig, 1907) and *Der Babylonische Gott Tammuz* (Leipzig, 1909) can still be used with confidence by the non-cuneiformist. In 1913, Hugo Radau published his *Sumerian Hymns and Prayers to the God Dumuzi: Babylonian Lenten Songs* (*Babylonian Expedition of the University of Pennsylvania,* vol. 30, Philadelphia, 1913), a pioneer work that contains numerous useful and at times even brilliant philological observations, but is seriously marred by the author's curious and erroneous ideas of Sumerian religion.

In more recent years, the late Adam Falkenstein has translated a number of passages in the liturgies with his customary care and reliability in *Compte Rendu de la Troisième Rencontre Assyriologique Internationale* (1954) (the paper was read in 1952), and *Sumerische und akkadische Hymnen und Gebete* (1953). The scholar who has been working most productively on the Dumuzi texts in recent years is Thorkild Jacobsen; cf. especially *Journal of Near Eastern Studies,* vol. 12 (1953) pp. 160-187; *Journal of the History of Religions,* vol. 1 (1961), pp. 189-213; *PAPS,* vol. 107 (1963), pp. 474-478. (The translations presented in these studies are superb; precise, penetrating, and reliable; the interpretations and etymologies, on the other hand, are to be taken with a sizeable grain of salt.) Altogether untrustworthy are Stephen Langdon's *Tammuz and Ishtar,* much of which was republished in 1931 in his *Semitic Mythology* (vol. IX of *Mythology of All the Races,* Boston, 1931, edited by L. H. Gray, J. A. MacCulloch, and G. F. Moore), and M. Witzel's *Tammuz-Liturgien und Verwandtes* (1935); the non-cuneiformist should not make use of them for his researches in any way since many of the translations are quite unjustified and erroneous, and most of the interpretations are superficial, unfounded, and misleading. (A sad example of the damage done by these two studies is E. D. Van Buren's "The Sacred Marriage in Early Times in Mesopotamia," *Orientalia,* New Series, vol. 13, (1944), a study which, in spite of the author's thorough and comprehensive knowledge of the archaeological material, is virtually worthless, because of its dependence on the Langden and Witzel translations and interpretations.)

47. The Dumuzi myth itself varied to some extent from poet to poet; cf., e.g., the variations on the theme of pursuit of the *galla* treated in this chapter. There are also indications that the *galla* carried Dumuzi off by boat; in any case there was a "man-devouring" River of the Nether World that had to be crossed (cf. *The Sumerians,* p. 133), although this is nowhere mentioned in "Inanna's Descent to the Nether World." There is therefore every reason to surmise that the tales concerned with the death of the deities, who in the course of time came to be identified with Dumuzi were neither uniform nor homogeneous. The god Damu, for example, is identified in some of the liturgies with Dumuzi and is designated as the son of Sirtur and the brother of Geshtinanna (cf. De Genouillac, *Textes religieux sumeriens du Louvre,* No. 8); in others he is correctly characterized as the son of Ninisinna and the brother of Gunura of Isin (cf. Zimmern, *Sumerische Kultlieder,* No. 26, vol. 2, and especially the Damu liturgy cited in note 45). Moreover, there was at least one dying god who, as far as is known at present, was not identified with Dumuzi at all in the liturgies, and yet the pattern of mourning by his mother and sister is virtually identical with that of the Dumuzi texts (cf. Thureau-Dangin, *Revue d'assyriologie,* 19, 1922, pp. 175-185). The name of this obscure deity is Lil, of the city of Adab; his mother is the goddess Ninhursag (also known as Ninmah) and his sister

is Egime. In this text Egime, the counterpart of Geshtinanna of the Dumuzi lament, pleads with her dead brother Lil: "My brother, rise from your grave, your mother would gaze upon you,/ Your mother Ninhursag would gaze upon you,/ Would give ear to your sweet lips,/ Would give ear to your gracious mouth, . . ./ Lad, do not let your mother sit weeping,/ Do not let your mother Ninhursag sit lamenting,/ Do not bring woe upon her, rise from your grave,/ Lil, do not bring woe upon her, rise from your grave." To which the brother replies pathetically: "Set me free, my sister set me free,/ Egime, set me free, my sister, set me free,/ Sister, do not scold me, I am no longer one who can see,/ Egime, do not scold me. I am no longer one who can see,/ Mother Ninmah, do not scold me, I am no longer one who can see,/ My grave is the dust of the Nether World, I lie among the wicked [?] ones,/ My sleep is anguish, I dwell among its evil ones,/My sister, I cannot rise from my grave. . . .

48. Note, for example, that in the early second millennium B.C. in Syria there was a month called Dumuzi (cf. E. Dhorme, *Syria,* vol. 25, 1946-48, p. 8) and the god Damu is probably mentioned in one of the Amarna letters dating from the fourteenth century B.C. (cf. Otto Schroeder, *Orientalische Literatur-Zeitung,* 18, 1915, p. 291). Nor is it unreasonable to assume that via Palestine and Syria, some of the motifs of the Dumuzi-Inanna myth spread to Anatolia, Cyprus, and Greece (note, e.g., that both Dumuzi and Adonis must remain part of each year in the Nether World), although it must be stressed that Frazer's facile identification of Dumuzi with Osiris, Attis, and Adonis is quite untenable. For recent discussion of this rather intricate problem, cf. especially Henri Frankfort, *Kingship and the Gods* (1948), pp. 286-294; Oliver Gurney, *Journal of Semitic Studies,* vol. 7 (1962), pp. 147-160; and Gottfreed von Lücken, *Forschungen und Fortschritte,* vol. 26 (1965), pp. 240-245.

49. Cf. Ezekiel 8:14. It is also interesting to note that to this day there is a month called Tammuz in the Jewish calendar, and that its seventeenth day is a day of fasting and lament that may originally go back to the wailing for the death of Dumuzi, although later tradition claims that it marks the destruction of the Jerusalem temple.

50. Cf. page 00 above.

51. Cf., e.g., "The Curse of Agade" lines 104-105 (see forthcoming *Supplement to ANET*); and note that when Gilgamesh, in preparation for his attack on the monstrous creatures that had settled in Inanna's *hulub*-tree, "donned armor weighing fifty minas about his waist," he handled it, according to the poet, as easily as if it were thirty shekels (cf. *The Sumerians,* p. 201).

52. One of the recurring epithets in the Dumuzi liturgies seems to be *nagar* "the divine carpenter" (it is always followed on the same line, however, by the epithet "Lord of the net," a phrase that hardly seems to go with carpenter).

53. This is explicitly stated in the Ninisinna hymn published by E. Chiera in *Sumerian Religious Texts,* nos. 6 and 7 (1924) (cf. No. 6, lines 11-28).

54. Cf. especially lines 75-79 of the Akkadian version of the myth (*ANET,* p. 108).

# *Glossary*

Abisimti: Mother of Shu-Sin, king of Ur.

Abzu: Sea, abyss, home of the water-god Enki.

Adab: An important city of Sumer, and its capital during the reign of Lugalannemundu. Part of it was excavated by the Oriental Institute in 1903-04; several thousand tablets were unearthed and are now located in Chicago and Istanbul.

Agade: A city in northern Sumer, founded by Sargon the Great, who made it his capital. For a time it was the richest and most powerful city in the ancient world. According to Sumerian tradition, it was destroyed and laid waste during the days of Naramsin, Sargon's grandson, and remained a city forever cursed. Following the reign of Sargon and his dynasty the land known as Sumer was called "Sumer and Akkad" (Akkad is a variant pronunciation of Agade).

Agga: A ruler of the first dynasty of Kish; one of the main protagonists in the epic tale "Gilgamesh and Agga."

Akkad: see Agade.

Akkadians: The Semitic inhabitants of Mesopotamia. The word is derived from the place-name Akkad (as written in the Bible). Akkadian is also the name of the Semitic language used by this people, the two main dialects of which are Assyrian and Babylonian.

allari: A type of love song.

Al-Ubaid: A mound near Ur that yielded some of the oldest archaeological remains in Southern Mesopotamia (see Ubaidians).

Amaushumgalanna: A by-name of Dumuzi; literally it seems to mean "The Mother, dragon of heaven."

Amurru: The Semitic people that infiltrated into Sumer, and gradually conquered it.

An: The Sumerian heaven-god; the word means "heaven."

Anunna: A general name for a group of gods who were probably originally "heaven-gods"; some of them, however, must have "fallen from grace," and were carried off to the Nether World.

Anzu: Probably the true pronunciation of the name of the mythological bird known in the literature as the Imdugud-bird (which see).

Arali: One of the names for the Nether World.

Aratta: An as yet unidentified city in Iran, to the east of Sumer, noted for its wealth of metal and stone, and for its skilled craftsmen; it was probably conquered and subjugated by Erech early in the third millennium B.C.

Ashnan: Grain-goddess, a sister of Lahar.

Babylon: The city in northern Sumer that was chosen by some of the Amurru as their capital at the beginning of the second millennium B.C.; hence the name Babylonia for the land known earlier as Sumer, or Sumer and Akkad.

Badtibira: A city in southern Sumer; the legendary seat of one of Sumer's antediluvian dynasties.

Bagara: A shrine of Ningirsu in Lagash.

balbale: A designation for a type of Sumerian poem or song; also used as a descriptive term for apples.

Baradurgarra: Inanna's temple in Nippur.

Bau: An important goddess of Lagash; spouse of its tutelary deity Ningirsu.

Belili: A goddess, to whose home Dumuzi flees in vain to escape "his demons."

Bilulu: A goddess killed by Inanna and turned into a water-skin for the benefit of travellers in the desert-steppe.

"Black-heads": An epithet of the Sumerians; its origin is obscure.

buranun: The original name of the Euphrates.

Damu: A god of healing identified with Dumuzi.

Der: A city in northeastern Sumer, whose god Sataran suffered a fate similar to that of Dumuzi.

Dilmun: A still unidentified land that was looked upon by the Sumerians as a blessed paradise.

Dumuzi: The "shepherd-king" of Erech who came to be known as the first ruler to wed the goddess Inanna in a Sacred Marriage Rite. Literally, Dumuzi means "Faithful Son."

Dumuzi-abzu: "Dumuzi of the Deep," an epithet of Dumuzi.

duru: A kind of lapis lazuli.

Eanna: Inanna's temple in Erech; its literal meaning is "House of An."

Eannatum: A ruler of Lagash who for a brief period became the sovereign of all Sumer.

Egime: Sister of Lil (which see).

Ekishnugal: The great temple of the moon-god in Ur.

Ekur: Enlil's temple in Nippur, the leading sanctuary in Sumer; its literal meaning is "Mountain House."

Elam: The country to the east of Sumer, and often in conflict with it.

Emesh: "Summer"; a protagonist in the disputation "Emesh and Enten" ("Summer and Winter").

Emush: A shrine in Erech.

Emushkalamma: A temple in Badtibira.

Eninnu: Ningirsu's temple in Lagash, rebuilt and restored by Gudea; its full name was Eninnu-Imdugud-babbar, a compound phrase of uncertain significance.

Enki: The god of wisdom, and of the sea and rivers, whose main seat of worship was Eridu; the literal meaning of the name is "Lord of the Earth."

Enkidu: The faithful servant and companion of the hero Gilgamesh.

Enkimdu: The "farmer" rival of Dumuzi, the "shepherd," for the hand of Inanna.

Enlil: The leading deity of the Sumerian pantheon (the literal meaning of the name is "Lord Air"); his main seat of worship was Nippur, with its temple the Ekur.

Enmebaraggesi: A ruler of the first dynasty of Kish; father of Agga.

Enmerkar: One of the heroic rulers of the first dynasty of Erech, celebrated for his conquest of Aratta.

ensi: The Sumerian title for the ruler of a city, who at times was as powerful as a king.

Enten: "Winter" (see Emesh, "Summer").

Enun: A shrine in Eridu.

Erech: One of Sumer's leading cities, still in process of excavation; the capital of Sumer at the time of its Heroic Age.

Ereshkigal: "Queen of the Great Below," the goddess in charge of the Nether World.

Eridu: A city in the south of Sumer now partially excavated; its tutelary deity was Enki.

Esharra: Inanna's temple in Adab.

eshdam: One of Inanna's brothel-like shrines in Erech.

eshesh: A religious feast about which little is known at present.

Etana: One of the kings of the first dynasty of Kish, celebrated in legendary lore.

gakkul: A special kind of lettuce plant.

galla: The cruel little demons of the Nether World.

gamgam: A bird as yet unidentified.

Ganzir: A by-name for the Nether World; meaning uncertain.

Gatumdug: A goddess of Lagash whom Gudea claims as his divine mother.

Geshtinanna: Dumuzi's sister; literally the name seems to mean "Vine of Heaven."

gian: An evil or unclean person unfit to live in a sanctified city.

Gibil: The god of fire.

giguna: A grove-like shrine found in Sumer's important temples. It is also the home of Inanna's temple in Zabalam.

Gilgamesh: A ruler of the first dynasty of Erech who came to be celebrated as Mesopotamia's leading heroic figure.

gipar: The part of the temple in which the high priest (or high priestess) lived.

Girgire: The robber-baron son of Bilulu.

gishban: A type of garment.

Gishbanda: A city in southern Sumer, as yet unidentified.

Gudea: The devout *ensi* of Lagash who rebuilt the Eninnu, a pious deed celebrated in a long hymn inscribed on two, and perhaps three, clay cylinders.

Gugalanna: The "Great Bull of Heaven;" the husband of Ereshkigal.

Gutians: A barbarous mountainous people to the east that overwhelmed Sumer toward the end of the third millennium B.C.

hahala: An as yet unidentified plant.

Hammurabi: The famous ruler and lawgiver of Babylon.

hulub: An as yet unidentified tree.

Huwawa: The monster who guarded the cedars of the Land of the Living; he was slain by Gilgamesh and Enkidu.

Ibbi-Sin: The last, pathetic ruler of the Third Dynasty of Ur, who was carried off into captivity by the Elamites.

Iddin-Dagan: The third ruler of the Dynasty of Isin, which followed the Third Dynasty of Ur; one of the documents from his reign is highly significant for the Sacred Marriage Rite.

idiglat: The original name of the Tigris.

ildag: Name of an as yet unidentified tree.

Imdugud: A mythological lion-headed bird that played an important role in myths and epic tales. According to most recent research, his name, although written with the sign of IM and DUGUD, should probably be read Anzu.

Inanna: The goddess of love, fertility, and procreation who was the tutelary deity of Erech, and the main protagonist of the Sacred Marriage Rite; literally the name means "Queen of Heaven."

Ishme-Dagan: Son of Iddin-Dagan.

Ishtar: The Semitic name for Inanna, the same as the biblical Esther.

Isin: An important city of Sumer, which became its capital after the fall of the Third Dynasty of Ur.

itirda: A kind of milk.

kalatur: A sexless devotee of the goddess Inanna; a mythological being created by Enki to help revive Inanna in the Nether World.

Ki: Mother Earth.

kisim: A kind of milk.

Kish: The capital city of the first dynasty after the Flood, according to Sumerian tradition.

kiur: Part of a temple, and particularly part of the Ekur of Nippur.

Kua: A place in the neighborhood of Eridu, where Dumuzi was at home before he became King of Erech.

Kubatum: A *lukur*-priestess of Shu-Sin; a necklace presented her by the king was excavated in Erech.

Kuli-Enlil: "Friend of Enlil," an epithet of Dumuzi.

Kullab: The sacred district of Erech.

kurgarra: A sexless devotee of the goddess Inanna, companion to the *kalatur*.

labi: An onomatopoetic word for "darling," see *lubi.*

Lagash: An important city in southern Sumer; the first Sumerian city excavated to a significant extent.

Lahar: Cattle-goddess, a sister of Ashnan.

Lamma: A guardian spirit and good genie.

Land of the Living: A still unidentified land noted for its holy cedar guarded by the monster Huwawa.

Larsa: A capital of Sumer in the early second millennium B.C.

Lil: A god of Adab who, like Dumuzi, was carried off to the Nether World.

lubi: An onomatopetic word for "darling"; see *labi.*

Lugalannemundu: An important early ruler of Sumer, whose capital was Adab.

Lugalbanda: One of the heroic kings of the first dynasty of Erech.

lukur: A priestess-devotee of Inanna who may have played the role of the goddess during the Sacred Marriage Rite.

Lulal: A god of Badtibira, the son of Inanna.

Magan: Probably the ancient name for Egypt.

magur-boat: A type of Sumerian boat used for transport of goods.

Magilum: A name of uncertain meaning.

Martu: Name of the Semitic tribes that infiltrated into Sumer early in the third millennium B.C.

mashgur: Name of an as yet unidentified tree.

me (pronounced "may"): The divine rules and regulations that keep the universe operating as planned.

Meluhha: Probably the ancient name for Ethiopia and Somaliland.

Mesannepadda: Founder of the first dynasty of Ur, and a contemporary of Gilgamesh.

Mesilim: One of the early rulers of Sumer, noted for his efforts to arbitrate a serious water dispute between the two cities.

Meskiagsher: Founder of the first dynasty of Erech.

Mishnaic times: Roughly the time when much of the Old Testament was canonized; Mishna refers to the older legal portions of the Talmud, the many-volumed compendium of Hebrew law and legend.

Nanna: The Sumerian name of the moon-god, the tutelary deity of Ur, and father of Inanna.

Nanshe: A goddess of Lagash, the divine interpretress of dreams.

Naramsin: Grandson of Sargon the Great; the defiler of the Ekur, according to Sumerian tradition, who brought an evil curse upon his capital Agade.

Neti: The chief gate-keeper of the Nether World.

Nidaba: The Sumerian goddess in charge of writing and literature.

Nina: One of the main districts of Lagash, where Nanshe had her main temple.

Ninagen: A canal leading to Nina.

Nindub: A deity in charge of tablets.

Ningal: The spouse of the moon-god Nanna, and mother of Inanna.

Ningirsu: A son of Enlil and the tutelary deity of Lagash, whose temple was the Eninnu of Gudea fame.

Ningishzida: The god of Gishbanda, who later came to be identified with Dumuzi.

Ninhursag: The Sumerian mother goddess also known as Ninmah, "The Noble Queen."

Ninisinna: The tutelary deity of Isin; the "great physician" of the Sumerian pantheon.

Ninmah: See Ninhursag.

Ninshubur: Inanna's faithful vizier.

Ninurta: A son of Enlil in charge of the South Wind; a storm and warrior god, also known as "farmer" of the gods.

Nippur: Sumer's holiest city, seat of its leading deity Enlil. Nippur was the seat of one of the great academies of Sumer, and most of the literary tablets excavated to date come from its scribal quarter.

Nudimmud: A by-name of Enki that probably refers to his part in the creation of man.

pala: A queenly garment worn by Inanna.

Rimsin: A ruler of Larsa who put an end to the dynasty of Isin.

sagkal: A kind of snake; Dumuzi was turned into a *sagkal*-snake to escape his demons.

Sargon: One of the great rulers of the ancient world; founder of the city Agade, and of the dynasty of Akkad.

Sataran: A god of Der who later came to be identified with Dumuzi.

shabra: A high official.

shagan: A type of vessel.

Shara: The tutelary deity of Umma, and Inanna's "valet."

shesh: A kind of grain.

shuba: A kind of semiprecious stone.

shugurra: Name of the crown worn by Inanna, literal meaning uncertain.

shukur: A kind of reed used by shepherds.

Shulgi: One of the rulers of the Third Dynasty of Ur, noted as a patron of literature and music.

Shusin: Son of Shulgi; a number of Sacred Marriage love songs involving this king have been excavated.

Sigkurshagga: The temple of the god Shara in Umma.

sikim: A kind of garment.

Sin: The Semitic name for Nanna, the moon-god of Ur.

Sirara-shumta: Probably a deity of Lagash, pronunciation uncertain.

Sirara-edin-lillu: The friendless son of Girgire.

Sirtur: The mother of Dumuzi.

Subarians: A people to the north and east of Sumer, who were often in conflict with it.

Sumugan: The god of the beasts of the steppe.

Surugal: A canal in the neighborhood of Erech.

Tammuz: The Biblical writing for the name Dumuzi.

Third Dynasty of Ur: The dynasty reigning approximately 2050-1950 B.C., a century commonly known as the Sumerian Renaissance.

tibu: An as yet unidentified bird.

Ubaidians: The earliest inhabitants of Sumer; the name is derived from Al-Ubaid, the site where their remains were first discovered.

Udug: A guardian spirit and good genie.

Umma: A city in southern Sumer in constant conflict with Lagash.

ummia: Sage, savant; head of a Sumerian school or academy.

Ur: The biblical Ur of the Chaldees, the original home of Abraham and his forefathers according to biblical tradition. This important metropolis, three times the capital of Sumer, was excavated in part by Leonard Woolley.

Ur-Nammu: Founder of the Third Dynasty and promulgator of the first law code recovered to date.

Urukagina: A ruler of Lagash, noted as the first known social reformer in the history of man.

Ushumgalanna: A shorter version of the name Amaushumgalanna (which see).

Ushumgalkalamma: The name of Ningirsu's soothing lyre in his temple Eninnu; the literal meaning of the word is "Great Dragon of the Land."

Utu: The sun-god, brother of Inanna.

Zabalam: A city in Sumer, not as yet identified with certainty.

zabalum: An as yet unidentified tree.

ziggurat: The stage-tower of temples, a hallmark of Sumerian architecture.

ziptum: A cord to bind captives and prisoners.